WHEELS UP

A NOVEL OF DRUGS, CARTELS AND SURVIVAL

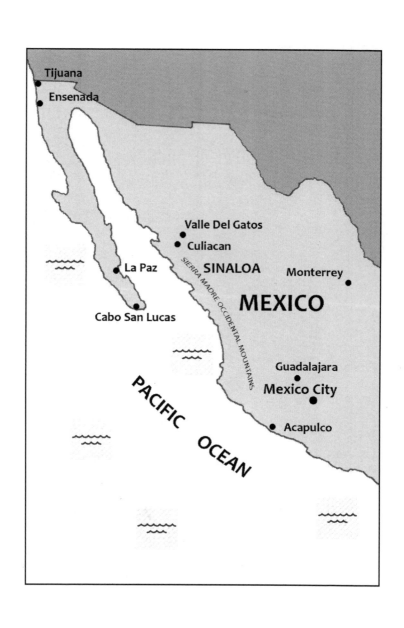

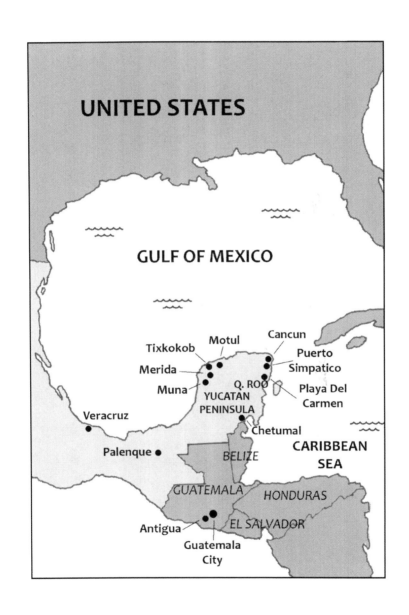

UNITED STATES

GULF OF MEXICO

Cancun

Tixkokob   Motul

Merida   Puerto
                             Simpatico
Muna   Q. ROO
          YUCATAN   Playa Del
          PENINSULA   Carmen

Veracruz

                    Chetumal

Palenque   BELIZE   CARIBBEAN
                           SEA

          GUATEMALA   HONDURAS

Antigua   EL SALVADOR

     Guatemala
     City

WHEELS UP

A NOVEL OF
DRUGS, CARTELS
AND SURVIVAL

JEANINE KITCHEL

Published by Jeanine Kitchel
www.jeaninekitchel.com

ISBN: 978-0-692-06469-6 (paperback)
ISBN: 978-0-692-09721-2 (ebook)
Library of Congress Control Number: 2018903960

Jill Logan's artwork Sensual Foliage has been adapted for the front cover, jilllogan.com
Cover graphic design by damonza.com
Maps by Steve Radziwillowicz at mayavision.com
Interior book design by Sun Editing & Book Design, suneditwrite.com

Printed and bound in the USA

Disclaimer: This is a work of fiction. All characters, names, incidents and dialogue in this novel are either the products of the author's imagination or are used fictitiously. Any resemblance to actual events, locales or persons, living or dead, is entirely coincidental.

Geography is destiny.

—*Napoleon Bonaparte*

CHAPTER 1

Yucatán Peninsula, Mexico
Present Day

The Gulfstream jet, loaded with two tons of Colombian cocaine, careened over dense Yucatán jungle as Layla stared out the compact window, horrified. If they weren't running on empty and destined to crash, it might have looked lush to her and beautiful.

Without fuel, the engines starved into silence, she heard only the whooshing sound of the aluminum plane as it cruised over mangrove swamps and fast-approaching mahogany trees. All thoughts of her hasty departure from Guatemala to escape Don Guillermo's wrath had vanished along with any hopes of safely landing in Cancun. They were going down.

Layla gripped the armrests, dropped her head between her knees, and prepared for the worst.

🔲🔲🔲

Three weeks earlier, Layla was sitting at the crowded bar in Bucanero's Cantina in Ensenada on Mexico's west coast while she waited for Clay Lasalle, Canada's biggest pot dealer, to show up. Carlos, her bodyguard and sometime lover, was with her, but rather than relieving the stress, his overbearing presence just added to the pressure.

With the recent recapture of El Patrón, her notorious drug lord uncle, Layla had catapulted to the top of the Culiacan Cartel as his replacement. Facing her first deal without her uncle's guiding hand, she was feeling on edge. Clay had set up the meeting with few details and she was eager to know what was on his mind. To calm her jitters she resorted to the one thing that never failed her: tequila shots.

"Don Julio, por favor!" Layla called to the paunchy bartender over the clamor of the rowdy, alcohol-fueled crowd—mostly tourists in shorts and Hawaiian shirts. Above the polished mahogany bar a framed poster-sized photo showed a nude blonde being ushered out of the century-old watering hole by two Mexican policia. Of course it's a gringa, Layla thought, Mexicans treaded more carefully in shark-infested waters. She waved a two-hundred-peso note as the bartender passed by with a tray of margaritas.

"Momentito!" he promised.

Carlos stepped away just as she downed her second shot. Though he'd given her his "cuidado" or "be careful" look before heading to the restroom, she ignored it. When a handsome gringo sat next to her and started talking, she was all in.

By the time Carlos returned, Layla was too busy chatting with her neighbor to worry about her bodyguard's glare. Carlos hated outsiders as much as seeing her drink, but she needed to chill. Tequila shots and flirting were a mindless diversion. The agave centered her, allowing her to distract herself without losing her edge before meeting Clay.

"You're from Chicago?" she asked. "I've been there."

The man gazed at the dark-haired Latina by his side. "What did you think?"

She gave a dismissive shrug. "Too cold." Her intelligent almond-shaped eyes were the color of charcoal. "I prefer

Mexico." A sardonic smile highlighted her cheekbones, making her face even more appealing.

Layla turned back toward her bodyguard and focused on the shot glass the bartender placed in front of her. Poor Carlos. Coming to Baja always rattled him. It wasn't only the jaw-breaking drive from Culiacan on dodgy Mexican roads. It was Ensenada—far from the safety of Sinaloa, well out of their comfort zone. But for Layla, Bucanero's Cantina qualified as northern Baja's one saving grace. The dive bar brought back memories of her wild, reckless early years. At thirty-five, Layla still had plenty of the right stuff. Her five-foot-six frame seemed mostly legs and Carlos's rare compliments always focused on her tiny waist. She emphasized her striking physique by wearing low-cut tops, but her most notable feature was the cascade of curly dark hair that spilled over her shoulders.

She downed her last tequila shot, scooted off the wooden bar stool a step ahead of Carlos and moved towards the empty dining room. The cantina was not the best place for a meeting, but it suited their needs: an easy landmark near the border with a back room for business. Layla slipped into the barely lit room, accepted a menu from the waiter, and handed him a two-hundred-peso note.

"Our associate arrives soon. We need privacy. Close the restaurant," she ordered. "Your manager knows."

He nodded, pocketed the bill, and turned towards the kitchen.

Layla walked across the worn wooden floor to a corner table in the back. She took a deep breath to steady herself before sitting down. Things would escalate into a full-scale argument once Carlos reached the table. She could already hear him whining, "Bosses keep to themselves, especially in public."

When Carlos had a bad day, everyone had a bad day. He could easily vie for title of most miserable man on the planet. Too bad the sex was so good. Hijole! He had the body of a male model but two sizes larger, with café au lait skin. So handsome but so disagreeable. Granted she shouldn't have given that gringo the time of day, but tequila made her bold.

Layla opened the menu, waiting for her bodyguard's interrogation to begin.

Carlos banged a cheap wooden chair against the table before sitting down. "What the hell do you care about Chicago? It's not Madrid, not even Barcelona! That guy was boring! Are you so starved for conversation you have to talk to a gringo?"

Layla silently perused the bill of fare.

"I've had it," he said, his voice rising. "I'm tired of my life. Am I just your bodyguard and nothing more? Everyone, *everyone*, told me to keep it strictly business, even your uncle. But I didn't listen. I thought it would be a drunken one night stand, and now I'm fucking chained to you because of this goddamn job!"

His powerful hands clenched into fists as he rubbed them over his knees. "If only I could've left you in Guadalajara. But I'd have never made it out of the city before taking a bullet from your uncle."

That was accurate. You didn't quit the cartel, the cartel quit you. She looked at the menu, avoiding eye contact, glad the waiter hadn't yet returned. "Should we order?"

He glared at her. "Are you acting like this conversation isn't happening? Do you want me to walk out of here, meeting or no meeting?"

Best not to test him. He'd do it, and then she'd be without a bodyguard. The drone of his voice, the bullying, started to sink in. Chinga! She had no trouble working the cartel mob, but Carlos ran her. He was as overbearing as her two brothers. Reynoldo, who should have been running the cartel had died trying, and Martín, her other brother, wasn't up to the task. Now with one brother and two cousins dead, Layla found herself atop the Culiacan Cartel.

She looked up and said in as soothing a tone as possible, "Carlos, let's not fight, okay? We're here for business. I need you with me. You're not only the man who protects me. I love you."

She did love him, though his bad attitude and barking complaints—usually aimed at her—were tiresome. He shifted his perfectly-proportioned body forward, staring at her with eyes she'd been lost in a hundred times. He surprised her by grabbing her hand, a little harder than necessary. They never touched in public.

"After this meeting, we'll talk about you and me." He scowled. "I don't know why you drink so much—and with strangers."

These macho men! "Okay, okay. I'll let up on the shots. One last Pacifico while we wait."

The waiter came and they ordered. She checked her watch, 10 p.m. Lasalle would be showing up soon. She'd met him once before in Miami and sparks had flown—there was no denying they had chemistry.

Layla changed topics. "So, what does he want?"

"Chinga! Who cares?"

She backpedaled. "Carlos..."

He gave her a cold look but couldn't hold back his opinion. "Routes for coke or pot."

The meal went smoothly. Layla pushed an enchilada around her plate and watched Carlos demolish an order of chilaquiles, three tamales, and a couple chicken enchiladas.

As he piled it in, a rare calm settled over him. He was well into his second beer when Clay walked into the restaurant. Layla saw him first but Carlos looked up the moment Clay crossed the threshold. As a bodyguard, Carlos's instincts were flawless.

The thirty-something Canadian smuggler was six feet two, a looker with brown shaggy hair and an easy smile. Though his frame was solid, almost hefty, he moved like a cat. Spotting Layla, he gave a nod as his long strides brought him across the room.

He let his knuckles graze the table as he flashed her a warm smile. "Layla, it's been a long time. Good to see you again. And this is..."

"Carlos."

"Carlos, hola. Clay." The Canadian extended a hand.

Carlos rose from the booth. "A pleasure." He spoke in Spanish. "I'll be close by," he said to Layla.

"Have a seat." Layla slid over to allow room for Clay. Not much had changed about the northern grower since she last saw him—still that laidback air even though he controlled the lion's share of Canada's pot sales.

"Something to eat?" Layla continued in English, though she knew Clay spoke passable Spanish.

He shook his head. "Just a Pacifico." She gestured toward her beer and the hovering waiter sprung into action.

"Long drive?"

"Not bad. Been waiting long?" Clay asked.

"No."

They silently watched the waiter set down the bottle of beer and retreat from the room.

"Salud," said Clay, raising his bottle. "Layla, I'm glad you could meet with me. I'll get right to the point. I want a partner to move a couple tons of coke to Cancun by air—

a regular run. I heard you lost a yacht recently, so a partner-ship could work out well for both of us."

How did Lasalle know about the navy seizing their yacht?

"Cocaine…"

"Boats are fine, but flying's faster and we can carry more. Plus I'm dealing directly with FARC. Gotta hand it to 'em. For a guerrilla army in the Colombian jungle, they know how to run those cocaine fincas. And we can get better prices from them than anyone's gotten before."

He took a swig of beer.

"Interesting," she said without emotion. "How will you manage those good prices?"

"A combined order with you." He paused and waited for her reaction.

She said nothing.

"The airport manager's on board," he said, "Already allowed some of my flights through."

She leaned back against the worn naugahyde booth, settling into the game of cat and mouse. "What kind of planes?"

"A Gulfstream and a DC-9."

Layla raised an eyebrow. "Who owns them?"

"A couple guys in Lauderdale run a shield for drug planes by providing American registration to the cartels. It's complicated—big money down, more than what the plane's worth. In return these guys maintain the plane registration, and hire Vietnam vets to do the cartel runs."

She nodded.

"If the plane's seized, the pilots deny responsibility. These hooked-up guys can reclaim the plane because their corpo-ration holds the lien," Clay said.

Layla slid forward, placed her elbows on the table and picked at the label on the empty beer bottle in front of her.

"How can they do that? Someone must hold the original papers."

"They disguise ownership by sheep-dipping it—you know, a fake identity—and pass it on to straw owners. It's a slick process, an old scheme used by the CIA."

"The CIA? Come on, Clay," she said with a slight frown. *Do I look naïve?* She flipped her dark hair over one shoulder. Clay's gaze shifted to Layla's long elegant neck.

He caught himself, looked away, and readjusted his long legs under the table before speaking. "These vets couriered traffickers from Colombia to Miami for the CIA. Talk about walking the line. They did time for trafficking, but they're back, and they're hotshot pilots."

"Your shipments came in with no problem?" Layla asked.

"Like I said, I have connections, and the players, they've worked it out."

"Does that include the Gulf Cartel?"

He nodded.

"Hmm. I've got to think things through," Layla said. "When's your next run?"

"Got a few details to sort out. I hear you're growing the European market—this'll get you a lot closer to that trip across the pond."

Layla gave him a cool smile. "If I didn't know better I'd think you were spying on me."

"Layla," Clay said with a chuckle. "I'm just trying to keep up with you."

She looked at him a second too long before she continued. "Can I get back to you?"

"Sure." Clay finished off his beer. "Let me know where and when."

⊡⊡⊡

Layla and Carlos left Ensenada immediately after the meeting, heading for the road to Culiacan. Carlos high-powered the black SUV through the moonless night while Layla closed her eyes and imagined the impact of bringing in new business on her own. In a four hundred billion dollar global industry, she could begin to stake out her territory.

"By working with us, FARC will see Clay as a real player," she confided to Carlos.

"Basta! Always business!" Carlos said, still in a huff.

Layla composed herself before responding. "Yes, it is. Business that allows you to drive a new Escalade, wear expensive suits and five thousand peso boots, and drink Don Julio and Dom Perignon. Let me remind you: My uncle's in prison and he's left me in charge. Get used to it!"

She leaned against the window, pulling as far away from Carlos as possible. *Always fighting.* She turned her attention to the darkness outside. It was a lonely two-lane road, not used much even in the daytime. Though she couldn't make out the mountains that surrounded them she knew they were there.

They rode in silence, absorbed in separate thoughts. Carlos concentrated on dodging potholes. Layla contemplated moving powder with Clay.

The rules were changing and in this game they all had to stay ahead of the curve. She was anxious to run the idea by El Patrón. But they had a long drive ahead.

CHAPTER 2

Mexico's invasion by foreigners began with the blue-eyed devil Hernán Cortés in 1519 and lasted until the early twentieth century when the US occupied Veracruz for six months during the Mexican Revolution. Even France tried her hand at dominating Mexico and failed. Twice.

Between the invading armies and the church's duplicitous missionaries, corrupt government, crooked bankers, and propped-up corporations, every Mexican citizen learns early on one explicit truth: Trust no neighbor, priest, politician, nor government official.

No small wonder why El Patrón chose Layla as his stand-in while he sat behind bars for the second time. In Mexico, only family bonds are sacred—all else fails.

Sinaloa, Mexico

Shortly before El Patrón's second capture, his third and current wife, Elena, reached out to El Zoyo, first lieutenant for the Culiacan Cartel, Patrón's right hand man.

"I need to see him," Elena said.

Zoyo sighed into his phone. "Impossible."

"It's been months." Elena, a former beauty queen, knew her effect on men; she usually got her way. But Zoyo, another of those fortunate souls who generally got what he wished for, was not one to fall for a pretty face.

Presumably a rancher in Sinaloa, Zoyo was one of the few drug lords with the audacity to clarify his "legal" business connections on television. The slender, dark-skinned trafficker had a clear penchant for showmanship, revealed by the way he wore his jet black hair—perfectly coiffed and a shade too long. Behind his back he was referred to as El Pelo, the hair.

Elena continued in a whining tone. "I know he comes down from the mountains. I can meet him in a safe house. His girls, the twins, don't even know they have a papa."

El Zoyo was getting bored. "Phones are dangerous," he said gruffly. "How did you get this number?"

"Don Zoyo," Elena said in a haughty tone. "Of course I can find your number. You know who I'm married to."

Zoyo changed gears. "Let me see what I can do," he said in the smarmy voice he used to silence others. He ran his fingers through his hair. "But do not call me again. I'll be in touch."

Elena was no stranger to the narco world; she knew the dangers. But she missed her husband. She wanted to see him and soon.

🔁🔁🔁

Patrón's first prison escape had lasted eleven years. Getting out of Alicante Grande proved the easy part. Staying free was harder; he spent no more than a night or two in any one spot. When he wasn't running from the feds or the scum-sucking DEA, he was dodging competitors who wanted more territory. To ensure his safety, he was always accompanied by a bodyguard.

Living on the edge was nothing new for a cartel boss and thirty years into the job Patrón retained his stamina. He made offers many of the smaller cartels could not refuse. The Culiacan Cartel was a powerful entity, the new Rome. Competitors had one chance only to accept his offer—el plata o el plomo—the silver or the lead. His bloody reputation preceded him. And his empire grew.

His last couple weeks of freedom had been especially trying. After attending a reunion with Zoyo in the mountains near Valle del Gatos, the destitute pueblo they came from, he decided to head to Culiacan and one of his six safe houses.

"Elena wants to see you," Zoyo had told him. "How long has it been?"

"I can't remember."

"Why not meet her at Angelina's?" Zoyo asked. "She's always willing to do you a favor, cabrón! The perfect ex-wife—grateful for her beautiful home and all you've done for her."

"Sure, why not?" the drug lord said. "Contact Elena."

A week later, Patrón was having lunch in Angelina's kitchen when a hammering sounded at the front door, then it burst open.

"Run!" his former wife called from the living room. "Federales!"

Someone had tipped off the authorities. El Patrón's bodyguard held off the feds long enough for his boss to slip through a carefully disguised trapdoor under a bathtub before agents filled the room. As the drug lord made his way through the tunnel below, all hell broke loose above him—Angelina's screams nearly overrode the sound of a sledge hammer destroying the tub.

In spite of the near miss, he escaped to Mazatlan to connect with Elena and the twins. Leaving the mountains with its network of remote back roads and protective neighbors could be a dangerous proposition, but El Patrón opted for it. He took up residence with his young family in a modest condo on the beach for a long-overdue reunion.

Two days later as the drug lord cooked breakfast for his wife and twins, another telltale knock came at the door. Mexican Navy troops stormed in. This time he didn't get away. Photos blazed around the world—the unpretentious condo, the beachside resort, close-ups of his daughters' matching pink suitcases. Now in a maximum security prison, El Patrón awaited sentencing by his government, the same one that had denied his extradition to the US.

ᘐᘐᘐ

Alicante Grande Prison, Mexico City

The metal prison door clanged against the grate as Layla watched her uncle walk down the hall with a prison guard tagging behind. Patrón looked nonchalant about being behind bars as he pushed the dark hair from his eyes. Of course, his prison terms were a far cry from those of his fellow inmates, not uncommon for narco mafia and other heavy hitters who paid off prison authorities in exchange for special favors. He had a chef, a suite of cells made up with a good bed and fine linens, even HDTV. He lacked nothing but his freedom.

"Tio," Layla said in a whisper.

El Patrón watched his stylish niece walk towards him, dressed in five thousand peso skinny jeans and a black designer jacket.

"Abrazos, mi amor," Patrón said as he embraced her.

Layla saw her uncle had aged since his recent incarceration. His dark, close-set eyes lacked their usual sparkle—she'd always thought he looked more like an overgrown schoolboy than a drug kingpin who'd committed horrifying crimes.

Usually fastidious, he hadn't even shaved. Maybe being in prison again was too much for him. He settled in at a table the guards had arranged as a makeshift office, designed for meetings with lawyers and cronies. Layla sat in one of the metal chairs and allowed Patrón to do the same.

"How are you, Uncle?"

"Ain't gonna be no Shawshank escape this time," he said, a sour look crossing his face. How well he remembered it, all those years ago, hiding in a laundry cart and being pushed out the prison gates to freedom. He turned to glare at the guard.

"Really watching me, but enough of that. How's it going, chica?" he asked, switching gears. "Any problems?"

"No, Tio. We've made progress in Chicago with heroin—we have a guy on every corner."

"Good. Cocaine?"

"The Zetas are making a move, pushing more product into southern Europe through Africa."

"So do you need help? Should I call Zoyo?"

"No!" Her protest was fast and emphatic. This was her first test. She had to push the envelope to stay in the elite circle. "I've got ideas. Clay Lasalle set up a meeting in Ensenada."

"The BC bud guy?"

"Si. He offered me a business deal." She lowered her voice as she glanced at the guard at the rear of the extensive room. She gave him a cold, hard stare, daring him to look away before continuing. "Moving coke from Colombia to

Cancun by plane. He cut a deal with FARC and he's getting pinche prices. Using a DC-9 and a Gulfstream."

Patrón raised an eyebrow. "Any problems with customs?"

"He got it cleared. The airport manager's on board and approved drop-ins."

El Patrón nodded in approval. "How 'bout moving product?"

"He has it set up with the Gulf Cartel. But we could skip them, use North Africa as a staging ground, then on to Europe."

"Better. Easier to buy off African officials. Hmm, the EU..." He paused momentarily. "But can you handle it?"

Surprised by the unexpected gibe, she spit out, "Of course!"

"You're not sitting behind a desk any more. No more accounting. You're a quick learner but I won't be around to fix your mistakes."

"There won't be any mistakes! You trained me." Though she felt like sulking, she masked her feelings, folded her arms across her chest, and changed the subject—a ploy she'd learned from her uncle. "Have we ever dealt directly with FARC?"

He gave her a long stare. "No, Escobar originally. We moved product in the eighties when Colombia couldn't get a shipment into Florida because the DEA had a microscope up their ass."

"So our routes are safer?" she asked, satisfied to have shifted away from competence issues.

"Claro. They couldn't get product to their biggest customer but we could, so we started charging in coke, not cash. A real coup." He settled back into his chair, a near smile on his face.

"What do I tell Lasalle?"

"We need numbers and turnaround from Bogota to Cancun. Who's he got flying?"

"Vietnam vets."

"The crazy gringos?" her uncle asked, surprised. "They're all loco from the war years. And always broke."

"He told me about some scheme, that the CIA works with the pilots," Layla said.

"Could be. The chingóns at the CIA and DEA are tricky. They traded coke for arms back then."

She twirled a long strand of hair around her index finger. "So it's true."

"Don't be surprised. They're part of the reason I'm here. And along with our federales they killed your brother in that goddamn ambush in Guatemala." Patrón placed a palm on his forehead. "Puta de madre! He took a bullet through the heart."

She hated talking about her long-dead brother but it was part of their dance, the Reynoldo fairy tale, homage to the fallen. "How could I forget?"

One pinche bullet had changed the trajectory of their lives. Losing his beloved nephew after being thrown into prison that first time had created a vacuum, with El Patrón leaning heavily on Zoyo, much to Layla's dismay. She well remembered approaching her uncle eleven years earlier. Then, as now, they'd sat across from each other in Alicante Grande Prison. El Patrón's effusive praise had given Layla every indication she could simply step into her older brother's shoes.

But when she'd broached the subject of when she would take over for Reynoldo, El Patrón had exploded in anger. Layla never saw it coming. Subdued by the unexpected outburst, she had whispered that her uncle had always told her she was like him, that with Reynoldo gone the cartel needed someone on the outside. He had shouted so loud it brought the guard running, while Layla floundered in raw emotion she was unable to hide.

Eventually, her uncle had overcome his anger and calmed down. She was not ready, he'd told her, not at only twenty-four, and a woman. She started to protest but he assured her he had promised her nothing. Seeing her ashen face, he began to console her. She was good, very good, she knew the organization inside out. But it was not her time. Not then.

That was a decade earlier, and even as the dead brother's promising younger sister, machismo ruled. Too young, and the kiss of death—female. Women were either Madonnas or whores. Jefes, bosses, dealmakers? No way.

Fast forward: an escape, a recapture, another vacuum at the top. Déjà vu.

Now, El Patrón placed his hands flat on the table. "So here we are again. You haven't had a lot of experience. Women in this business can't afford to be weak. You sure you're ready?"

She nodded. What choice did she have?

"While I'm in here, it's best to keep things with the families—ours and Zoyo's. He'll continue with heroin and meth, and handle the muscle. You'll be in charge of pot and coca."

"Have you talked to Zoyo about Little Beto?" Layla asked, referring to Zoyo's son.

For a split second her uncle looked away. "No. What's to say? Sure, it's bad luck Little Beto was taken down. What're ya gonna do?"

"Is there a link between Beto's capture and your capture now, Tio? He's Zoyo's kid but that doesn't mean he's squeaky clean." She began to warm to her subject. "He's been sitting in a prison up north for years. Who knows what deals he's been offered?"

Patrón shook his head in warning. "Don't even think about it. Zoyo and me go back to Valle. We started out together in that shithole." Patrón scratched his left ear. "And I don't need a turf war, not with me on the inside." He waved his hand, dismissing the subject. "Now, this Canadian. What'd ya think?"

"He looks young for the power, but you were, too, when you took over from El Padrino."

Her uncle nodded. Everyone knew Mexico's legendary cartel boss, a godfather-like figure, had trusted El Patrón enough to give him the chance to succeed.

"They tell me Lasalle's a Buddhist, and he's into martial arts. Sounds crazy, but he doesn't play games," Layla said. "The Canadians, they're different from the gringos."

"Listen, I trust your decision, Layla. You're family, and family is *all* that matters. If his prices are good we'll cut costs and time in getting it to Africa, then Europe. This could be your piece of the action, chiquita. Our growth. Your future."

"We're on then?" she asked, willing her voice to sound self-assured.

"Yes! Oh, one more thing. I want you to see Zoyo at the ranch. Make sure you're completely coordinated with him, okay?"

She looked away. An order was an order.

"Yes, Tio."

Chapter 3

Vancouver, BC, Canada

When Clay wasn't doing drug deals he hunkered down in the same prime pot-growing country east of Vancouver where he'd first learned cultivation as a teenager. Back then in the 1990s, it hadn't taken him long to realize that growing sweet sensimilla was his life's calling.

In his twenties, as a protégé to a dealer named Minh with connections to the Red Dragons, an Asian organized crime syndicate, Clay was tutored by the Vietnamese national in Aikido and eastern religions. Clay wasn't dabbling, he was going at his spiritual overhaul seriously, from every angle. His introduction to the martial arts opened a porthole to a different world. After studying Buddhism, he got the idea of reinventing himself—he yearned to become a samurai.

Clay eventually broke with Minh to grow his business and found his own organization, the Rainbow Tribe. He modeled it after the Red Dragons and held Asian-inspired initiation ceremonies for his gang. He became the part—he was the samurai.

After a decade growing the best marijuana on the Northwest coast, having earned the nickname Mr. BC Bud, Clay decided to break into cocaine. He set his sights on Mexico. In Mexico a kilo of coke was only eight grand versus the twenty grand it commanded in Vancouver. And one product Mexico lacked was high-quality bud even though a strain called pretendica had surfaced. But to a pot connoisseur it was just that—a pretender to the throne. All Clay needed was a connection.

Rumors floated around that the cartels coveted his bud. He had one Mexican contact, a friend of a friend, who'd gone to school with Little Beto, son of El Zoyo, first lieutenant to none other than El Patrón, head of the Culiacan Cartel.

Beto was a second generation narco with ivy league credentials and their first meeting took place in Mexico. Clay was at the top of his game with demand for his bud at an all-time high.

"Is it true you use helicopters and snow mobiles to bring pot across the border?" Beto asked.

"Hell, yes! RVs, choppers, anything with wheels or wings. I'd use huskies with sleds if the dogs could pull a half ton."

"Your bud is huge, man, bigger than Humboldt County." Though he usually refrained from smoking, Beto accepted a joint from his new associate. "We can make arrangements," Beto said after taking a hit. He handed the joint back to Clay. "No one has the primo sensimilla you got. We'll do a trade—your bud for my coke."

He dealt with Beto for a while, but Mexico was just a stepping stone and Clay's quest for the best and cheapest coke eventually took him to the source, Colombia. Through networking, with his reputation preceding him, he met the right people. By going direct to FARC he cut out any middlemen. Next up came transportation and the task of shipping product. His FARC contacts suggested he piggyback onto the Gulf Cartel's loads until a better plan came along.

That's when Clay stumbled onto a couple Vietnam vets in Bogota who piloted Learjets and flew contraband back and forth from Colombia to Mexico.

"We can take it from Bogota to Cancun," the pilot named

Donavon told him after a brief introduction from Clay's local Colombian contact. The rangy, dark-haired vet looked like an aging athlete who still had the physique and stamina, but just barely. He dressed like a surfer and came with another guy in tow. Clay later learned it was his little brother, Jake. They met at the Club Mocambo, a popular expat hangout.

"From Cancun, getting coke north depends on routes the Mexicans developed decades ago. But we have contacts. Your product will be safe with us," the pilot assured him.

Clay was running out of options. Discreetly checking around, he vetted the vets. Donavon, he was told, had extraordinary flying talent. Granted he'd had issues with alcohol and substance abuse, but that could apply to almost anyone in the business. Sources claimed he was currently clean, and that Jake kept close tabs on his older sibling. Clay's first shipments with the Gulf Cartel had gone without a hitch, but it was time to break out on his own. He contacted the brothers and made them an offer.

Clay had learned early that communication was the ultimate Mexican litmus test. One figured out what was happening, or one could find oneself without a head. In Mexico, justice was not only blind, its eyes were gouged out. The unofficial count on drug-related deaths since President Calderon's War on Drugs began in 2006 was one hundred and seventy-five thousand, though journalists claimed it was more like two hundred thousand and climbing.

Instinctively, Clay maneuvered through it all, somehow managing to end both cartel relationships without losing his head or his standing in the drug world. He had a sixth sense for self preservation and relied on intuition. If anything came up in his proposed arrangement with Layla that he couldn't handle, he'd call on the Vietnam vets. With their help, he'd figure it out.

CHAPTER 4

With El Patrón behind bars, El Zoyo typically managed daily operations of the Culiacan Cartel. Zoyo was chiefly occupied with heroin and the meth business, revolutionized by El Patrón years earlier. With a US crackdown on the sale of pseudoephedrine, meth soon became Mexico's number one export. Throughout the mountains of Sinaloa, Jalisco, Michoacán and Nayarit, El Patrón constructed large meth labs and rapidly expanded his organization. Then it was time for the cartel to set up shop in the States and they chose Chicago as their headquarters.

The cartel bosses knew a rebirth in the use of heroin was coming fast on the heels of a new American trend—an addiction to prescription narcotics. The Chicago market for an opiate substitute overshadowed even that of New York, and Zoyo stepped up to fill the void.

With Zoyo mired in Chicago's heroin demands the coke trade needed assistance, and Layla was ready. Already heading up marijuana sales, the old standby that nearly handled itself, she yearned for a bigger challenge—cocaine was just the ticket.

Though Patrón had downplayed the fact that Little Beto was languishing in a US federal prison for years, Layla knew that he, too, had an uneasy feeling about Zoyo's son. Could Beto remain mum after all these years?

Before his confinement, Beto was a top player. The kid

was whip smart and responsible for coordinating multi-ton cocaine shipments from South America through Mexico into the States. His out-of-the-box thinking proved what a first-rate education could pull off. He had tried every transportation angle: 747 cargo jets, narco-subs, container ships, fishing vessels, buses, rail cars, and even eighteen-wheelers once NAFTA got rolling. His savvy grew the cartel into a serious organization on the scale of a Fortune 500 company, landing El Patrón a spot on Forbes' list of richest billionaire businessmen. Twice.

With the exception of Patrón and Zoyo, the new cartel overlords were second generation, schooled in the States with degrees in business or economics. They wore Polo shirts and designer jeans, and looked more like grad students than drug bosses. The narco juniors earned the right to be involved by their DNA and stayed in the game because it was the family business, no different from a cattle ranch or chain of department stores. With their prestigious educations, old school dogma flew out the window and over-the-top profits poured in. Cartels could afford cutting-edge technology in any field—from submarines to high-tech tunnels under the border. And when these narco hot shots got into the groove, their know-how commanded the largest market share of all drug sales on the worldwide stage. Ever.

To retain key player status, Layla had to find cheaper product and more efficient transit. Time to prove what she could do for the cartel, no matter where El Patrón spent the night—in the mountains of the Sierra Madre Occidental or behind prison bars.

Bogota, Colombia

Clay had to make a trip to Colombia to pay off a shipment and see that an airstrip was carved out of an anonymous jungle near Bogota. A FARC lieutenant had told him of a small town a hundred miles north where peasants could strip out foliage long and wide enough for his needs.

"You think you've seen tight landings?" Donavon bragged to Clay while out on the town one night in Bogota. "Back in the day I was king of the short runway. Love those old prop planes."

But these days Gulfstreams and DC-9s ruled. High-tech aviation was smuggling's new wave. The jets came equipped with adjusted wing design, torqued fuselages, gravel pit attachments, and beefy tires designed to take outback landings. With sixty years of flying under their collective belts, the brothers knew how to land aircraft. Vietnam training had given them all the right stuff: a surplus of daring and a wariness that translated into that proverbial sixth sense. In their world night landings were the norm, with nothing but flashlights to beckon a plane from the sky.

"Good GPS is key, but most important," Donavon said, "is flying low, under eight thousand feet. Don't want air traffic control to get their panties in a twist."

Clay knew the markups he could command in the pot trade, but he was amazed at the excessive markups on coke. Payments to the peasants who ran the fincas were included in FARC's price—a mere five thousand dollars per kilo. After transportation costs, it was pure profit.

Sure, there were start-up costs such as the outlying airstrip. But the gringo vets had a line on a plane so he didn't need to lay out that chunk of change.

He was lucky to be Canadian. The Colombians had no

anti-Canada sentiments. Hell, who did? Canadians were the Boy Scouts of the western world, the maple leaf kings. No apple pie or stars and stripes for him. Pure maple syrup all the way.

🔲🔲🔲

A week after his meeting with Layla, Clay stood in a newly tamped-down field bordered by meter high brush, one hundred miles north of Bogota. Donavon insisted it was an airstrip, Clay expressed doubts.

"Can a plane really land on this?" he asked, looking around.

"What do you think, my man?" the pilot chortled. "Jeez. I've seen a lot worse!"

Clay was still shaking his head when a Colombian peasant came up behind him. "Señor? My jefe says any time you want to use the field, it is ready for you."

Clay turned to Donavon. "What about tires? Can they handle these bumps with a full load?"

"They're souped up for dirt fields. I may have been born at night, but not last night."

"Hmm. I don't know," Clay said, shaking his head.

Donavon patted the Colombian on the back. "Our Canadian here has a fear of flying. This isn't United, Clay. You were expecting LAX?" He cracked up, coughed and spit onto the dirt. "We'll do a trial run. Get over it! You're in South America now, amigo, not Vancouver."

For the first time in a long while, Clay questioned his instincts. He was on a distant continent with a recovering cocaine cowboy who flew Learjets as though they were bucking broncos. He hoped to hell Donavon knew what he was talking about.

Chapter 5

Rancho Verde, Sinaloa, Mexico

Mornings at Rancho Verde began with the sky bursting into fiery hues as the sun blazed its way over the Sierra Madre Occidental Mountains and lit the valley beyond.

Layla dreaded going to Zoyo's ranch, but it was a duty that needed attending to. She hated Zoyo, with very good reason. When Carlos came down with food poisoning that morning she nearly canceled, but decided it was best to just do it, even without a bodyguard. She talked herself into a power pose, amping up her feeling of control by dressing impeccably in skinny leather pants by Valentino and a Helmut Lang blouse of cream-colored linen.

After passing through elaborate gates at the guard house and being waved through by a young man in a dark blue uniform, Layla drove up the half mile tree-lined drive that led to Rancho Verde. Alongside the paved asphalt, Kentucky blue grass lay like a soft green carpet on the other side. Ficus and towering royal Poinciana with large boughs in full green splendor grew between the occasional King or Queen palm. In all those years since she'd last been there, it hadn't changed much—still the impressive entrance leading to immaculate grounds bordered by white slat horse fences.

She tried to purge the wretched memory from her mind: the worst remembrance of all—the one she had kept secret

26

from everyone—that day in the horse barn with Rosalia, her favorite of Zoyo's horses, and the new filly.

Layla had been twelve years old that year. She was visiting Little Beto and his sister at their father's ranch for a week, the same as every summer, a time she looked forward to.

One night after supper "uncle" Zoyo asked if Layla wanted to see Rosalia's new filly. Her love of horses was well known, and her childlike excitement at the offer was obvious. They walked outside the rambling villa and under a pergola lined by sweet-smelling Flor de Maya trees towards the horse barns in the distance. Zoyo was a trim man in his thirties who'd always shown a strong interest in pleasing his partner's pretty daughter. He told her Rosalia was in a different barn now because she was nursing.

"Which one?" she asked.

"Over there," he said, motioning with a slight upward movement of the chin, so typical of this man who conserved his energy as though it were a non-renewable resource.

She ran across the carefully raked dirt that surrounded each barn and entered the one Zoyo had pointed out, searching for her special horse. Though the stables appeared deserted, she heard stamping in the straw at the end of a long row of quiet, closed stalls. On approaching, she saw the roan mare. Beside Rosalia stood an exact replica, in fuzzy miniature.

"Can I go inside?" she asked Zoyo who was soon beside her.

He nodded. "Si, mi amor, por supuesto." Yes, of course, my love.

Zoyo smiled at the young girl he had groomed into a budding horsewoman. He took full credit for teaching her all there was to know about horses and their habits.

He stepped up to the red cedar stall and unlatched

the gate, allowing the musky aroma of straw and horse to escape. As the door creaked slowly open, Layla entered the stall where Rosalia and the new filly stood together, watching her from the far corner.

A low nicker emerged from the mare. The horse knew the girl yet she moved in front of her foal, either as a protective measure towards her offspring or to greet her friend.

Layla was dazzled and turned to look at Zoyo who watched the scene with satisfaction. She moved closer to Rosalia and touched the underside of the mare's soft mouth and rubbed her scratchy whiskers. She ran her hand over the mare's coat and at the same time, gazed raptly at the filly. Layla watched, enthralled, as the newborn animal nuzzled against its mother's flank.

After a minute, Zoyo spoke softly. "Okay, mi dulce, Rosalia needs to feed her little one. Let's go back to the house. It's getting dark."

The girl, still caught up in wonder at the scene, allowed Zoyo to take her hand in his as they stepped out of the stall. Dusk had faded to night and the barn was dark save for a dull yellow light at the far end of the structure.

As they walked towards it, Zoyo's soft hand in Layla's squeezing lightly, he said in a low tone, "So lovely, very lovely, Layla, wasn't it?"

"Yes," she said, squeezing back.

They walked closer to the light. Then he stopped. "Wait a minute, come in here." He ducked into one of the open stalls. "Let's stop for a moment, just a moment." Two bales of fresh straw sat in the empty stall. "Here," he said, motioning. "Sit down."

Layla and Zoyo sat side by side, her hand resting comfortably in his. "Layla." His voice was soft and husky, almost a whisper. "Do you know how special you are to me?"

His other hand now moved to her arm, and he shifted her body ever so slightly towards his.

"Yes, Zoyo," the girl said, feeling pride.

"Mi dulce, I can never tell you how much I love you, how beautiful you are to me."

The girl blushed in the darkened barn, unsure of what to say. "I know ..." she said.

"No, my darling, you will never know how much."

And then he slid his hand from her arm and put it on her knee. He pushed her short dress aside and moved his hand up her leg. Layla wasn't expecting it and became alarmed, but didn't know how to respond. This was her father's friend, their family friend, Zoyo. She tried to push his hand away but it was firm, and then his hand was well up her skirt, high up her thigh.

She went totally numb; for a moment it felt like her heart stopped beating. Frightened, she didn't know what to do—he'd caught her off guard. He slid her off the bale onto the prickly straw that covered the stable floor. He dropped down beside her, one arm now on top of her, overpowering her. She struggled, but he was much stronger and easily dominated her.

"No, no, no, not right!" she cried, pushing against him with everything she had, hitting him, sobbing. "No!" she screamed to the empty barn, fighting him, his body now on top of hers. "Help! Help me! Help me!"

"Easy, girl, easy" he said softly, as though quieting a frightened horse.

And that was all she chose to remember.

🔄🔄🔄

Layla sighed, trying to push away the uninvited girlhood memory that had niggled its way back into her thoughts, the day that changed her life forever. Gaining control she shook it off, aware she was far from alone in what she'd experienced. She knew of other girls who had been molested by uncles, neighbors, or family friends like Zoyo. The problem crossed all social and economic boundaries. It wasn't talked about much. But whispered secrets spilled out with many a tear from girls who confided in sisters, aunts, or friends.

Being molested by Zoyo nearly broke her. Forced to keep an unholy secret, Layla carried a shame she couldn't express or ignore. She lived two lives: one in which she embodied goodness, as though trying to outwit what fate had dealt her, and in that other life she took wild chances, tempting the gods to punish her for the mistake she felt responsible for.

Now, years later, even hearing Zoyo's name disgusted her, but she had to deal with the dreaded scum on a business level.

As she drove up the driveway, a lone vulture flew high in the cloudless sky above the ranch's manicured grounds, circling in wide concentric loops, no doubt searching for an animal that lay dead on the ground far below.

Layla pulled to a stop in the parking area next to a four-car garage where a uniformed valet stood waiting. She glanced skyward through the car's open window and straightened the classic blouse over the waistband of her leather pants.

She swung one perfect foot, clad in a red Valentino pump, out of the navy BMW 7 Series sedan, then the other. She planted both feet on terra firma and stood, shaking off a shiver in the warm country air. It was time to face her demons.

CHAPTER 6

The maid opened the metal-encased front door and showed Layla into the foyer. At first glance she remembered it all: the lofty ceiling with hefty beams, wrought-iron chandelier, chalky stone walls with tiny pebbles stacked on end, carefully shoved into grout lines, like layers of memories.

Layla forced a smile at the diminutive woman in black maid's uniform who stood before her.

"Buenos dias, señora. He is waiting for you in the study," the maid said.

Oh, the hallowed study, with the arched boveda ceiling of rounded red brick and a library, as though Zoyo ever read a book.

Layla's leather heels clicked on parquet floors as she followed the maid down the darkened hallway. The mahogany study door swung open and she spotted the pendejo sitting behind a desk, smoking a hand-rolled cigar. Probably Cuban, even though Mexico now cultivated some of the world's finest tobacco. Zoyo pushed his chair back and stood as the maid ushered in his visitor and quietly exited the room.

"Layla," he said in the voice she had once found soothing, so many years ago.

"Hola." She hated this asshole as much as she hated the smell of lingering cigar smoke that hung like a cloud in the

31

well-appointed room. El Zoyo, still polluting the world.

"How are you?" he asked.

Layla gave a curt nod, indicating she had no intention of going overboard with this reunion. She found it difficult to even look at the man.

"Sientate," he said in a commanding tone, picking up on her resistance as he motioned to a leather chair not far from the desk. He sat down like a king on his throne attending to a commoner. Layla sunk into the chair, crossed her legs, and finally her arms.

In no mood for small talk she jumped right in. "As you know, Patrón wanted me to see you about my handling cocaine. I'm mostly up to speed thanks to Julio in Culiacan but I want to know more about the Colombian end on purchase and distribution."

"Well, we've started to buy coca fincas directly from FARC," Zoyo said, eyeing her carefully to gauge her reaction.

"What?" She caught herself just short of shouting. "When did that happen? Does Patrón know?"

"No need to tell him before he went inside, and production hasn't slowed. No doubt Julio's figures confirm that. We divided up the territories while you were still sitting behind a desk. Surely Patrón must have explained it to you," he said, giving her a confident stare.

"About the territories—yes—but he said nothing about FARC!"

"It's been in place more than a month now," Zoyo said. "We were looking for new Colombian partners since we lost the Respeto clan. Things are all stirred up down there. We needed to strengthen our supply line. Patrón was busy trying to stay out of the feds' way and his freedom was more important than new ops since he was on the run. No time to consider new deals. He told me to handle anything that came up."

"But why is FARC selling off their fincas?"

"They've decided to cooperate with the government by getting rid of coca production facilities. And they're doing it by selling them directly to us," he said.

"That's ridiculous! The Colombian government will know they're pulling a scam."

"You know the Colombian government doesn't give a damn as long as it looks clean. They'll report to the pinche gringos that they don't have those FARC fincas in their possession, and still get War on Drugs' dollars. It's all a game—I don't have to tell you that, chica." His smile made the hair on the back of her neck quiver.

In a cocksure manner, he brushed his fingers lightly over his hair. Layla stared at him as he postured with the insane mane he labored over with so many beauty products it would keep a telenovela star occupied for weeks. *What a fucking idiot.*

"Hijole! We're bringing in two tons of cocaine by air. I've arranged for Lasalle, the Canadian bud guy, to do a run for us. It's a two-million-dollar deal." She chewed her lower lip, a nervous habit she'd abandoned long ago.

"Really? I hope it's with FARC fincas that still fall under their protection or he could have trouble," Zoyo said.

"What kind of trouble?" she asked.

"The government could be watching to see if some cabrón is stealing from them right after the deals have been made. You know how these things happen."

"Jésus y Maria. What fucking timing!"

Zoyo smirked. Layla knew he couldn't be happier that she was running into trouble, getting sabotaged on her first solo deal.

"Where's it coming from? Your load?" Zoyo asked.

"Lasalle set something up in Bogota, then to an airfield

north of there and onto Guatemala."

"FARC connects with part of their faction in Guatemala, too," he said. "It's a new alliance, close to Mexico without as much trouble. The cartel there is very capable. They clear the run for final destination to Cancun. This'll be huge for us, owning the fincas. We'll have full control."

"I've got to warn him about the changes," Layla said, more to herself than Zoyo.

"When's the shipment arriving?"

"Soon."

"I hope it's worthwhile, stepping outside the box," Zoyo said, baiting her. He looked first into her eyes before giving her a thorough once over from head to toe. She read his vile thoughts, re-crossed her legs, straightened her back, not giving an inch. Again she straightened her blouse over her slacks, willfully ignoring his lecherous gaze.

"It'll be worth it. How many fincas will change over?" she asked.

"We have no way of knowing. They plan to take it one at a time. See what will appease the feds. Could be a lot, could be a little. There's sure to be corrupt officials who sign off on these things. Depends how capable our FARC friends are in their dealings with those they've set up."

"Why didn't you tell me sooner?" Her voice was a low growl. "You're withholding key information! I need to know these things immediately." She wished she could pulverize him with her stare and rid the world of the despot. "So in the future, where do I get my info? From you?"

He slid open the center drawer of his desk and nonchalantly rummaged around until he found a sheet of ivory letterhead with Rancho Verde embossed at the top in dark green lettering.

"He'll give you all information in Mexico *and* Guatemala,

should it come to that," Zoyo said, with an arrogant look. He jotted down a name and number and leaned slowly across the desk offering the paper, making her reach in so close she could smell his repugnant cologne. He held onto it just a moment too long once she'd grasped it, to throw her off guard.

"But this is not my problem," he said as he let go of the stationery.

She glared at the psychopath before her, willing her face to remain impassive.

"Oh, a word of warning." Zoyo paused dramatically before continuing. "The Colombians and the Guatemalans, they're both competing for our business. Don't get caught in the middle."

CHAPTER 7

Layla gunned the accelerator on her BMW as she tore down the asphalt driveway, away from Rancho Verde, away from Zoyo, and away from her toxic memories.

Of all the pinche luck. FARC decides to win over the Colombian government now, just as she and Clay plan to bring coke into Cancun. Back in Culiacan, she vowed to herself, she would sit down with Julio and go over each and every aspect of the cocaine end of the business ad nauseam. No more second-hand news.

She pictured Zoyo and his disgusting manner. Hijole! She'd rather spend a week with Carlos in a foul mood than a minute with that lech. What was it with the men in her life? Zoyo, Carlos, even Reynoldo when he was alive, God rest his miserable soul. *Are all men pendejos, or do I attract them? Will I always be surrounded by men who treat me as though I'm a goddamn doormat? Orale! I'm in charge of a goddamn cartel. I'm no lightweight! What's going on?*

When she was well away from the ranch, Layla pulled over on a deserted berm and stopped. She gulped for air as she slammed her fists against the steering wheel. She needed to think, and more importantly, breathe.

Her plea came fast and furiously. *Save me Lord! I need help.* But how? It might be time to see Our Lady of Guadalupe at the Basilica of the Virgin. Do penance to Mexico's patron saint; prostrate herself in front of the Virgin like hundreds of thousands did at the shrine in Mexico City every year, pleading for guidance. Maybe she'd gain strength from Guadalupe. *Prayer works for others, why not me?*

There was another option, very popular in the drug world of Culiacan. She could pay homage at the shrine of San Malverde, the patron saint of narcos and smugglers. Before deals and dangerous jobs, drug lords and their henchmen beat a path to the unassuming church in an obscure neighborhood, praying for luck, money, and their very lives before the grave of the former bandido, hanged as a robber in 1909. His legendary shrine always overflowed with flowers, beer, rum, cash, and cigarettes. *Can Malverde deliver for me?*

Lost in thought, she recalled a mystical reading given to her by a Nahua shaman after traveling all day with her mother to a faraway pueblo. She had been a young girl at the time but she could see the man, Don Cuauhtemoc, like it was yesterday: his precious stones, his gentle manner and his invocations to the gods of lightning and wind.

"The woman is coming..." That's what the shaman said. That was the message her mother had put so much faith in. Layla had dreamt many times since then about the old man positioning his stones and seeds on the slab table in his twig hut as he divined her future, all the while gazing at her through half-closed eyes. *Can his mysterious message help me now?*

At that moment, something ignited within Layla, not unlike the lightning bolts summoned by the mystical shaman so long ago. A flood of emotions bathed her body and she felt warm all over. An unknown entity seemed to inhabit her and she felt a surge of pride in her sense of self and who she was. A fervent feeling overtook her.

In a flash, Layla realized what was happening. She was holding her own in a world filled with men: strong men, corrupt men, evil men, ruthless men. Men who had mocked, belittled, and abused her.

She didn't need the Virgin's help, though her blessing would be welcome. No need to light incense at Malverde's smuggler's shrine. And dwelling on the shaman's puzzling assertion—*the woman is coming*—was no longer necessary, because now she had the answer.

She knew who she was. She was her uncle's niece. She would prevail. It came to her like a streak of lightning. She'd been hit—as though the diviner was standing right beside her, drawing energy from the sky and directing its force to her alone. She needed no religion nor dumb luck from a narco shrine to make her way in this world, to conquer all who stood in her way.

She needed only herself. She had the willpower, the drive, and the listo—the readiness—to do it all. She would triumph. At that moment, Layla took a private sacred oath and that oath was this: The woman *is* coming.

CHAPTER 8

Culiacan, Sinaloa, Mexico

Layla dwelled on how to contact Clay, but he didn't expect to hear from her until Cancun. He'd already left for Bogota—she was sure of it—where he planned to do the drug deal with FARC before traveling north. Once Clay made the purchase in Bogota, the coke would be loaded by FARC personnel into the Gulfstream jet stashed at El Dorado International Airport.

Layla needed to connect with Clay in Guatemala City, to smooth things over just in case there were any loose ends with the Guatemala Cartel. She wasn't sure if Zoyo's heads up would be a blessing or a curse.

🔁🔁🔁

Bogota, Colombia

"Donavon! I tried you at your hotel all day yesterday. No answer. You know that makes me nervous, man," Clay said.

"What's up?" Donavon asked, yawning into the receiver.

"Looks like the drop will happen this weekend." Clay said, breathing a sigh of relief.

The Bogota trip had been a balancing act. Dealing with FARC proved a breeze in comparison to convincing the

Vietnam flyboys to stay out of trouble—it was like keeping a house dust-free in a sand storm. For Donavon in particular, Bogota's temptations had proved too tempting. Rumor had it the pilot had fallen off the wagon—scoring powder was now his endgame. Bogota being Bogota, his dance card was full of names he could rely on.

"Great," Donavon said. "Just got up."

"What the hell? It's two o'clock."

"Late night. Hey, can you hold on a minute?"

Ice cubes clinked into a tumbler followed by the soft sound of liquid being poured. Cocaine wasn't Donavon's only vice. "I'm back," Donavon said.

"You don't do coffee?"

"Sure, after a little pick me up. Gotta get rid of this headache. Hair of the dog and all that," Donavon said as he stifled another yawn.

"Damnit, Donavon! You know as well as I do ya gotta keep your nose clean twenty-four hours before takeoff. No alcohol, either. Are you gonna be straight enough to fly?"

"Never had a problem yet...I could fly that baby blindfolded."

"Christ, cut the crap! We gotta meet tonight so I can explain where we're flying, how the loading'll take place, and about the touch down at the secondary field." Donavon had explained his flight plan would include stopping at the bush airstrip in northern Colombia as many ranchers had remote fincas in outback regions and were known to use private jets to fly back and forth to Bogota. This would dispel questions that might arise with a plane landing in the middle of nowhere.

"Sure, the Mocambo? About nine?"

"Bring Jake, too." Clay said.

"Yep. Over and out, amigo." Donavon signed off.

Clay said a silent prayer. If Donavon could just stay clean, it'd all come together. Once FARC and the pilots were taken care of, he could relax. In a matter of days it would all be a done deal.

In the trade, considerable down time was the ruin of many a dealer and mule. Clay knew that for a fact. Donavon was no exception. Clay didn't snort but he liked his herb, and wherever he went, he always scored, to take the edge off while waiting long hours or longer days for a deal to come down. Of course his Aikido training and his meditation practice helped. His devotion to Buddhism made him an oxymoron in the drug world, but he found being a Buddhist was a working asset. He never lost his cool and if he was "present" when he did deals, everything progressed smoothly. His mental state set the tone, even when dealing with unhinged nut jobs.

It had been a tense few days waiting for FARC's final confirmation. Clay's contact scheduled a meeting at a different location with a new lieutenant serving under FARC's chief drug dealer, the Fatman, since this run was so much more substantial.

Now, in barrio Cuidad Bolivar—mega slum—home to Bogota's poorest population and a hotbed of gang activity associated with the narco-mafia, Clay was to meet the Fatman's lieutenant, reputed to be a wiry little guy named Emil.

He parked the rental car outside a dilapidated warehouse surrounded by a four-meter cement block wall with a chain link gate. A manic junkyard dog announced his arrival with non-stop barking. Clay rang the number he was given, meanwhile watching the over-excited canine enforcer run full speed to the end of its chain, stumble backwards, and begin all over again.

41

Emil picked up and asked Clay to wait. Moments later he poked his head out the steel door.

"Hey! Silencio!" the lieutenant bellowed at the dog, as he walked to the thrice-locked gate to allow Clay entry into the yard. Introductions made, they moved towards the warehouse. On entering, they passed through a narrow room and then into a private area in back barricaded by another heavily armored door. A desk, two beat-up chairs, a rumpled cot, a few battered file cabinets, and a small corner kitchen occupied the vast space.

Emil's appearance was deceiving. Due to his slight stature and a shock of unruly hair complete with cowlick, he looked like someone's hapless younger brother rather than a FARC lieutenant. Looks aside, he spoke passable English and eagerly shared info on how FARC got into the drug trade. He was either supremely bored or hopelessly stupid, a tough call. But why point fingers? Clay was in the thick of it in Bogota, down to a funky warehouse and new FARC lieutenant as contact. He wasn't packing, probably should've been, but he had no clue where to buy a gun in Colombia. Up north he relied on martial arts to get him through, stashed a knife in his boot as backup, and rarely carried a firearm.

But he was here now. His price break was significant thanks to the Culiacan Cartel's additional ton and FARC seemed eager to work with him. They took seats at the desk, Clay on one side, Emil on the other.

"You brought cash?" Emil asked.

"Of course. Doesn't everyone?" Clay said in a joking manner.

"No. Not really. Some Mexican cartels demand our cocaine on consignment."

"You gotta be kidding! Consignment?"

"Yes, you know," Emil said. "You get money after the buyer sells it."

"On cocaine?" Clay asked.

"Si. Loco, no? FARC sends product to Guatemala for shipment to Mexico. But the Colombian cartels, they say they never receive the money and they don't send no more."

Clay shook his head. Rule number one in drug dealing: Get the cash. "How much coke?"

"Oh, more than just a few kilos. One time five hundred."

"Five hundred kilos?" Clay let out a low whistle. "How long do they have to wait?"

"Forever?"

That wasn't so unusual, the being stiffed part. But who would front anyone cocaine? He'd spent enough time in Mexico to learn not to trust Mexican promises. Even mañana didn't always mean "tomorrow," it simply meant not today.

"FARC sells cattle now," Emil said.

Clay scratched his head. "Cattle? Why?"

"We need money to finance the movement, and no drug money comes in. We wait and wait, but no money. For fifty years FARC has fought the government," he said, searching Clay's eyes to see if the Canadian realized how significant this was. "First we made money with drugs and now FARC steals ranchers' cows and sells them."

Selling drugs in and of itself seemed a bad way to finance a revolution, but cattle rustling? No wonder FARC was eager to work with him. He was a paying customer, willing to pony up cash in exchange for product. Old school.

"You know this is a cash deal. Now, when will I see product?" Clay asked.

"Soon. They usually bring it in from the fincas twice a month. It's ready this weekend."

"How about packing it into the plane?"

"They will do that for you. We have people at the airport," Emil said.

"Well, let's start counting. Fifty percent right here and the balance at the hangar. You'll give me a call when to meet you there?"

"I will contact you very soon, Señor Clay," Emil said, a smile on his lips as Clay opened the briefcase. Hundred dollar bills peeked out—so new you could almost smell the ink—banded and evenly stacked. All systems were go.

CHAPTER 9

Culiacan, Sinaloa, Mexico

On the outskirts of the city limits, Layla's BMW cruised to a stop on the shoulder of a deserted road just as the sun was going down. She rummaged in her purse, located Clay's cell number, and pulled an old-fashioned satellite phone from the back seat. It was a relic but her whereabouts would remain untraceable as long as she changed locations immediately after a call was made. She dialed. Clay picked up on the second ring.

"Hola, Clay!" she said, speaking loudly into the receiver.

"Layla?"

"Si. I need to talk to you, something important."

"What?"

She heard the tension in his voice. "FARC is selling off their fincas to us. Rather quickly. They want to pretend they're cooperating with the Colombian government and this way they'll get cash from both land and lab sales and also make up with the current administration. They're two-thirds of the way through an overall peace agreement."

"How does that affect us?" he asked.

"We'll worry about the rest later, but for now I want to make sure you get the product you've paid for from FARC. I need to meet you in Guatemala."

"Christ," he said. "I'm scheduled for the drop in two days."

"Good," Layla said. "That probably means no hold-up. They're paid?"

"Half down, half on receipt. Why do we need to meet in Guatemala?"

"Zoyo told me FARC's working with us *and* the Guatemalan cartels. We use the Guatemalans to grease inroads to Cancun and assure all goes without a hitch. Standard operating procedure, a formality. I want to make sure they know you're working with us."

"That makes sense. I expect to get hold of it soon like I said. If you don't hear from me tonight, it's on. I'll tell the pilots about the change in the flight plan. You and I will meet in Guatemala City. You have the call numbers on the plane?" he asked.

"I do, plus your number. Stay in touch if anything changes."

"Sure. Over and out."

Layla drove past the guarded entry of the gated community and into a world of graceful trees and manicured gardens. Everyone she knew or associated with in Culiacan lived here. They were her tribe, this was her territory. It was her girl in a bubble mode, she had once joked to Carlos. After her father died, Patrón brought Reynoldo, Martín, Layla, and her mother here to live until her death. Layla didn't see much of Martín though he was on the payroll.

Layla shared her house with Carlos and in spite of his infuriating personality traits, she was glad to have the company. Threats to narco families were common and Carlos's constant presence was a necessity, plain and simple.

Early on Patrón had shielded her from reports about cartel mayhem. With her finely tuned logistics skills, she hunkered down in the office, a loner, as she dealt with statistics, income, the books, far removed from details on how cartel muscle worked. She tried to avoid learning about the escalating violence that began with bloody shootouts in TJ and Juarez—bad enough—and progressed to include torture, beheadings, and hangings from bridges. She realized how valuable her life had become. Though conflicted, she kept quiet. She knew the score.

She had booked two first class seats on Aero Mexico into Guatemala City for Friday. No time to see Patrón beforehand but she had clearance. She'd make a call to Zoyo's reference, an attorney named Eduardo Suarez, and get as much info as possible from him to ensure that her shipment got to Cancun from Guatemala with no problems.

She wound her way through the gated community's immaculate streets, a brightly lit lamp post on every corner and the occasional garden planted with sego palms and succulents. What a duality—all serenity on the outside though the teeming endurance game taking place behind closed doors paved the way for the largest drug organization in the world.

She pulled into the three-car garage and let out a sigh. Sometimes it was too much to think about. Coming home to Carlos was a welcome escape. Yes, they made more war than love lately, but it took her mind off the reality of the dangerous game she was involved in—like the unforeseen clash over Colombian fincas, with Clay sitting right in the middle.

Clay was no innocent, far from it, but she didn't want the Canadian caught in the cross hairs through a series of unfortunate events. She should have had the information, should have known the cartel had designs on FARC labs and fincas. She screwed up, plain and simple.

It may have started with Zoyo withholding information, but it came back to her. In the future she would dig deep for anything and everything that applied to all deals she was in charge of. Now the wheels were set in motion. It was time to give Eduardo Suarez a call and get a contact name she could rely on when they arrived in Guatemala. With Suarez's help and Layla's penchant for following protocol, all would go as planned, or so she hoped.

CHAPTER 10

Guatemala City, Guatemala

The three-hour flight from Culiacan to Guatemala City went without a hitch. Suarez told Layla that Guillermo Muñoz would be her contact in Guatemala and he'd advise all who needed to know of her arrival plans. Suarez explained that, as cartel captain, Muñoz managed all contraband moving through his country to Cancun and onward, though the famous tourist resort was usually the final destination for anything illegal passing through the Guatemalan terminal.

They exited customs into the crowded arrival salon where touts, taxi drivers, and tour guides stood holding name signs. Layla spotted hers, held up by a young man of indigenous descent dressed in jeans and a Guatemala soccer t-shirt who balanced her name sign while trying to clean his nails with a pen knife. She walked up to him with Carlos in tow.

After brief introductions were made, their greeter grabbed Layla's Louis Vuitton carry-on from Carlos and they followed him outside La Aurora International under a daunting sun. The air was thinner here at high altitude, unlike sea level, where it was always heavy with humidity.

"Señor Muñoz requests that you meet him at his villa in Antigua," the young man, Estefan, said as they walked away from the terminal. "I will drive you there now."

"Fine," Layla said, "but first I have to contact my partner. He's here at the airport. Give me a minute."

Layla stepped off the patchwork sidewalk away from Carlos and Estefan and pulled out her phone. She punched in Clay's number.

"Clay," she said, happy to hear his voice. "It's Layla."

"You made it." Though he didn't actually sigh, she detected a tone of relief.

"Yes. Where are you?" Layla asked.

"At Hotel Dos Lunas, not far from the airport. Been here since late yesterday. Me and the boys are hunkered down, waiting for instructions."

"The pilots are at the hotel, too?" she asked.

"No, they're with the plane at the airport. Someone needs to watch the company store."

"Right... Well, our Guatemalan contact wants to meet me at his villa in Antigua. You want to join us?"

"Sure. Can you pick me up at my hotel? You're close. I'll call the boys and let them know we'll be heading out tomorrow."

"That's the plan," Layla said. "Can Carlos and I hitch a ride with you to Cancun?"

"Sure thing. See ya in a few," Clay said as he hung up the phone.

"Estefan," Layla said as she walked back over to the two waiting men. "We need to stop by Hotel Dos Lunas. Do you know it?"

"Si, Señorita Layla."

🔁🔁🔁

Clay's hotel wasn't far. Layla could see him standing in the lobby when the black Mercedes pulled into the hotel drive. He spotted the car and headed out the door as the sedan pulled to a stop. Greetings were exchanged and he got into the front seat alongside the driver.

As Estefan maneuvered across twenty-two sprawling barrios in a city of two million, Guatemala's capital lay before them like a rumpled blanket spread over a valley surrounded by snowcapped volcanoes. Though far from beautiful, Guatemala City, or Guate, as locals called it, was the country's largest city.

Guatemala's abundant population of indigenous natives gave the city a feel similar to Chiapas, Mexico, home of the Lacondón and Quiché Maya. Colorful clothing in bright reds, blues, purples, and greens flashed everywhere. Back in the eighties, before he was convicted of genocide against his own people, dictator Rios Montt prohibited indigenous women from wearing their native dress under penalty of death. Now, thirty years later, women were ablaze in vibrant rebozos and traditional embroidered huipiles, balancing baskets on their heads laden with fruit or packages. Men carried backpacks stuffed with tools and firewood. The city buzzed with a fast-paced awareness.

Beamers and SUVs crowded alongside an army of rickety cars held together with duct tape, Bondo, and sheer ingenuity. The black sedan navigated through the boisterous city and Layla and the others settled into air-conditioned comfort, though a nervous silence hung in the air. Meeting Muñoz, head of the Guatemala Cartel, was uncharted territory, a journey into the unknown. Eduard Suarez's minimal contact with the Guatemalan capo was the closest anyone in Layla's circle had come to meeting the mystery man. Estefan, either unaware of their concerns or merely concentrating on traffic, appeared unfazed by the lack of conversation and drove south towards Antigua as tuk-tuks beeped, dashing through the maze of vehicles.

Antigua, also known as old Guatemala City, was roughly forty kilometers away. They progressed in a slow motion crawl over narrow streets and wide boulevards and eventually came to the outskirts. About an hour after they'd picked up Clay, Estefan exited the highway. The rural side road was rutted from recent rains, but the car traveled steadily onward as civilization receded into the distance.

Ten minutes later, Estefan paused at a lane with an unexceptional entry. It looked deserted but when the Mercedes pulled to a stop in front of the nondescript gate, two men in jeans and faded t-shirts appeared. Estefan put down the window and spoke quickly in Spanish to the taller of the two who peered into the vehicle to take a quick inventory. He spoke a few words and then tapped the rear of the car. Layla checked over her shoulder as they departed and saw him speaking into a walkie-talkie.

The road wound upwards. After traveling another half kilometer they came to an archway with a guard house, the entrance to the estate itself. Another gate awaited. This time the uniformed guard barely glanced at them before he waved them through.

Towering royal palms stood like sentinels on either side of the road with flowering red hibiscus shrubs interspersed between. They soon arrived at a long gravel driveway and a two-story rose-colored Spanish villa came into view. Expansive wings on either side graced an imposing entrance with monumental carved doors laden in ornamental iron work. A chauffeur and house man stood waiting at the horseshoe drive. When Estefan stopped the car, the chauffeur jogged over to open doors all around.

Layla stepped out into the warm afternoon air. It smelled fragrant, like flowers, though she couldn't identify the variety. Estefan opened the trunk and retrieved her carry-on. Carlos grabbed the briefcase and took Layla's Louis Vuitton from the driver while Clay waited by the car.

At the entrance, a fussy-looking maid appeared, clearly anxious to unload the car. "Bienvenidos á Casa Madrona," she said in a hurried monotone. Welcome.

She asked if she could take their bags. Layla nodded and Carlos relinquished her Louis Vuitton to the maid. Layla asked where she would find it later. To her dismay, the maid summoned a third servant. Layla followed it with her eyes as far as a waiting room off the foyer.

"Señor Muñoz is waiting in the library," the maid said in Spanish.

Layla took in the villa, its trappings, the maid, and the circumstances. A sense of dread tiptoed into her consciousness. The grand manor was all too reminiscent of Rancho Verde, El Zoyo's hacienda in Sinaloa.

They walked single file on terra cotta floors down a hallway bordered on either side by dark oil paintings of thoroughbred horses and Spanish missions. At the library door, the maid stood aside and motioned for them to enter. "Adelante," she said, more a directive than an invitation. She turned on her heel and departed.

Gazing out an oversized picture window facing away from the door stood Muñoz. On their entrance, he turned. Layla had no idea what to expect but it was definitely not the man in front of her: late fifties, graying sideburns, a flabby face with a dark drooping mustache and hanging jowls. His barrel chest extended over a burly body that seemed to be held in place by a thick leather belt adorned with a sizable silver buckle. To counter what heredity could not alter, he was immaculately dressed in brown slacks and an expensively tailored shirt; on his left wrist was a chunky gold Rolex.

His unyielding look at their entrance conveyed it all—he didn't give a damn. He said not a word but his cavalier, brutish airs filled the entire room. Layla had the uncomfortable feeling an unspoken challenge had taken place, as if they were two gladiators circling an arena.

He looked at the two men dismissively, and at that, she spoke, her hackles up, unwilling to condescend.

"Buenas tardes, Don Guillermo. Mucho gusto. Layla Navarro Almada. A pleasure to meet you. Carlos and Clay are here with me," she said, continuing in Spanish.

With a nod, she left the two men and crossed to the other side of the spacious room, so she and Don Guillermo could speak in private.

"I assume you knew I'd be coming with my bodyguard. I took the liberty of bringing my partner along, too. I'll introduce you in a moment."

Layla's candor caught him off guard. "Cartel meetings are usually held in private but you're El Patrón's niece, Sinaloa *royalty*," he said with a touch of sarcasm, a cardboard smile pasted on his face. "Forgive my old-fashioned Spanish ways."

She nodded. She'd set the tone. He had, after all, invited her to come to his villa to meet him.

"Don Guillermo," she said in her most charming voice though her heart wasn't in it. "You know I'm moving product from Colombia to Cancun. My partner is Clay Lasalle, a Canadian." She nodded at Clay across the room. "He's lined up two American pilots. They've worked with Mexicans and Colombians for years."

Don Guillermo said nothing.

"Thank you for your help moving our product," she continued. "Clay has used FARC in Colombia before, but Zoyo told me just this week we're buying fincas from them. I wasn't aware of this when we set up the deal. Forgive me if I've overstepped boundaries or caused you any inconvenience."

He looked at her for a long moment before speaking. "Señorita Layla. First, it's a pleasure to assist you. I am your willing servant. Whatever your needs, I will gladly lend a hand. Now, how can I be of service?"

His direct about-face softened her. First appearances could be deceiving. Maybe she'd read him wrong. Of course it was mere Spanish protocol to be obsequious, but it worked for her.

Layla continued, "The jet is at La Aurora. We plan to leave early tomorrow but fuel up first."

"Certainly, no problem."

"How do we arrange that?" she asked.

"I will make contact for you. At the airport proceed to the main hangar and then to the office of Guatemala Civil Aviation. It's clearly marked. The name you want is Hernando Morales. Estefan will have his phone number for you. When will you leave?"

"Early."

"Do you have your flight plan?"

"I assume we do. The pilot has a lot of experience."

"You absolutely must show it to aviation control before takeoff."

"Por supuesto. I wanted to make certain there would be no problem due to FARC's recent changes. With us buying up their fincas, you'll no doubt see us again in the future."

The capo shifted his sizable frame. They'd remained standing for the entire conversation. "El Patrón has been more than fair to us. No doubt he or El Zoyo told you what a strong alliance we have. Lately we've dealt with Zoyo since Patrón has been—unfortunately—detained."

Layla gave a rueful smile. "Of course. And that's why we're meeting."

He nodded. Everyone knew Patrón's capable niece was now in charge of cocaine and all shipments for Culiacan. Rumor said she was good with numbers, had a calculator for a brain. "So, we are all set. Now, introduce me," he said.

Layla walked to the other side of the room where Clay and Carlos were sitting like two school boys in detention and introduced them to Guillermo Muñoz.

Don Guillermo cleared his throat, and, in a move that seemed totally out of character, said, "Why not stay for dinner? Before Estefan drives you back to Guate."

Layla looked at Clay then Carlos. Carlos, as always, displayed no emotion; she couldn't read Clay either. Her business sense understood it would be a huge affront to turn down this generous, though last minute, invitation.

"Certainly, we'd be delighted," Layla said, with a smile as bright as though she'd been invited to the Vatican by the Pope himself.

"Why not freshen up first, have something to drink on the terraza? In an hour dinner will be served. Now, please excuse me, I have a matter I must take care of," Muñoz said.

Then he shook her hand, nodded at the men, and was gone from the room.

CHAPTER 11

Casa Madrona, Antigua, Guatemala

The trio sat in wrought-iron chairs on the terraza gazing at the picturesque Antigua valley and watching the sky turn dusky while the day wound down to its inevitable end.

Layla sipped a soft drink and twirled her straw in the ice, wondering what Clay was thinking.

He spoke first. "It looks like you've covered the bases, Layla."

She half closed her eyes and stared into the distance. Finally she looked at him. "Uh-huh."

"You seem hesitant."

"Oh, it's nothing. I'll just be glad to be back in Mexico tomorrow."

That seemingly innocent statement conveyed much more than the words actually spoken. To Layla, it felt as if they were at a wake rather than sitting in an elegant Guatemala manor awaiting a gourmet dinner. What was it about Guillermo Muñoz and this place that made her feel on edge? It wasn't quite a sinister castle from a creepy horror story. But still...

"I'm going to find a bathroom," she said, deciding action of any kind would be good.

She got up, stretched—it had been a long day—and walked towards the open French doors that led back into the villa. Inside, she took a moment to appreciate the elegance of the manor, so perfect it could have been lifted from the pages of Architectural Digest. She realized she had no idea where she was in the mansion and no clue how to find the services. The maid was nowhere to be seen. An ornate hardwood staircase curved up to the second floor. From her vantage point below she noticed a number of doors. One had to be a bathroom. With that goal in mind, she moved towards the winding stairs and began her ascent.

Once at the top landing—it was a dizzying height-—Layla looked down at the foyer and the set of French doors she'd just come through. Doors and more doors, upstairs and down, but still no one in sight.

Alone, she could do a little more exploring, take a personal tour of Guillermo's grand villa. The hushed solitude of the manor made her feel wary, so she tip-toed across the magnificent polished floors. The Guatemalan mahogany occasionally creaked, and with leather soles she had to be careful not to click as she walked.

She opened the first door she came to. A quick peek indicated it was an office, complete with desk, computer, leather chairs and shaded reading lamps. She closed the door and moved on. Next appeared to be a guest room, decorated in Spanish colonial style with twin beds adorned in maroon velveteen duvets. Dark floor-to-ceiling drapes blocked the sunlight which gave the room a sinister feel.

She pulled that door shut and moved on. The next door she chose was what she'd been looking for, a bathroom. Finally.

The lavish bath screamed opulence—it was the size of a bedroom. The shower enclosure, lined with modern glass tiles and gleaming shower heads, was nearly the size of her entire bathroom. Layla used the services and prepared to exit, ready to continue her tour of the capo's fortress.

She looked at the door on the opposite side of the room. Why not check it out? She'd come this far.

She stealthily pushed open the door and saw a blur of movement inside the heavily draped room. As her eyes adjusted to the dark, something moved again on one of the beds. Fearing she'd disturbed someone sleeping, Layla started to shut the door when she heard a soft moan. She closed the bathroom door and flicked on the light. Stretched out on the bed lay a dark-haired young girl. The girl sat up and wiped her eyes. She'd been crying.

"Sorry to wake you," Layla said, turning to leave.

"Help me," the girl said in a whisper. "Please help me, señorita."

Layla stopped and narrowed her eyes. "What? Who are you?"

"Lupita." She looked around furtively and then went on in a whisper. "They stole me! Me and my sister. And now she's gone."

"What do you mean?" Layla asked, not daring to move.

"They took me from the street near my home, and I'm all alone."

"Who took you?"

"Men. Two men. They took us from Antigua. They stole us."

"What? Stole you? But surely you can go back. No one's guarding you," she said. The door wasn't locked.

"I tried to run away and they put me in this room and took away Carmen, my little sister. They said the next time I try to run away they will hurt her. So I stay."

"What do you mean hurt?" Layla moved closer to the bed.

"They do bad things to us, all the time. Those men."

Layla snapped to attention. She sat down on the edge of

the bed. "What's your full name?"

"Lupita Ortiz Gonzalez. My sister is Carmen."

"How old are you?"

"Twelve."

Layla's pulse quickened. *The same age I lost my innocence.* Her throat constricted; she felt short of breath.

"Should I talk to Don Guillermo and ask him to help you go back to your home?"

"No!" the girl cried, trying to muffle the sound by putting her mouth on her arm as she sobbed. "No! He will hurt us both, like he hurts the others."

"Others? What others?"

"There are many of us. They steal us from barrios, schools. They take us and do bad things. The men say I'm lucky. A lot of the girls have to go to dirty places and work with a lot of men every day. I can stay here and only Don Guillermo touches me. But sometimes they do, too."

Layla let out a low sigh. "Oh God, how long have you been here?" She placed her hand on top of the girl's and stroked it lightly while her stomach did somersaults.

"I don't know. I haven't seen Carmen for a long time. I'm so scared."

"Do you think she's here in the house?" Layla asked.

"I don't know."

"Have you seen the other children?"

"No, but the men talk about them. About stealing them from barrios or the streets."

"Where do they take them?"

"Maybe Guate—maybe far away."

Layla dropped her head onto her chest as she suppressed a silent scream. "When did you last see your family?"

"Long time."

"Is it just you and your sister who are here?"

"I don't know." The girl started to cry again. "I don't know where anyone else is. Please help me."

Layla's heart was breaking but she tried to focus—was this girl, her sister, and the others she spoke of a mere pleasure for Guillermo or was he moving girls—children—as in sex trafficking? She took the girl in her arms and stroked her hair, trying to give the traumatized child some sense of calm. "Listen good, Lupita. These are very bad men who have hurt you. I want to help you, I really do ..." There was a long pause before she got it out. "But I can't help you today."

The girl started to shake uncontrollably. "What do you mean? Please, please. Help me!" She sobbed out the words, "Take me now. Please. Take me with you."

"Lupita, listen! We are in a large house that's like a fortress. If I try to take you with me now, they'll make me a prisoner, too. Then I can't help you."

Layla knew it was unlikely that Guillermo would abduct her, the niece of El Patrón, but she had to make the girl realize help was not coming today. Her heart sank at the thought of the fate that awaited this girl.

"You know I am going to help you, right?"

Lupita nodded as she gripped Layla tighter around the waist.

"Okay, then you have to be very strong. You have to believe me. Look at me."

The girl shifted around to look into Layla's eyes.

"You will have to wait until I can come back for you. Do you hear me? Lupita?"

Lupita let out another long moan. "No, no please don't go! Don't go!"

"Lupita!" Layla shook her once, firmly. "I promise I will save you. But I cannot help you tonight. The bad men will get us both if I do. You have to promise me that you will be strong."

"No, please, please don't go!" the girl began to cry, her entire body shaking, now in spasms.

"I have to go, and I'm so very sorry, but if I don't go back downstairs they'll start to look for me and if they find me with you, then we will *all* die." All Layla could think to say came out like idiotic lines from a melodrama. "I'll get you some water."

The girl nodded, obviously distressed.

What else can I do? I'm powerless. She removed the girl's arms from around her waist and went into the bathroom. She brought a glass of water to Lupita who gulped it greedily. *What have I uncovered? What have I stumbled into?* She felt like crying. *No, I must remain strong, for her.* She held the girl at arm's length, to memorize every detail of her tear-streaked face: the penetrating, pitch black eyes, the soft eyebrows, narrow yet perfect nose, and high forehead.

"I am so, so sorry," Layla said as she held Lupita.

The girl seemed spent. She fell back on the bed and stared off at nothing.

"Lupita! Lupita! Look at me. I have to do this."

The girl turned her face towards Layla, but her eyes were blank.

"I will save you, I promise," Layla said again, outwardly calm. Inside she was seething.

Chinga de madre! It couldn't be any more fucked up. She trembled in disgust as a distant memory surfaced from long ago, compliments of Zoyo. *How can I save her? I couldn't even save myself.* She took the girl's limp hand, but it was as unresponsive as a doll's. Layla sighed and pushed herself off the bed.

Lupita's eyes were closed when Layla spoke. "Lupita, remember. I am coming for you."

Layla backed away from the bed. The girl lay still as a stone. She could do nothing more. Not now. Layla opened the door to the bathroom, entered, hit the light switch, and grasped the granite countertop so as not to collapse. She felt like throwing up.

Her heartbeat raced as though she'd run a marathon and her mind felt like it would explode. How the hell was she going to save that girl and her sister? And what was going on with Guillermo? Was he alone involved with humans as contraband, or had the cartel branched out, forgetting—yet again—to keep her in the loop?

CHAPTER 12

Her body was still trembling as she turned on the cold water and let it run for a minute while she mechanically moved her hands back and forth in the flow before she splashed it on her face. She took a towelette from a ceramic tray next to the sink and dried around her mascara-smeared eyes. She leaned in closer to the mirror. How the hell could she save that girl and her sister?

I'll expose it—tell Carlos and Clay.

Her decision came as an epiphany. There really was no other option. A new resolve hit her like an arrow finding its home in the center of the bull's eye. She grabbed the brass handle of the bathroom door, and let herself out into the stillness of the hallway.

She walked straight down the center of the hall, no longer creeping along the sideboards. She had a mission that would take her beyond safe limits. A mission with a purpose, far outside the boundaries of her cartel home, the bubble that promised power and wealth, but that also came with velvet handcuffs that would forever restrict her. She jogged down the stairs.

Lupita's plight and that of the other innocent children kidnapped and used as sex slaves tore at her heart. Cartels had branched into kidnapping and human trafficking because it was a renewable resource, unlike drugs that could be sold only once. Humans could be sold over and over again.

By helping the girl she'd be performing a selfless task. The thought brought her the same strength of purpose as when she sped away from Zoyo at Rancho Verde, after she'd flashed on the memory of meeting Don Cuauhtemoc so long ago.

At the downstairs landing Layla walked through the room that led to the terraza and strode across the deck where Carlos and Clay still sat alone in the evening dusk. Discovering Lupita had heightened her senses; she could feel their tension.

At the sound of her approach they turned in unison, Carlos with a reproachful look—had she been gone that long?—and Clay with a look of relief. Nearing them, she shot a quick glance over her shoulder to make certain she hadn't been followed. They were alone and outdoors, where no one could eavesdrop on their conversation.

"Hola." She pulled up the chair she'd been sitting in before her life had changed.

"Hi," Clay said with a smile. "Guess you finally found the bathroom."

"I found more than that," she said. "I have to talk to both of you, now."

Her tone had altered. Carlos's expression was wary with distrust, while Clay was wide-eyed.

She looked around again before speaking. In a whisper, she said, "Guillermo's trafficking children. I found a twelve-year-old girl locked in a room upstairs, one of his sex slaves."

"Puta de madre, Layla!" Carlos nearly shouted. His eyes had gone to black, his irises dissolving into the pupil. "What are you doing sneaking around this guy's house?"

"I used the bathroom and another door led into a bedroom and that's where she was."

"What the hell! You were looking into the bedrooms?" he asked in a fury, his hands grasping the wrought-iron table so hard that his veins looked close to popping.

"I found a girl, Carlos, a young girl. He's trafficking *children*."

Carlos pushed himself away from the table, nearly spilling his empty drink glass. "It's no concern of yours! Who are you now? Mother Teresa?"

Layla stared at him, speechless. She'd never seen him this upset about anything other than their personal dramas.

Clay stepped in. "Carlos," he said in a tone that was calm yet firm. He leaned in to get the bodyguard's full attention. "Hold on. Layla's concerned about this young girl." He turned to look at Layla. "How do you know he's abusing her?"

"She told me," Layla said.

"Chinga! You had a conversation with her?" Carlos said, his voice rising again. "Listen. We gotta be careful. We're not in Mexico, Layla. We're in Guatemala and we're in Don Guillermo's house. We can't fuck around, we gotta get out of the country with the drugs. We can't worry about *anyone else* right now. Do you understand? I have to protect you. You're not making it easy. You're way outta bounds."

"Carlos, I understand," Layla said in the softest voice she could manage. "I'm sorry. I know my safety's your number one concern. But if it was your little sister, what then?"

"Stop it, Layla. I can't feel sorry for that little girl because I have a job to do. *You're* my job. I promised El Patrón I would protect you, not some chica who was in the wrong place at the wrong time. Put all this talk on hold till we're safe in Cancun."

Still struggling to be the mediator, Clay said, "Wait a minute, Carlos. I understand what Layla's saying. She's concerned about a girl who's being kept for sex, used as a tool for some old guy right in this house. But Layla, even if we wanted to do something, what could we possibly do tonight? We don't have a car, plus we're in a compound with two sets of gates —both well-guarded—between us and the road. How far would we get if we snatched that girl?"

"I know, both of you, I know," she said as she grabbed Carlos's hand and gave it a squeeze, trying to make an appeal. "Please Carlos, don't be mad. It's a long story and I can't tell it to you now—not tonight—but sometime soon, I am going to save that girl."

"Hijole! We're the Culiacan Cartel, not Amnesty International. When did you get religion?"

Wrong approach. Layla was steamed. "Carlos! How dare you?" But he doesn't know about Zoyo, Layla reasoned, trying to keep her temper. What does he know about what women face?

"Listen," Clay said in a beseeching tone. "Cool it. Carlos is right, Layla. We're in a delicate situation. Our main goal is to keep things calm with Guillermo and get the hell out of here."

Layla started to interrupt, but Clay put up his hands. "Let me continue. Your heart's in a good place. But we have a dinner to get through and Carlos nailed it. We have to be careful."

Layla heard footsteps in the adjacent room that led from the hallway to the terraza.

"Do you read me, Layla?" Clay asked, reaching over to touch her arm.

"Loud and clear," she said, hastily turning to the door and flipping her hair over one shoulder.

To build a case she would need more time and that wasn't available at the moment. The maid approached the table.

"Dinner is served. Follow me." A sand crab had more personality than this woman did.

They stood, each of them searching the others' faces for signs of complicity, solidarity.

But what about the girl? It was *not* her fault. She hadn't tried to cross the border; she hadn't run away. She was being a kid in her neighborhood, and they simply grabbed her and her sister.

Layla shuddered. It could happen any place, at any time. To any woman or child in any country. Human trafficking is far too common. In Guatemala, Mexico, or even the United States of fucking America where thousands of women and children are missing. In that glorified land of promise and plenty. It even happened there.

Her thoughts were a jumble of right and wrong, good and evil, but mostly a growing hatred for Don Guillermo.

CHAPTER 13

Casa Madrona's dining room was ablaze in lights, from the softly glowing wall sconces to the brilliantly lit chandeliers. Dozens of flickering candles sat on both a sideboard buffet and the dining table, creating an intimate warmth in the cavernous room.

It would be a quiet evening, a dinner for Guillermo and Layla's group alone, the high gloss table set for only four. As a rule, bodyguards didn't attend dinners with principal players. Their realm was the less lofty terrain of back rooms or caretaker cottages. But since the Sinaloans were far from Mexico and that country's protocol, rules could be bent. Carlos was seated beside Layla.

"Clay, next to me, sit," Don Guillermo said as he motioned to the chair beside him.

Though the evening began with the false pretense of all going well, Clay sensed trouble. Though he hadn't known Layla long, he could tell she was wound tight, on high alert.

Layla's discovery of an underage girl held against her will in Guillermo's villa was bad timing as far as Clay was concerned. Since he'd been involved in the drug trade, he'd learned the new normal was lies, rip-offs, short loads, and outright cons.

Clay would never run his Rainbow Tribe in that manner, but he knew that the entire dope business reeked of violence and betrayal, and with big money came big risk.

Death, or the possibility of it, carried its own particular odor: the smell of fear. And to the Mexican cartels, murders and assassinations, though heinous, were routine. In Mexico not many small time players survived more than five years in the business.

If any part of the trade was innocent, it was pot cultivation. Clay believed everyone had a right to light up some herb, and pot was just that, an herb. It came from the earth, born of soil, sun, and rain. Mother Nature smiled on it.

Not until Clay started dealing with cartels did he learn how far what he'd believed to be true about the drug business was from the reality of it. The Gulf Cartel and their terrifying spin-off, Los Zetas, had branched into murder for hire, kidnapping, and human trafficking. The Culiacan Cartel didn't need to stoop to those levels. They stuck solely to drugs until recently when they began robbing Pemex, Mexico's nationalized oil corporation. Pemex claimed cartels punctured twenty-five hundred pipelines, mostly across the Texas border where shale oil was king.

Stealing carloads of limes and avocados was left to lesser cartels from Michoacan—La Familia and Knights Templar. They hijacked produce trucks and targeted local farmers, threatening to kill them and their families if they didn't cooperate. The farmers became vigilantes in retaliation. Things got so out of control the Mexican Army was called in to referee. But kidnapping and human trafficking, that was the bottom. No wonder Layla was agitated.

🔁🔁🔁

Don Guillermo had changed for dinner and looked relaxed in a fresh cotton shirt and tan slacks. The others in the party hadn't had that luxury. Layla and Carlos, who started out early that morning in Mexico, still wore their travel clothes. Clay had been up since sunrise on Guatemalan soil, worrying how their plans would unfold.

Their host motioned the butler over. "Roberto," he said. "Do the honors, pour our wine."

Guillermo had become a convivial host—a far cry from the scowling hulk that had greeted them an hour earlier.

"This comes from my vineyards in southern Guatemala," he explained as the waiter poured wine into Waterford crystal glasses. He lifted the delicate goblet towards his guests, "Salud."

Glasses high, everyone drank. "I'm delighted you could join me for dinner," Guillermo said, with a nod to Layla.

Layla acknowledged her host, and said, "Gracias, Don Guillermo. It's so kind of you to welcome us here at Casa Madrona."

Carlos caught her sarcastic tone and tried to get Layla's attention with a sideways glance but she ignored him. He more than anyone knew her mouth could get her in trouble.

The butler returned, poured more wine and motioned to a server standing near the sideboard to bring on the first course. Appetizer size empanadas arrived, along with a spicy cream sauce.

Eschewing small talk, Layla turned to their host. "Don Guillermo, Guatemala has so many recent immigrants from El Salvador and Honduras, why?"

"Well, Honduras and El Salvador are considered the murder capitals of the world, in that order," Don Guillermo said as he tucked into an empanada. "People from those countries run to Guatemala as a way to get to Mexico. And from Mexico, they hope to get to the States."

"Why is there so much crime in El Salvador and Honduras?" Layla asked.

"Gangs, lots of them, most not related to the cartels. In the nineties, the US sent Salvadorans back to their homeland. The flaw was most of these tipos had been in prison where they created monster gangs. They fight constantly over turf. Innocents get caught in the crossfire."

"Doesn't a lot of Colombian coke go through Honduras?" Clay asked.

"Three-quarter goes through Honduras, the rest through Guatemala, then to the US. For a while it even went through Costa Rica. There's always problems." He shrugged.

"I've heard the gangs prey on children," Layla said.

"One moment, Layla," Don Guillermo said as he motioned for the butler to serve the main course, standing rib roast with dark gravy, small golden potatoes, and steamed squash.

"Now," Guillermo continued after the meat was served, motioning for more wine all around though he was the only one drinking. "Do gangs prey on children in Honduras and Salvador? They—"

"And here, too?" Layla asked. "Mexico's not perfect, but we have the gangs under control."

"Of course Mexico does—because of the cartels. Cartels are very strong in your country, almost a military presence. And many of the police are on the cartels' payrolls, so individual gangs could never survive. It's easier for them to join the cartels."

"I've heard that here in Guatemala gangs prey on children as young as five, and contract them as runners. Many are orphans with no other options," Layla said.

"Not so much here as Honduras and Salvador. Honduras is barely holding on, though world news will never report that. They never recovered from Hurricane Mitch in '98."

Layla picked at a small potato with her fork. "So what

about these kids?"

"For many street kids it's their one chance at survival unless they get past Mexico to the US border, but most are caught and turned away by immigration. The gringos make certain of that. Now, back to dinner. Do you like the beef? It's from my ranch south of here, all grass fed."

The look on Layla's face was impassive. "Tasty," she said though she'd barely touched it. Epicurean delights weren't the main course on *her* menu.

Carlos, in stark contrast, dedicated his entire being to dissecting the enormous portion of meat in front of him. Food calmed him and he may have sensed that a heavy dose of carbs and calories would be required to make it through the night.

"What about the street kids who don't make it across the US border. What happens to them? Are they used for human trafficking?" Layla asked.

"Well, human trafficking actually began by moving hopeful immigrants across the border, for a price. In the past we called it using a coyote. Much cheaper just ten years ago, three to six hundred US. It's up to three thousand dollars or more. Inflation."

"I have heard many of those waiting to cross don't have that money, so the coyotes, who are now cartels, say they can pay them back once they get across, with their first month's wages."

"You're very aware, Layla. That's exactly what happens ..." Don Guillermo turned to Clay, motioning to the platter of beef. Clay declined with a slight shake of his head.

But Layla had not yet made her point. "And those amounts, I hear, are wages they could never earn, not for many months, if ever. So the women and children are forced into the sex trade, to pay off the debt."

An uncomfortable silence settled on the group. The only sound to be heard was Carlos's fork and knife scraping his plate, savoring what he no doubt believed might be his last supper.

"Hmm. You've been doing your homework. You're definitely El Patrón's niece, my dear," Guillermo said, managing to keep an upbeat inflection in his tone.

Layla waited a beat and asked, "Are you involved in the sex trade?"

Guillermo's fork stopped just short of his mouth. He forced a self-conscious laugh. "What kind of question is that? Such an unpleasant topic, when we're enjoying such good food."

"I'd like to know," she said, in a commanding tone. "It's my understanding the Culiacan Cartel isn't involved in sex trafficking or kidnapping. Perhaps you know different."

Maybe the wine had been flowing too freely because Don Guillermo shocked his guests by answering. "Since you ask, and are so insistent, I think at times we may have, let's say, assisted with moving people across the border. On very rare occasions of course."

"What about the sex trade?"

"We would always take a cut, like a vig, on whatever was moved. We get a percent of the cash, or the product. You know how it works."

"But if you're taking part of the profit with moving people across the border, and those people can't pay, that's slavery. You're making them slaves."

Carlos finished and pushed away his plate, ready to give full attention to the conversation.

"It might happen once in a while," Don Guillermo said, "but as I said, it's very rare."

"Does El Patrón know about it?"

The eagle had landed.

"Layla, I don't think we should discuss this right now," Guillermo said in a conciliatory manner.

"I asked," she said, her voice an octave higher, "if Patrón knows."

The room stood still. In a flash Guillermo's enormous face turned from a soft shade of healthy pink to beet red. What had started as a mere blush peeking out from under his bespoke shirt had gone full-blown rojo, bordering on rage, in seconds.

He was good at what he did though—staying in control. He cleared his throat and said calmly, "Let's say El Zoyo is aware of it."

Bingo. Zoyo had partnered with Guillermo in trafficking, leaving Patrón out of the loop. Both knew her uncle would never approve of a third-rate business in the land of golden opportunity.

"What about that girl in the upstairs bedroom?" Layla asked.

Guillermo stood up abruptly, nearly spilling his wine. His silverware clanked against the dishes as he pushed back his chair, throwing down his napkin as he glared at Layla.

"What are you talking about?" his voice was gruff, a lion preparing to roar.

"Lupita. The twelve-year old, third door down, just off the bathroom."

"What? You have no right to talk to me like this. Have you been snooping around?"

"I was looking for the bathroom," Layla said. She was as composed as Guillermo was agitated. "I opened the wrong door, my mistake. She said she's being held as a sex slave, stolen from her barrio. Her and her sister."

"What right do you have to talk to me like this in my

house? It's time for you to leave. Our business is finished!" He spoke rapidly to the butler. "Tell Juan to have Estefan get the car, take them back to Guate. Now!" The butler turned to go and Guillermo followed him.

Halfway out of the room, Guillermo pivoted, eyes on Layla. "And I will say this to you—everything is not always as it appears. Don't jump to conclusions. You'd best tread lightly with what you think you know." He gave her a look so vicious, Carlos started to rise from his chair. "Call off your bodyguard! Roberto! Dinner is over."

With that he strode out of the dining room, leaving a palpable feeling that a pin had been dropped from a hand grenade, whereabouts unknown.

"Hijole, Layla!" Carlos hissed when Guillermo was definitely gone. "Chinga! Are you trying to kill us all?"

CHAPTER 14

Layla looked triumphant as she rose from the table and motioned to Carlos and Clay. "We're outta here. Let's find Estefan. She moved towards the dining room door, not in the least unhinged. Clay and Carlos were right behind her, with Carlos carrying the briefcase.

"I have to find my valise," she said. "Where's the maid when you need her?"

As if on cue, the woman appeared. She excused herself and entered the side room where Layla's Louis Vuitton was stored and returned with it in hand.

"Estefan will bring the car," she said as she moved closer to the door, opening it wide and ushering the trio in that direction as if trying to drive out a bad smell, clearly aware something awkward had occurred over dinner.

Banished from the manor, the trio huddled on the villa's threshold in the dark, anxiously waiting for Estefan. The maid hadn't even bothered to turn on the outside light. Barely a word had been spoken since leaving the dining room, each entertaining their own private thoughts.

Moments later the black Mercedes arrived. Estefan jumped out, as much in a hurry as they were. No words were spoken as he opened the back door for Layla and Carlos. Clay let himself into the passenger seat upfront.

Estefan dropped into the driver's seat, released the hand brake, and gunned the motor. There would be no pussyfooting around getting back to Guate—they'd hit the ground running.

🝊🝊🝊

Layla woke from a troubled sleep. It was not yet five, but time to rise and see what the day would bring. Her heart felt heavy and she had no idea what collateral damage her outburst had caused. She'd been so preoccupied thinking of the fallout from her dinner conversation that she'd forgotten to ask Estefan for the number of their contact at the airport. She'd have to call to make sure they could get the necessary fuel needed to make their final run into Cancun.

What was wrong with her? She rarely acted out, never overstepped boundaries. She was the Stepford wife of drug dealing: perfection, perfection, perfection. Patrón kidded her about it. This was unprecedented, outing a rogue like Guillermo, and on his own turf. But her moral compass—working at odds with her safety barometer— was going berserk, reminding her Guillermo had been double-dealing Patrón, as had Zoyo. They'd sidled into an independent operation—one she knew Patrón would never condone.

She went into the bathroom and ran the shower, hoping Carlos would stir once he heard water running. Letting herself be pulverized by the stinging drops, she prayed it would wash away her fears, right any wrongs she'd committed. This would be one ball buster of a day. Bienvenidos á Guatemala. A few moments later she stepped out of the shower and toweled dry. By the time she put on fresh clothes and a little make-up, Carlos was sitting up in bed.

He gave her an incriminating look. "What happened last night, Layla? Why the hell did you go for the jugular?"

"Something snapped. Seeing that girl, knowing Guillermo's dirty intentions."

"It's not your job to deal with it. Not now. Hijole! We have to get back to Mexico. I have to keep you safe. Chinga! I hate this job." Always Carlos first.

"Pobrecito! You don't care what *I'm* going through! How do you know I don't hate *my* job? You just complain. Fuck you! Too bad you hate it, but it *is* your job. I'm your job and I'm your boss. So shut up, buck up, and while you're at it, *get* up. We've got a big day ahead of us."

He stared at her. She never reproached him. A single syllable escaped his lips before he clamped his mouth shut.

Layla madly scoured the room. "Where's my fucking phone?"

He shook his head, slid out of bed, and headed to the bathroom, closing the door behind him.

Retrieving her phone from under the bed, Layla called Estefan to get the number she forgot to ask for the previous night. She dialed. One ring, two rings. Finally—a voice.

"Buenos dias," she said with a brightness she didn't feel. "Good morning, Estefan."

"Hola. Quien esta?" Who is it?

"It's Layla. Sorry to bother you so early but last night I forgot to get the number for our contact at the airport. Don Guillermo said you'd have it for me."

A pause. "I have no number for you, sorry." he said.

"Wait, wait! What do you mean?" she asked.

"Don Guillermo told me to tell you to contact him. He'd have information."

She heard the click of the phone. Round two, with the ball in Guillermo's court. She searched her phone for his number and called.

He answered on the second ring. "Bueno."

"Buenos dias, Don Guillermo," she said. "Last night I forgot to get the number from Estafan."

"Well, I have no number for you, Layla, but I do have some information. You don't have to worry about your little upstairs friend any longer."

"What are you talking about?" she asked.

"She's dead."

"What? No!" Layla let out a wail. Her cries brought Carlos from the bathroom in a towel. "Chinga! What did you do, you fucker?"

"Let's just say she died peacefully." He hung up.

"Oh God! Oh, Carlos, I've killed her." She smashed the phone against the wall, then threw herself on the bed, weeping uncontrollably.

"Layla! What happened? Tell me!" The bodyguard quickly crossed the room and put his arms around her, lifting her up, holding her as her frame heaved up and down in wrenching sobs.

"He killed her—Lupita, the girl," she said. "It's my fault. My fault. I called him, I called Guillermo, to get the number and he—he told me she was dead. He killed her!"

Carlos pushed her back, staring hard. "Did you get the number?"

"No," she said, shaking her head. "But what does it matter?"

"Layla! Listen! It matters! We need the number to get fuel and get out of here."

"I know, I know, but he fucking killed her."

Carlos shook her. "Layla, fuck that! We have to concentrate. *You* have to concentrate. Call Clay. Get going. We need to move, fast." His instincts clicked in and he moved around the room like a fireball, packing what little they'd brought with them. This is what he was paid for—to think under pressure.

Layla's body had taken on the look of a listless rag doll. "Call Clay," he instructed her again, a firmness in his tone. "Tell him what's up. Now."

Her phone had ricocheted onto the bed. He picked it up. "Now," he repeated, jaw clenched, arm outstretched, phone in hand.

Her hand was shaking as she scrolled the phone to locate Clay's number. He picked up on the first ring. "Clay, we're outta here in five minutes. Gotta leave."

"Did you get the number?"

"No."

"So what happens now?" he asked.

"Call the pilots. Tell them we're coming over—immediately. They said we had enough fuel to get to Cancun. You told me."

There was a moment of silence before Clay said, "Barely, Layla. They said just barely."

"We have no choice." Her voice was robotic.

Long pause. "Okay, I'll see you in the lobby." Clay hung up.

Layla shifted her attention to Carlos. "You're right. Let's go. We'll have the desk call us a taxi, get to the hangar with Clay."

"What about the fuel?" he asked.

She gathered her purse and bag, merely going through the motions. "The vets will think of something, that's what we're paying them for. They've been getting out of tight spots for thirty years. What's one more?"

CHAPTER 15

The sky was still dark when the taxi pulled up outside the hangar. *Our getaway under cover of darkness*, Layla thought.

"Are they expecting us?" she asked Clay.

"If they're not expecting us, they're expecting something."

What kind of answer was that?

The only thing separating the trio from the facility in which two tons of contraband cocaine was stored in a Gulfstream jet was a ragged chain link fence. A lone security officer, or someone pretending to be one, heard the cab pull up and dragged himself to where they stood.

He stared at them through sleep-deprived eyes. "Si?"

Layla had composed herself and was in form once again. "We're here with the Gulfstream," she said. "Leaving now."

"Okay," the man said, slowly unlocking the gate so they could enter. He didn't ask who they were, checked no IDs. Guatemala security was even laxer than Mexico's, or Colombia's for that matter. Not even a junkyard dog.

The security guard led them to the hangar door. Thirty feet high and bulky, it was made of corrugated metal, on rollers. He started to pull on it. Clay lent a hand as did Carlos and it moved, a loud squeal shattering the night's silence.

"I just remembered," Layla said while watching the hangar door roll aside. "Guatemala Civil Aviation, Hernando Morales."

"What?" Clay asked, looking back at her. His tone was clipped.

"That's our name. It just came to me. Maybe the vets know him," Layla said.

"At least we know where to go to get outta here," Clay said in a low mumble.

They entered the darkened warehouse and heard the sound of another door opening.

"Amigo!" Donavon's voice came from the far side of the building. "What's happening?"

"Hola!" Clay's voice echoed in the near-empty hangar. "We're here and ready to roll."

Layla heard Donavon climbing down the jet's metal stairs, and immediately he was on the hangar floor moving towards them.

"Early day, huh?" he said, looking at Clay. "What time's take-off?"

"Well, there's been a hitch," Clay said, shifting his glance to Layla. "Layla, this is Donavon."

"Mucho gusto, Donovan," she said.

"Same to you, ma'm."

"Sorry for the lack of communication, but we're in a hurry today. Long story."

"Aren't they all? So what's the plan?"

"Can you get us to Cancun without fueling up?" she asked in English.

"Say what? Now I didn't think that was in the plan."

"It is now," Layla said. "We have the name of the person in flight control, Hernando Morales, but we had a little hiccup last night. Fuel's a problem."

Donavon nodded slowly. He knew better than to ask for details—they wouldn't be forthcoming. Last minute changes weren't unusual in his business. He wasn't working for General Electric. This was as freelance as it got.

"I've got the flight plan all set up. There's not a lot going on here before sunrise, so if we head over to aviation control, we can adjust the departure time and take off early. They're loose on protocol. But I don't understand the no fueling deal."

"If we wait to fuel up, it could affect our safety. We have to take off as soon as possible. Once we get to Cancun, we'll refuel, no problem," Layla said, trying to sound nonchalant in spite of her veiled message.

"I'm sure we can make it to Cancun. I just like the cushion, but with less fuel we'll get there faster," Donavon said, not in the least rattled. The laidback pilot rolled with the punches, a consummate veteran of the drug game where change could come at any time, for any reason.

"Is Jake ready?" Clay asked.

"We've been ready, just waiting for you all to come. Now, you'll be flying with us, too, right?" Donavon asked. "You and …"

"Carlos," Layla said hastily, realizing they hadn't met. "He works with me."

"Mucho gusto, Carlos," he held out his hand and Carlos grasped it. "Okay, sounds like we got a condition here, so let's head over to flight control, change our plan, and get airborne."

"Bueno," Layla said. All of a sudden it seemed as though things might actually work. They'd get out of Guatemala with the drugs. She was in capable hands.

꙾꙾꙾

The plane taxied down the runway as the sun began to rise on the eastern horizon. La Aurora International wasn't a big airport—few flights even when the sun was up. Donavon resubmitted the flight plan with no explanation needed. It was all very low-key, exactly as promised.

Nearly airborne. Layla sat next to Carlos, with Clay across the aisle, the only seats remaining in a jet otherwise loaded with contraband—coke, blow, Bolivian marching powder, or whatever the media currently called it. Tightly wrapped kilos had been inserted into jumbo black garbage bags—the dealer's packaging of choice.

Lift off. Well, they were airborne now, just another bird in flight. *We made it.* We escaped that wretch Guillermo—if we'd waited for fuel, no doubt we'd have met up with him, she thought.

With the Gulfstream safely in the air, Layla had a free hour to ponder her reaction to finding Lupita and exposing her. Time to consider the irreparable damage she'd done. The girl was dead because of her need to come off like a savior, but one with no escape plan. She had the blood of an innocent on her hands.

It wasn't only Lupita on Layla's mind. What recourse was needed due to Guillermo's double dealing, entering the human trafficking trade along with Zoyo? What a muddy pool. She hated the killing and payback part of the business. She pretended she wasn't involved in that messy end of the industry, and early on that was easy. Patrón and others shielded her well.

She knew, however, that she was far from exempt. She was complicit, a silent partner in the killing machine that defined not only the Culiacan Cartel but all Mexican cartels. In her early years, she considered herself lily white, dealing only with numbers and logistics, leaving the dirty work to others. Such a Mexican way of dealing with the ugly side of life—glossing over facts, promoting half-truths, and pretending things were what everyone else pretended they were.

Muscle mattered. If another cartel strong-armed your territory and got caught, it meant torture and death. If a competitor pushed for bigger percentages, their main guy could end up in a ditch with two bullets in the head. That was an honorable death—no cock in the mouth, eyes gouged out. Everyone knew what that implied.

She made it her business to know what was happening. She was good at what she did, just as Patrón said. She was like a Stepford wife. Or had been until last night. Why had she called out Guillermo? What had flipped in her head? At dinner she came out blazing, conveniently ignoring the fact that she and Clay had two tons of stashed product at the airport and were counting on Guillermo's help to exit the country. Her job was to get that shipment to Mexico, that was her only reason for being in Guatemala. Nada mas. Nothing more.

They were airborne now. Only an hour from Cancun. She couldn't wait to see the turquoise-blue Caribbean. Wheels up.

CHAPTER 16

Layla rested her head on Carlos's shoulder with a sigh. "Carlos," she said softly.

"Si," he said, with no judgment in his eyes.

"Thank you for this morning, for getting me started." She relaxed against him as the plane reached cruising altitude.

There was a long pause before he answered. "This is your first time out. You shouldn't be too hard on yourself. You did it, Layla."

Coming from Carlos, the words were a coronation. *He is with me all the way.*

"Mi amor," she said, a mere whisper into his left ear. "Thank you for everything." She nestled further into his comfortable, bulky shoulder.

"No problema," he whispered back, taking hold of her hand.

🔲🔲🔲

From her sky-high perch, Layla spotted dense mangroves near the border of Belize and Mexico. Low to the ground, these tree-filled swamps absorbed both salt and fresh water in a unique eco-system no other life form on the planet could manage. The rain forests of southern Mexico were so different from those in Guatemala's highlands, where towering mahogany and cedar hardwoods stood hundreds of feet above the forest floor. In stark contrast, the rainforest in the Mexican Caribbean was dense and low.

Occasionally Layla spotted a lone Maya hut, far from civilization. Small puffs of smoke appeared, too, due to sporadic fires. She knew the methane created by rotting vegetation often sparked spontaneous combustion; these flare-ups were simply nature's way and usually extinguished themselves, so prolific were the waterways that surrounded them.

Mexico—this proud, diverse land, was her land. Though she hailed from another coast with its own unique set of natural wonders, the view out the window mesmerized her. Soon they'd be circling Cancun International Airport. Donavon said he'd flown this route so many times, it was permanently etched in his memory. As they neared the control tower he'd contact Cancun Civil Aviation Control, and they'd be cleared to land.

"Layla," Clay said from across the aisle. "Get ready for landing."

She leaned around Carlos, still clasping his hand. A slow smile spread across her face, the first in twenty-four hours. "I'm so happy."

Flying high above the glitzy hotel zone, the Gulfstream took a wide curve over the Caribbean. Layla spotted the runway, but then felt a slight hesitation in speed, as though the Gulfstream paused in mid-air. A lapse, followed by acceleration. A second later the cockpit door flew open and Jake called out, "Listen up!"

"What's happening?" Clay yelled back.

"Trouble, big trouble! Fasten your seatbelts! Donavon says we're not cleared for landing." The panic was apparent in Jake's voice.

"What? What the fuck does that mean?"

"Exactly what he said!" Donavon shouted from the cockpit. "The mother fucker is denying us landing rights!"

"That can't be!" Clay shouted back. "We were cleared!"

"Well, we ain't now! Seatbelts!" Donavon's demand came out loud and clear. Hastily, they all buckled up.

"What are we doing?"

"We need another spot to land—a jungle airstrip, a long stretch of road, anything, anything—between here and Merida!"

"That's nearly two hundred miles," Clay said.

"It's *only* two hundred miles and that'll be the last of the fuel. With no fuel we may have a chance of not frying alive. Fuck! Left engine's flared out!"

"Orale!" Layla screamed. "What's happening?"

"We're going down!"

A thousand random thoughts flashed through Layla's mind—Patrón, Lupita, Clay, that pendejo Guillermo, her mother, small memories of life. She tightened her grip on Carlos's hand and he squeezed back.

"Damn! Second engine just quit. Gonna happen fast, prepare for crash landing! Heads down!" Donavon's voice boomed from the cockpit.

The trees were rapidly approaching, rushing up to meet them. That was her last thought before the jet skimmed the tops of jungle hardwoods, shaking it from left to right like a bad day at the car wash. There was a horrible rumbling noise as the plane snapped the tops off the tall sentinels—the only thing between them and the ground. Donavon's skilled piloting managed to keep the jet level before they hit.

Layla gripped her armrests, head down, and prepared for the worst.

Layla didn't know how long they'd been on the ground. Outside the shattered window was total destruction: toppled palms, a broken wing from the jet, stray aluminum parts, steamy vapors wafting up from still-warm engines, and hundreds of black garbage bags strewn in hodgepodge fashion, as though an explosion had gone off. Total chaos. She was still strapped into her seat with shattered glass fragments covering her arms, legs, hands, and shoulders. Luckily she'd covered her face.

She began lightly brushing herself off as she shifted her gaze to the back of the plane, now in parts—the fuselage had broken in two, sheared off at the wings. Thank God Carlos was there with her. But something was wrong. *Very wrong.*

"Carlos!" She shook him. His head was heavy, slumped on her shoulder. "Carlos!"

With his bulk nearly on top of her she couldn't move. Their seats had meshed together in the crash and she sat slightly beneath him. She could see Clay on the other side of the aisle. It looked as though he was stirring. She turned to look at the cockpit—the door was missing.

"Carlos!" she yelled louder now, shaking his shoulder.

That jolted Clay into an upright position. "Layla! Are you all right?"

"Clay, it's Carlos. Something's wrong!"

The Canadian struggled to undo his seat belt. He, too, was at a weird angle. The impact had separated the seats from the floor and they'd found new homes at odd angles in the debris. Palm fronds stuck through broken windows and a huge tree trunk jutting up from the center of the aisle had come very close to nailing them. The plane shuddered, one final gasp at life, before collapsing a few feet closer to the jungle floor. Ragged metal screeched loudly, shattering the jungle stillness as it protested its new position.

Layla screamed again, now pushed further still under her bodyguard's weight. She called out to Clay. "Can you tell if he's breathing?" she managed to gasp.

"Let me get out of this seat. Donavon! Jake!" He called to the pilots.

No answer.

"Oh, Christ, I wonder if they're okay," he said. "Goddamn it to hell."

Clay freed himself from his contorted position methodically, checking his limbs to see if everything was working before trying to make his way over to Layla who looked engulfed by Carlos's bulky body.

"Layla," he said, as he heard her soft sobs. "Layla."

"I killed Carlos. I killed him."

"Layla, hold on now. It's a plane crash, for Christ's sake. You didn't kill anyone," Clay said.

"You don't know about the girl. I didn't tell you about the girl."

"You're not making sense, Layla."

"The girl's dead, too. Guillermo killed her. He told me this morning when I called."

"Oh Christ, Layla, darlin', please don't cry. I'm coming."

She was sobbing, holding tight to Carlos, clinging to him even though his weight was crushing her.

"Help!" a voice called from the cockpit.

"Donavon?" Clay asked.

"Help me!"

"Donavon! I'm here, buddy. Be right there. Just gotta get to Layla."

Clay crossed over the aisle, pushing through the debris to reach her. Layla was halfway under Carlos, trapped by the seats and his weight. Clay crawled sideways alongside the two and reached over the big guy's body to grasp Layla's hand.

"Darlin', you're gonna have to be strong now. Show me what you're made of. Head of the cartel—I want to see it."

Layla was sobbing raggedly. Just twenty minutes before the crash, it seemed like she and Carlos had reconnected. "Clay, he's gone. I know he's gone."

"Layla, I think you're right. Not sure what happened, but his head looks pretty banged up. I'm checking his pulse. Next I'll pull him off you, okay?"

"Okay," she said as a muffled sob spilled out.

A moment later Clay said, "No pulse, Layla. I'm so sorry. Listen, I need to get you out, and then I gotta help Donavon, okay? I can't believe we didn't burst into flames."

"No fuel. He said no fuel, no fire."

"Right. Now don't try and help me, but I'm going to pull Carlos over to the side and I want you to try and climb over him. Think anything's broken? Are your parts all working?"

"I think so."

"Now I'm pulling, and I'm gonna lay him down in the aisle. You crawl around him, on the other side, okay?"

"Si," she said as she slowly removed herself from the entanglement of Carlos's limbs.

"Clay!" It was Donavon.

"Coming buddy, just give me a minute. Almost got Layla out, then you and Jake."

"Jake's unconscious."

"Oh, Christ," Clay mumbled.

"What?" Layla crawled past Carlos's lifeless body.

"Nothing, darlin', nothin'. Doing good, keep coming."

She was nearly in the aisle, past the hulk of her former bodyguard, a man she'd wished dead a thousand times, and who now, had finally obliged her.

"Oh, Clay," she sobbed as she reached him. "Please hold me, just hold me."

"Just for a moment—gotta help Donavon," he said, as he engulfed her in a bear hug.

She moved out of his arms quickly. "Oh, sorry, of course. Let me help."

"Layla, just sit here for a second, all right?" he said, as he took off his jacket and covered the top half of Carlos's body, avoiding Layla's eyes as he did so. "I'm gonna help the pilots."

Clay's six-foot-two frame wasn't meant to fit in the Gulf-stream before the crash, and afterwards he had to stoop further still, unable to stand in the demolished plane. Not only had the fuselage broken in two, but toppled trees had crushed in the roof. He made his way to the cockpit in a slow motion shuffle, shoving random debris out of the way.

"Clay!"

"Coming, Donavon," he said. At the open portal where a door once stood, he saw Donavon still strapped into his seat. Jake was in the co-pilot's seat, head cocked at a weird angle. Clay moved towards Donavon. "Does anything hurt, man?" he asked.

"Everything hurts," Donavon said, in an attempt to sound like the cavalier voyager the world knew him as. "But my leg really hurts. Might be broken. And my seat belt's stuck."

"Don't worry, buddy. Umm, I mean, we'll get it figured out."

"Did Jake make it? Haven't heard him," Donavon asked. His pilot's seat had shifted towards the left in the crash, facing him in the opposite direction of his brother and co-pilot.

"I don't think so, man."

"Goddamn fuck it to hell!" Donavon yelled, completely

out of control. Then, still more out of character, he let out a long low sob. "Oh, God, oh God. No!"

"Oh, Christ, man," Clay said. "Christ, Donavon. Listen to me, please." He continued inching his way to him. "Right now, we can't do anything for Jake, but we can do something for you, my man. Hold steady. I'm getting to you," he said as he crawled through the overwhelming amount of debris that separated the survivors.

"Oh, man. My brother and me flew together thirty years. Thirty fucking years!"

"Listen, man, listen," Clay said. "We gotta concentrate on what we *can* change right now, not what we can't change. You hear me?"

Donavon's air force training kicked in. "Yeah, yeah."

Clay reached him, and began to untangle the seatbelt straps that wrenched the pilot into an extremely tight spot. "Which leg hurts?"

"The left one."

Clay looked above Donavon where the window had crashed in. The framing that once held it together had collapsed onto the pilot's leg.

"How bad does it hurt?"

"Bad," Donavon said.

"I know a little about broken bones. Let me pull you outta here first, then find a spot to lay you down. It's gonna take a bit."

"I can't look at Jake, man. I just can't."

"Then don't," Clay said. He began the slow process of working the beam off the pilot's leg.

"How's the other two?" Donavon asked.

"Layla's okay but the big guy didn't make it."

"Shit," he began to shake his head. "Christ, I couldn't find a spot to land, then the engines just quit on me."

"Listen, listen, we're gonna do what we gotta do and get out of here. We're lucky it's daylight. Thankfully, we got an early start."

Clay pulled the seatbelt from around the pilot's waist, and Donavon let out a low whimper. As Clay lifted the beam off his friend's leg Donovan whined, "Ow, jeez."

"I know, man. But I gotta see what's up with the bone," Clay said, as he gently adjusted Donavon's leg. "Looks like a fracture. Gonna cut the khakis, free it up. Got a first aid kit?"

Donavon pointed behind him to a small closet that had remarkably remained intact. Clay found the kit, took out scissors, rolls of bandages, disinfectant, tape, and a small splint.

"Hey, I'm gonna try to straighten your leg, then tape it up. First I'm gonna clean it, disinfect it. You're probably in shock, so we're gonna fix you up by using the white powder and water on a bandage roll like a poultice, to numb the pain. Can you move the other leg?"

Donavon nodded.

"Layla! You okay?"

"Yes."

"Hang in there. I'm helping Donavon. His leg is broken," Clay shouted from the cockpit.

"Can I help?"

"Let me know if you can get outside. But before you do that, can you get to one of the bags and bring me a kilo. Gonna numb this old vet's leg."

"All right," she said, glad for something to do besides stare at Carlos's body.

Layla stood on wobbly knees, holding onto one of the seats to steady herself and moved away from Carlos. Metal debris was everywhere, jagged pieces of steel that looked like body-piercing javelins. She was surprised they hadn't been beaned by the two tons of coke in back, with some of the cargo still piled behind their seats in mountains of black garbage bags.

From the aisle near Carlos's body, Layla climbed to where the fuselage had fractured. Their load, a jumbled mess, was a far cry from the orderly stacks she'd seen on first entering the plane. She grabbed a bag, struggled to tear it open and managed to break out a kilo.

"Got it." She yelled in Clay's direction. "Should I bring it up to you?"

"Yeah. Can you make it?"

"Yes."

Thus began her careful crawl towards the cockpit. She hurt everywhere. What a thrashing they'd taken. But she knew others, Carlos and Jake, felt nothing at all.

Layla pushed aside palm fronds, stepped over tree limbs, small debris, odd metal parts that crunched under her feet. She reached the open door to the cockpit and saw Jake's lifeless body strapped into the co-pilot's seat and Donavon stretched out halfway across the narrow aisle while Clay hovered over him with a grim look of despair.

Clay recovered quickly when he saw Layla, having no desire to further dampen her already fragile spirits.

Layla stared at Donavon who looked whipped, barely responsive, a different picture from the brash pilot who'd entered the cockpit just an hour ago.

"Hola," she said in a whisper.

"Hi." With hand outstretched, Clay said, "The key."

Layla passed him the tightly wrapped cellophane package. Clay reached into his pocket to extract the Swiss Army knife he'd used to cut strips for bandages for Donavon's leg. He sliced through the packaging, exposing the white powder they'd just risked their lives for.

"Donavon, this will lessen the pain. We know the power of the powder. But I want to tell you both what our plan is gonna be. Are you ready?"

The Canadian's usually laidback exterior radiated total focus. The pilot nodded first, the cartel leader followed suit. No doubt who was alpha dog now.

"We lost Carlos and Jake, a terrible disaster. We're alive, but we're a long way from being okay. We have to get to safety and the only way that's gonna happen is by getting ourselves out of this damn jungle.

"Now, Donavon, for me and Layla, it's gonna be easier because we're pretty much in one piece. But with the help of the powder, you're gonna feel like you are, too."

Donavon nodded again. The man was no stranger to the active properties of cocaine.

"I don't care how we do it, if we have to walk, run, or end up crawling—and it may come to that—but the three of us, we will get out of this jungle," he said, staring directly into Donovan's eyes, then turning to Layla.

"You got it? Both of you?" he said, waiting again for nods of agreement. "We're lucky we took off early because we have time on our side. It probably won't be long before someone—a peasant, a woodcutter—notices there's some gigantic broken thing in their jungle.

"Actually, we'd be lucky if it was a local. Because we all know this: We were denied landing rights in Cancun, so someone knows we're within a two-hundred-mile stretch between Cancun and Merida. I don't want to scare you, but we know the business we're in."

Clay saw Layla's eyes go wide.

"First things first. Layla, you need to find me some water somewhere, so I can make a paste to put on Donavon's leg.

"Donavon, I'll affix the splint, tape you up good as new,

make a crutch, and give ya a couple lines to take the edge off. I'm gonna drag you off this plane. Then we're gonna walk to civilization."

"Which way are we heading?" Layla asked.

Clay gave a quick shake of his head. "Doesn't matter. First thing is Donavon's leg. Next, outta the plane. Got it?"

"What can I do?" Layla asked.

"After the water, sit by Donavon, hold his hand while I'm fixing the splint, play nurse."

"You ready?" Clay asked. "Cause we're gonna give it our best shot."

CHAPTER 17

"I need a minute with Carlos," Layla said to Clay as he ushered a limping Donavon out the plane's cockeyed door with one hand, machete in the other. He nodded and returned his concentration to the needs of the wounded vet.

Alone in the wreckage of the jet, Layla knelt beside Carlos's body. Pulling aside the jacket that covered him, she gazed at her bodyguard. Even death couldn't dim his rugged beauty, but it was hard to look at the now impassive face. "Oh Carlos, my love," she whispered in Spanish.

She never dreamed she'd be crying because he was gone, but she was. How many times had he caused her to break down in tears? And quite a few of those times she had wished he was out of her life.

Layla stood, rubbed the wetness from her cheeks and pulled her Vuitton bag onto the remains of Clay's seat and rifled through it. She grabbed the shoulder-strap valise, passport, phone, and a stack of pesos. In Carlos' briefcase she found more pesos, his phone and passport. Clay had retrieved Donavon's passport along with Jake's before leaving the plane.

"Don't want these left behind," he had told her. "Plus I'm hoping we need them."

She grabbed hold of the seat and pushed herself up and away from her lover. "Carlos, Carlos, how will I live without you, you pinche cabrón?"

She wiped tears from her face with her right hand, bent down a last time and rubbed the tear drops along Carlos's right cheek, making the sign of the cross on his forehead. She re-arranged the jacket over him. When she reached the door, she turned for one last look at her lover's body.

Now she was ready to leave.

The mangled stairs of the jet led onto a down-trodden mat of oozing foliage—definitely jungle. The dank smell of plants and rot permeated every pore of Layla's body. Before her lay a surreal masterpiece of an environment in chaos. Mid-center sat a mauled Gulfstream jet amidst a toppled forest of palms surrounded by hundreds of intact black garbage bags. All that shiny aluminum juxtaposed with the deep, psychedelic green of the tropics. In a matter of days federales would be streaming through the jungle, marking the territory with yellow tape used to identify crime scenes, as evidence of a drug deal gone bad. How absurd. The only crime she could think of was some asshole airport manager in Cancun denying them landing rights after promising precisely that.

Bright sun should have streamed into her eyes, but the Yucatán's low forest ceiling shielded the light from her face. Probably just as well—with humidity, it had to be pushing ninety. Thankfully, they hadn't landed directly in swampy mangroves or poisonous snakes surely would have posed a problem. She was wearing sturdy Teva sandals, but the straps offered no protection against snakes like the deadly cuatro nariz or other amphibious creatures. She'd worn pants and not a skirt that morning, so at least her legs were covered, though her arms were bare. She'd decided not to change into a long-sleeved shirt due to the heat.

She joined Clay and Donavon on the jungle floor. Her eyes shifted to the pilot. Poor Donavon. The vet had been a basket case before Clay laid him out a couple healthy lines. Who could blame him? Crash-landing in a jungle, his brother dead, his leg broken, and no help on the way. But the powder did its magic and got his mojo working. Along with the hastily-prepared crutch Clay had crafted out of some piece of wood—a dowel from the pilots' coat closet?—it looked as though they were ready to continue their expedition, though one under considerably less steam than earlier. When would it end? Poised to set out from smack dab in the middle of nowhere, she felt she was living the warning posted over the Gates of Hell from *Dante's Inferno*: "Abandon all hope, ye who enter here."

🔲🔲🔲

It was decided: Clay would lead the way, Donavon in the middle, and Layla pulling up the rear. Unsurprisingly, she couldn't get a signal on her phone—and forget GPS. Though the sun was tough to spot from beneath the canopy of trees, Clay gauged it as best he could and set a direction in which they'd walk.

Even though Clay swore he hadn't racked up any Boy Scout badges or the equivalent in his Canadian childhood, he claimed to have a good sense of direction and he clearly had some survival skills. Donavon exhibited a marked change, his spirits bolstered by the powder. He appeared alert and as ready as Clay and Layla for the bizarre survival competition they'd entered by accident.

At present, all that mattered was initiative and action. Their mantra: keep moving. Towards what, no one had a clue.

"So Donavon," Clay said. "How many clicks outta Cancun before we went down?"

"A hundred or so."

"Any pueblos nearby?" Clay asked, as he placed a walking stick he'd crafted from a tree branch in front of him. They were inching along, but moving.

"We should be pretty near one of those villages about sixty miles from Chichen Itza."

"Not very populated?"

"No, even though Chichen is a tourist mecca, you get a few miles away from the pyramids and there's nothing. Piste, the closest town, has maybe a thousand people, if that."

As they talked, they carefully trod through forest jungle. Clay led them in a westerly direction. They all hoped to locate a village, a place to rest, where they could figure out what they were doing.

For the moment, survival was the only thing on their collective mind. Eventually, they had to put some distance between themselves and the Yucatán Peninsula and return as quickly as possible to Mexico's west coast.

Someone blocked us at the airport. Was it the Gulf Cartel, Guillermo's long reach from Guatemala, or some political snafu they'd inadvertently sidestepped into? In the drug world, anything was possible. And as for the now derailed transport of two tons of coke, so be it. Funny how a life and death situation changed one's perspective on the previous significance of loss of cash and product transfer.

Clay looked at the sky through a tangle of trees. "It can't be more than nine," he said. "That gives us nearly nine hours of daylight."

Thank God for that, Layla thought. Maybe that would be enough time to find someone to help them get out of the jungle, closer to civilization, and salvation.

CHAPTER 18

Cancun, Quintana Roo, Mexico

José Chan Canul was freaking out. As Civil Aviation Director of Cancun International Airport, he had prevented a Gulfstream jet from landing. He'd looked around at the others in the control tower, trying to gauge their reactions to the blunder they'd witnessed, but no one gave anything away. That was so Mexican. The world could be falling down around them, and they'd pretend everything was perfectly fine. Ojala. Isn't that what his Maya mother said? By the grace of God. Chinga! He was going to need that and more. The jet he just denied landing rights to was carrying product for the Culiacan Cartel. Why hadn't he said no to those first couple shipments a month ago? Why?

Then it had been the Gulf Cartel, but did it really matter which cartel it was? Though the money was nice, it was more that he feared not complying with their demands wasn't an option. The cartels never took no for an answer. El plata o el plomo.

Last month, immediately after he'd allowed the second drug-loaded jet to land, the DEA came down from the States. The DEA! Puta de madre! No one wants to be seen anywhere near those guys. And it wasn't like they laid low. You could smell their sick craftiness, sniffing around for this or that. The slightest wrongdoing and it was like they had radar, as if they already knew you were guilty. How did they hear everything, and so fast? Some mole no doubt— someone snitching.

José had no way of disguising the arrival records, that was the sad part. If he'd known the DEA was going to come calling, he could have forged new documents. But he had no time to do that once they showed up. One day they were simply at his office, demanding a meeting and asking for the password to his computer. His password, for God's sake.

It didn't take long before they identified the two out-of-sequence flights—private jets. And then it got heavy. They escorted him out of the building while his co-workers looked on. The DEA ushered him right into a waiting car and whisked him off to the Cancun hotel zone for the grilling, the interrogation, the demands. At least that embarrassment took place away from the airport and the prying eyes of, well, everyone.

During the questioning, things heated up. "Mr. Canul," Agent Smith, began, smiling, like the nice guy he pretended to be. Why did they always do that good cop, bad cop routine? "We need you to answer a few questions, and then we'll let you go back to business as usual."

Like that was an option.

"We know you approved two private flights, arriving from Guatemala, for landing here in Cancun last month— two flights that didn't have proper paperwork to make an international landing. Why did you allow that?"

All nicey nice. He sure could talk pretty, and in Spanish!

"No, Señor Smith. They had proper authorization. Our guidelines state that an international non-commercial private air transport for non-profit purposes is acceptable for landing as long as their first stop is on Mexican soil; Article 28 in Mexico's Civil Aviation Code."

Bad cop now, Jones. "Oh, come on, Canul. That's bullshit and you know it. They had no authorization from your Minister of Communication and Transport. Plus we know for a fact you were aware those planes were carrying very important cargo—tons of cocaine—that belonged to the Gulf Cartel. Whose payroll are you on?"

"No one's, Señor Jones, just my job," José said, a line of sweat forming on his thin upper lip. "Of course they had proper paperwork. All our planes do."

"Okay, how long are we gonna play this game with you?" Bad Cop again. "Frankly we don't have time to sit here and chat. If you don't 'fess up and fast, we'll drag your ass back to the States. We can have extradition papers worked up in forty-eight hours, no problem. Then you get to say goodbye to Mexico, your family, and your freedom. You'll do about twenty in a US federal prison. How's that sound?"

That's how it went. They wore him down in record time. He was no match for them. He wasn't a mobster or a gang member. He was just a civil aviation guy who knew how to administrate and on a good day, manage. Nothing more. He was forty-three years old with an engineering degree from UNAM, a wife, and two kids who played soccer on the weekends. He just bought a house in Playa del Carmen. He worked hard, six days a week. Cancun was growing and there were rumors another runway was in the works. Plus the tourists kept pouring in. Couldn't stop them. They were in love with Cancun. Fucking gringos. If they weren't so into their damn drugs, he wouldn't be sitting in the hot seat right now. It was the gringos' fault, all the demands due to their addiction to the powder, and for some stronger stuff lately—heroin, or junk as they called it up north.

Chinga! Mexicans didn't do drugs. Man, they barely drank alcohol. Did you ever really look at what Mexicans drank when they were eating out? Not a single beer bottle on the table. What they were addicted to was Coca Cola. It was the running joke: Mexico used more coke than any nation on the planet. But the liquid kind! The country was addicted to sugar cane, not cocaine.

Day to day, the average Mexican didn't drink alcohol or smoke cigarettes. Why? It was never their nature in the first place. In a survival mode lifestyle there's no room for addiction. Plain and simple, they have families to feed, or themselves. None of those excesses for los Mexicanos. Life didn't allow it.

Now the gringo? Every addiction in the world! Canul had friends who worked in fancy hotels—from Cabo to Cancun —and they told him all tourists asked for two things: marijuana and coke. Well, Mexico could certainly comply. So here *he* was being grilled by two DEA agents because of those damn gringos and their need for speed. And the investigators were applying pressure. They threatened him—if he allowed even one more unauthorized landing, they'd nab his ass so fast he couldn't even spit out "hasta la vista" before they extradited him to the land of milk and honey.

This was only the beginning. Next they'd ask him to inform on his boss or wear a wire.

So a Gulfstream called in—a gringo, he recognized the pilot's voice—and asked for clearance.

"Denied," José said.

There was a lot of crackling on the line, but he heard, "Fuck, what?"

"Denied."

He switched off the radio. He didn't need to hear any more. Why make it more of an issue, when his co-workers were right there overhearing every word he uttered?

From the tower he could see the plane dip, then elevate and straighten out. It looked like it was going to head due west, towards Merida. Maybe they'd allow him to land there. For the sorry son of a bitch's sake, he hoped so.

José walked away from the tower, returned to his modest office, shut the door, closed the cheap vertical blinds, sat at his desk, put his head in his hands, and wept.

CHAPTER 19

Yucatán Jungle, Mexico

By noon Clay was fighting his way through forest so thick the machete he'd grabbed before departing the ruined jet was getting quite a workout. Leading the way, he hacked a narrow path through vines and creeping foliage for his followers. Donavon and Layla were holding up well under the circumstances. With little water to supplement them, they'd forged ahead, no complaints. Clay decided it was time for a break.

"I see a log up ahead," he yelled back. "We'll take five."

Layla was glad to hear it. The heat was killing her and she couldn't take her eyes off the slippery uneven ground for a second or she'd trip. She had no idea how Donavon was coping. She dripped with sweat and smelled like she hadn't showered in a week. The musty jungle odor no longer bothered her, but those damn mosquitoes! In an air-conditioned gym, she could pump iron, run circles around others, fast track on the treadmill, and even take in a yoga or Pilates class afterwards. A true city girl, she'd never been anywhere near a jungle. In fact, the outdoors in any form was not her specialty. And the humidity was killing her.

But Layla was no complainer, and when times were tough, she rose to the occasion. She'd been coached by the best, a long line of underdogs who clawed their way to the pinnacle. Now, she sat at the top. Leaders didn't complain, they acted.

"Sit here, Donavon," Clay said, as he helped the wounded vet down onto the damp hardwood log. "First have some water, my man, then I'm gonna fix you up a line."

From a gray backpack he'd been carrying since they began their Guatemala trip days earlier, Clay brought out an aluminum water container and handed it to the pilot. He unzipped a front pocket and took out a puffy packet filled with coke.

"Layla?" he asked, nodding at the powder.

She shook her head.

"Just wanted to make sure," he said. "Donavon needs this to keep going. I think you and me are working on sheer adrenaline."

She nodded. "Can I have some water after Donavon?"

Clay waited for the pilot to drink, handed her the container, and set about crafting two beefy lines on the back of a hotel note pad, scraping them together with a credit card. He handed the pad carefully to the vet and pulled out a two-hundred peso note.

"How's the leg feel?" Clay asked, as he rolled the bill into a tight cylinder.

"It'll be better after this." The vet's face wore a pained expression and it was obvious the earlier infusion had long since worn off.

"I know it's hard," Clay said, watching the pilot closely as he handed him the bill, "but we've been walking almost two hours. I know we're gonna reach something soon. Trust me. I'm an old country boy and I get these hunches."

Layla felt hopeful in spite of herself. Even if he was bull-shitting, it made her feel good.

After snorting the first line, the vet seemed to believe him, too. "You think so?"

"Why not?" Clay said, getting into his own version of a sales manager building the team. "Those Maya are everywhere around here, aren't they? Christ, they say their civilization is lost? Forgetaboutit. Every time I've been to the Yucatán, all I see are Mayans. For being lost, there sure are a lot of them."

Layla gave a little laugh and even Donavon managed a smile.

"Okay. Coffee break's over. You ready?" Clay asked, now wearing his forest ranger hat.

"Sure," Layla said, getting up and stretching. She handed back the water container.

"Well, all righty. Hut-two-three-four. Donavon knows what that means."

In a few minutes, the small group was on the move again, ready for their adventure into the unknown.

CHAPTER 20

Cancun, Quintana Roo, Mexico

March had started off as a good month for former army colonel Geraldo Montoyo Alcazar. His new position, recently offered by the Cancun Police Department, came unexpectedly. In truth, he didn't want to leave Mexico City. But Quintana Roo in general, and Cancun in specific, presented a man with his background a range of benefits in one or two years far beyond what could be attained in the country's interior. He couldn't afford to say no to a posting in Cancun.

Revered for his hardline approach on crime, Alcazar planned to parlay his no-nonsense policy into a take-no-prisoners stance with the drug cartels that were methodically breaking into Mexico's number one tourist destination. Not only had they carved inroads with drug imports, they'd created a sophisticated money-laundering network using hotels as decoys for cash flow.

His good friend Enrique had compared Cancun to the wild west when they met at a reunion in Cuernavaca a few months earlier. Geraldo, Enrique, and several other friends, all tennis players who knew each other from school, still got together every couple years to compare notes on their lives and families. Now in their early fifties, most came from privilege and had retired from industry or family businesses. In fact, Geraldo was the lone working stiff amongst them.

Having shied away from his father's lucrative warehouse business in Mexico City, he chose to make his mark in the military, against his family's wishes.

"Geraldo, do come to Cancun," Enrique said, as they sipped Cuba Libres on the terrace of a friend's Cuernavaca villa. "It's the closest thing to heaven on earth. Absolutely gorgeous. The sea is turquoise, with tall coconut palms lining the white sand beaches. And if you're willing to gamble, there's money to be made in land and real estate."

"Really?" he'd asked. "Can I get clear title?"

"Por supuesto," Enrique said. "Most of it's titled now. Some ejido tracts are still left, but for the most part, the government gave ejido land to the chicleros, you know, those tree tappers for Wrigley's Gum. They granted fifty-hectare parcels in the jungle to populate the territory back in the sixties, trying to displace the indigenous Maya. Beachfront property is still for sale, too—farther down the coast."

Quintana Roo, Mexico's thirty-first state, came into being in 1974, a few years after the Mexico National Tourist Corporation deemed the spit of sand on a narrow island extending out from the mainland to be a bonafide world-class tourist resort.

A computer chose the destination after feeding basic requirements into the program: good beaches, perfect temps, short flights to the US, and few if any hurricanes. Cancun's location was on Mexico's eastern seaboard, in what was then the unruly territory of Quintana Roo. The population consisted of a few fishermen, a handful of chicleros, and one coco plantation.

According to Geraldo's friend Enrique, Cancun's bountiful land was its main attraction. A killing could be made by anyone motivated enough—or reckless enough, depending on perspective—to invest.

"Why do they call it Cancun?" Geraldo asked.

"It's a Mayan word. It means nido de culebras."

A shocked look crossed Geraldo's usually placid face. "Nest of serpents?"

"Not to worry, amigo," Enrique said with a dry chuckle. "The translation sounds horrible but Maya culture reveres serpents, so really, island of the enchanted serpent is more like it. I just wanted to rattle you a little. And believe me, the place *is* enchanted. Come visit."

Not long after the reunion, Geraldo departed for Cancun. His new position at the Cancun Police Department began with a personal promise to the Chief of Police that he'd be tough on crime, a not so secret code meaning he would deal with the cartels head on. To the outside world he was known as Public Works Security Director, but within the department his unofficial title was Commissioner to End Cartel Violence.

On Geraldo's arrival, the police chief supplied the former military man with a bodyguard who also served as driver. He gave him one of his most trusted men, a Maya local named Ricardo from Leona Vicario, a small agricultural town west of the city.

One night a month later, at around 11 p.m., Geraldo and Ricardo departed headquarters and were driving on Av. Rodrigo Gomez, a four-lane boulevard that runs across Cancun from east to west. They'd left the stoplight in front of the Costco shopping center when a black SUV approached on their left and forced them off the road. Another SUV appeared in front of them blocking their path. Shots rang out.

In moments Ricardo was slumped over the wheel and Geraldo's dead body lay on its side in the front seat next to his driver. He'd taken fifteen shots, mainly in the head and neck. Geraldo had been on the job in Cancun barely a month.

The cartel message was clear: Don't mess with us.

Por Esto and Novedades, two Cancun newspapers, kept coverage short. " 'They were fired at less than a half hour after they left the building," a spokesman for the deceased man's department said. "We don't know how many shots. We can't see a motive. He worked in an office planning public security. He wasn't on operations and had nothing to do with investigating drug cartels.' "

Just the facts. What the newspapers failed to mention was how busy that street was, day or night. That particular evening there were no other vehicles on the road departing Costco, Home Depot, or Comercial Mexicana. Though police put out a request for any piece of information, not an eyewitness could be found.

CHAPTER 21

Yucatán Jungle, Mexico

C lay thought he heard something in the forest jungle other than the noise he and his friends made as they struggled along, man against nature. Besides their careful treading on slick fallen leaves, they had to step over countless branches, palm fronds, and the occasional tree trunk. Each encounter made a sound, small or large.

There it was again. Something in the distance gave off a soft *whack, whack, whack.*

"Layla!" Clay put up a hand and turned to look at her and Donavon. "Did you hear that?"

"Yes," she said. "Maybe a machete or an ax?"

"You think so?" Clay asked.

Even Donavon got in on it. "A wood cutter?"

"Could be," Clay said, "Let's listen."

The trio abruptly stopped and tried to tune in to what they hoped was the sound of civilization. By now it was well into the afternoon. They'd been walking for hours with very little sustenance, the exception being grit, something all three had plenty of. But each step posed a potential problem, and poor Donavon with a busted leg and shaky crutch was not having an easy time. At least there were no longer large predators in Yucatán jungles. Jaguars had once roamed freely, but the Maya killed them off long ago for their hides and talisman properties. The biggest enemy so far—aside from the heat—was insects.

"It's coming from that way," Clay said. He was motioning with his right arm, pointing in the direction they were facing. "I'm gonna go look for that guy. You wait here for me. I can go faster on my own!" he said with an energy he hadn't shown since they left the wreckage.

"But will you be able to find us again?" Layla asked. The very idea of being in the jungle alone with only Donavon, no machete, and little water, terrified her.

"Layla, I told you I'm a country boy. I grew up hunting and tracking up north. I know how to backtrack my own trail, don't worry."

Donavon joined in. "He's gotta go, Layla. We could never make it fast enough, the three of us," the pilot said, referring to his own compromised body. "And what if the guy leaves? Who knows when we'll get another chance?"

Clay chimed in. "We may only have this one shot."

Put that way, it made total sense. "You're right," she said. "Better hurry."

Clay flashed her a smile before he said, "I'm leaving the backpack with you guys. Layla, can you lay out a line for Donavon? Think it's about that time."

Clay turned away and grabbed the machete with a tighter grip as he started to cut a swath of foliage before him. An arduous task, but one that now whispered hope.

Layla felt flustered as she took the pack, trying to concentrate on anything other than Clay's departure. She looked around for a feasible spot for the two of them to rest while they waited, hoping she could find a place where the mosquitoes would be less annoying than on the trail. Not to mention the army ants, which were beyond aggressive.

"Donavon, let's go sit over there," she said in English, and helped him to the base of one of the taller trees that looked drier than anywhere else. "How about a little water?"

"Sure," he said. "And it's time for my meds." He tried to crack a smile.

"Does this remind you of Vietnam?" she asked. "I mean, the jungle?"

"Well, I didn't see a lot of jungle from this perspective. I was usually flying above it," he said out loud. Under his breath he muttered, "and dropping a shitload of bombs on those poor motherfuckers."

"What?" Layla asked.

"Ah, jeez. Just thinking about the war. Like the bombs weren't bad enough, then we—well not me—sprayed the villages with Agent Orange. What a fucked-up war!"

"Okay, Donavon, time to change subjects." Layla said as she unzipped the pack, pulling out the water container. "Here's the water."

The pilot accepted the offering and took a quick gulp before passing it back. He waited expectantly while Layla pulled out the packet with the coke, located the note pad and rummaged in her purse for a credit card to scrape the lines together. The Mexicana did this all as if she had experience.

"Do you ever do coke?" the pilot asked.

"What? Don't tell me you believe that *Scarface* bullshit?" Her look put that thought to rest.

Two sizable lines emerged from the pile of powder. Layla handed them over to the vet. "Momentito," she said, then continued in English. "Gotta find that peso note."

She rummaged again in the pack and found the bill. She rolled it tight following Clay's example and passed it to the pilot.

"Mission nearly accomplished," Donavon said as he snorted the first of two lines. He placed a thumb under his numb nostril before quickly inhaling the other. His entire body went into a brief moment of temporary relaxation, a pause before the rush as the incoming buzz exploded in his cerebellum.

She watched the pilot surrender to the powder before asking, "How's your leg?"

"Can't really feel it. Think the poultice Clay made fixed me up. I'm just really wiped out, but that little hit was like pure adrenaline. Don't want to think about the tiredness."

"No, of course not."

"But say," Donavon said, feeling bolstered by the blow. "What happened back there? Why didn't they let us land in Cancun?"

She shrugged. "I really don't know. Maybe Guillermo. Maybe the Gulf Cartel, or the feds."

"Speaking of Guillermo, why didn't we fuel up in Guatemala this morning?"

"Long story."

"I think I deserve to hear it. Ain't going nowhere." The drug had obviously renewed Donavon's confidence. He was starting to act like his former self.

Layla let out a sigh. "Yes, you do. And you're right, even though you didn't say it. This is my fault. All of it. I am so sorry, Donavon. Truly I am. About Jake and Carlos," she sighed again as she took a deep breath. "About the fuel, your leg, the crash."

"What the fuck happened?" Donavon flipped into commando mode, with an edgy tone. His fingers drummed on his khaki-clad thigh in a rhythmic manner. The powder had found its mark.

Layla knew it was time to come clean. Why keep secrets when you're one of two survivors lost in the middle of nowhere? And who was she to withhold information from a guy who'd tried to save them by landing a plane in a jungle and lost his brother in the process? Carrying her fucked up shit. She reassessed the vet. He could be the last person she spoke to on God's green earth. Keep it real.

She rearranged herself against the trunk of the tree. "It started at Guillermo's villa last night —it's way outside of Antigua. The place was in total lockdown and the whole situation had a weird vibe, but he works for us, so I didn't think anything about it."

"Go on," Donavon said.

So she did. Beginning with her innocent search for a bathroom, and telling him the whole story of finding Lupita and what she'd heard from the girl.

"It was the hardest thing I've ever done. Leaving her. Something in me snapped. I couldn't control myself when we got to his grand dining room and that fat cabrón comes in acting like he's king of the world. I called him on it."

"On the girl in the room?" Donavon asked, startled. "What happened?"

"He lost it. Told us to get out. Had his driver take us back to Guatemala City."

"That's why we left so early?"

"Yeah. Because I stupidly hadn't gotten the number of the guy in civil aviation who was supposed to let us fuel up. So I called him this morning and ..." She trailed off.

"Guillermo? What did he say?"

"He said he didn't have a number. Then he told me—" her voice cracked. She stopped for a moment while the pilot waited for the punch line. She was trembling and her mind had taken a brief detour. She pulled herself together. "He told me the girl was dead."

"What? He killed her?"

"I don't know who killed her, but I think it was him."

"Oh, fuck," Donavon said. "Layla. I'm so sorry." He

reached for her arm to give it a sympathetic squeeze. "That's so wrong."

"I know it is. It is. But all of it, Lupita—that was her name—her death, and Carlos and Jake dying, the crash and us being here in the jungle, it's all because of me. Because I couldn't focus on what was happening. I blew it, and I am so, so sorry."

She started to cry.

"Hey, hey," Donavon said, massaging her elbow lightly as her tears came. "Listen, Layla. Shit happens, bad shit. Today I lost my brother. You lost Carlos."

"But I screwed up, and I'm in charge."

"Hey, you can't control the future. You should know that by now. The business we're in, it's a motherfucker. Anything can happen, to anyone, at any time. We all know the risks."

"Yeah, I know," she said, wiping her runny nose with the back of her hand.

"But if I learned one thing over the years, it's you can't obsess on anything too long—the killings, the deaths, even the madness. You can't do that and keep your sanity. You gotta buck up. That's what your uncle would tell you, isn't it?"

She nodded, unable to speak.

"I'm really sorry about the girl and about Carlos. He seemed like a good guy."

"He was." She was still crying. "Donavon, I'm so sorry about Jake."

He looked at her long and hard before speaking. "Say, why don't you lay me out one more line. We'll say it's for the road, and maybe that'll bring Clay back with help. How about it?"

"Excellent idea," she said, going for the pack, glad to have unloaded her burden on the pilot's sympathetic shoulders.

CHAPTER 22

Time seemed to move backwards while they waited for Clay's return. Layla fixed up a semi-dry spot for Donavon to recline under the tree so he could take the pressure off his leg. Every few minutes the pilot shook off an ant attack. Along with the dratted ants, they slapped at a multitude of buzzing insects and stayed on high alert for anything that moved. Both survivors continued to return their gaze in the direction where they'd last spotted Clay, hoping to manifest him like Juan Diego's glimpse of the Virgin Guadalupe. Talking petered out and Donavon dozed off in spite of the massive amounts of coke he'd ingested.

Layla pondered the situation they'd be in if Clay didn't return. By the time they figured out he wasn't coming back, it would be nightfall. She tried not to think about what happened in jungles after dark. They didn't even have a machete for protection.

Layla stopped looking at her watch every fifteen minutes as it did little to speed up time. When she finally did sneak a peek, Clay had been gone over an hour. Maybe the noise they'd heard had been farther away than it sounded. Or perhaps by the time Clay got to where the sound originated, the creator of the noise had already departed, his or her mysterious mission accomplished.

If she continued along this line of thought, Layla knew she could go crazy. Was this similar to being stranded on a desert island? It was basically the same thing—not surrounded by water, but instead encircled by a dense, equally daunting forest. Maybe she was already going mad. In her world, she had no time to ponder life—she just lived it. But here she was, stranded with a disabled pilot in a jungle and not even a jacket to cope with cooler night temperatures.

Just as she began her descent into hell, figuring that dying was easy, it was living that scared her, she thought she heard something far off down the path Clay had cut.

Should she wake Donavon?

Another far-off noise kept repeating. It sounded like rustling or chopping.

It had been a while since Clay's departure and neither Layla nor Donavon had wanted to entertain anything other than hopeful thoughts. Layla checked her watch, three p.m. It was early spring and the sun would still sit high in the sky for quite a long time, but because they were under a tapestry of trees, darkness would fall sooner rather than later.

"Donavon, do you think it's Clay?"

He'd awakened as if on cue. "Who else would it be?" the pilot said, trying to sound flip.

The noise came steadily closer. Layla longed to investigate by following the crude path Clay cut, but hesitated, knowing Donavon—though bolstered by the amount of powder he'd snorted—was in precarious shape.

They looked at each other trying to pretend all was well, but Layla felt a tinge of terror. What if it *wasn't* Clay? To take the edge off, she needed to do something.

"Donavon, how about another line? This time, really for the road?" Layla asked. "I think there's just enough powder for one last bump."

"You're an angel, amiga." A relaxed smile softened his angular features. In his younger years he must have been a good-looking guy, she mused. Classic tall and dark, though not truly handsome, Donavon had an aloof yet alluring quality that women would notice. No doubt he'd given his share of women their fair share of trouble. Layla was sure he'd stopped more than a few hearts in his day. But she got the feeling the only heartbreaker Donavon ever flipped over was waiting in Clay's backpack. One of Eric Clapton's famous tunes ran through her mind and it wasn't "*I Shot the Sheriff.*"

The pilot finished off Layla's last line.

Layla tidied up the note pad, put the credit card back in her wallet and stuffed the now-empty packet into her valise. She stared up at the trees, trying not to look at Donavon and not to feel edgy, as they waited to discover what the sound was. She sensed Donavon, though high as a kite, was probably attempting to feign nonchalance as much as she was.

"Layla! Donavon!"

"Oh, Christ!" Donavon shouted. "Clay! Where are you?"

"Coming, coming!"

"Clay! Thank God!" Layla grabbed Donavon's arm. "Maybe we'll be okay after all."

"Yes! I got places to go, people to see!" Donavon's tormented face broke into a grin.

In seconds, both were in a silly mood that bordered on slapstick, hoping Clay was bringing someone with a sense of direction who could save their sorry dehydrated asses.

꧁꧂꧃

Five minutes later Clay emerged from the brush. He looked like the wizard of Oz accompanied by a munchkin. The woodcutter with him was diminutive but seemed to propel himself through the jungle as though he was an active part of it, an extension of the foliage.

Nearly as wide as he was tall—in a stocky, hard-body way—the Maya local didn't look like a first responder, but Layla knew he was the right man for the job.

The closer he advanced the more real were his hobbit-like features. He looked old to be hanging out in the jungle, but he didn't appear winded or bothered by the journey.

Layla hailed from Mexico's west coast, but she knew all the Maya tales. Not only were they naked eye astronomers who had built impressive step pyramids and created a written language, they'd kept Caucasians and Mulattos out of their territory Quintana Roo—at that time not yet a Mexican state—for nearly one hundred years. The Caste War of Yucatán lasted until the 1930s after the Maya had endured centuries of suffering by Spanish overlord landholders.

And Maya could survive in the jungle. They lived on the land and knew what vines supplied water, what trees provided nourishment. They were chroniclers of the jungle and lived alongside it, never taking too much, only what was needed. And what was needed most was firewood. The Maya man had a machete in hand and a rough-hewn rope pack on his back. Empty.

"Clay! You're here!"

"Yes, along with Juan! Couldn't have done it without Juan," he said, beaming at the back of the advancing Maya. The two men entered the clearing Layla and Donavon had called home for the past couple hours. Clay lay down his machete and Juan did the same.

"Hola," Layla said to Juan. "Layla."

"Donavon," the pilot said.

"Mucho gusto. Juan Balam," said the hobbit-like person. He averted his eyes in a shy manner.

"He speaks Spanish? Have you talked to him?" Layla asked, looking at Clay and smiling at the Maya man.

"Not much. Just told him we had a plane crash, two amigos were dead, Donavon was hurt. That's all I had to say. He put down the wood he was chopping and was ready to find you guys."

Layla grasped the man's hand, and said, "Muchas gracias, señor. Muchas gracias."

Obviously embarrassed by the attention, he withdrew his hand, looked down again, then glanced upwards. He pointed at the sky. "Oscuro." Dark.

That was all they needed to hear to propel them into the last push of their accidental journey. Layla handed Clay his backpack. Donavon stood up, shaking badly.

Juan's eyes locked on the pilot, watching his slow, unsteady movements. He looked over the makeshift cast Clay had pieced together and concentrated his attention on the pilot's strained face.

"Bien?" He moved closer and lightly touched Donavon's leg.

"Si," Donavon nodded, wiping rivulets of sweat from his forehead with a piece of ragged khaki material. He looked at Clay. "Layla's been mother's little helper while you were gone."

"Good," Clay said. "Recently?"

"Yeah, we were having an early celebration when we thought we heard you in the distance. Layla got me all set up. Now seeing Juan, I could walk on water as well as through this damn jungle! Bring it on!" He let out a raspy laugh but his face contorted into a grimace as he spoke.

Juan stared at the pilot in disbelief. Gazing upward again, he motioned to Clay with his hand, indicating small talk was over; it was time to move on.

CHAPTER 23

Motul, Yucatán, Mexico

Juan Balam led the bedraggled group to the edge of the dense jungle where his stash of firewood awaited. Clay helped him place the wood in the rope sack on his back and stuffed kindling into his own durable backpack to lighten the Maya's load.

The day was drawing to a close but that no longer posed a threat. Juan was there to help, and they followed blindly along, Layla behind Juan, and Clay assisting Donavon who was struggling to keep up.

After walking another thirty minutes, they emerged from the jungle into a clearing. Juan stopped in front of an unpainted cinder block house with a palapa roof. No other homes were nearby. Chickens ran free in a dirt yard where two limón trees grew alongside a few tattered maize plants. A chaká shrub fence surrounded the property.

"Motul." Juan took off his hat exposing a thick shock of graying hair. He rubbed a hand across his brow.

"Motul?" Clay asked.

"Si, mi pueblo, Motul. Casa de mi sobrino." His town and his nephew's house, he explained as he pointed at the small abode.

"Manuel!" Juan shouted. He rested his hardened palms on a lopsided wooden gate. "Manuel!"

A moment later a slender man in his twenties with

raven-black hair stuck his head out the screen door. He looked surprised to see his uncle with such an unlikely group.

"Tio!"

The young man bolted out the door and in an instant was through the fence. He embraced the older man, all the while taking stock over his uncle's shoulder of the ragtag strangers in his midst. An exchange took place and in moments Manuel was caught up on the day's events.

"My nephew lives here in Motul," he told the group in Spanish. "He weaves sisal for Panama hats and can put you up for the night, maybe longer."

"We'll pay him," Clay said, in a gracious tone. The Maya local had come through beautifully, finding them a reasonable spot to land while they tried to find a doctor for Donavon.

"What about Donavon's leg?" Layla asked Clay in English.

Donavon had faded fast once they left the jungle, even with Clay helping him along.

Manuel looked at the wounded pilot, shaking his head. The jerry-rigged crutch and makeshift splint had barely held together in the Bataan-style march through an inhospitable jungle.

"Don Ramon?" he asked of his uncle.

"Si," Juan nodded.

Manuel dashed around the group then sprinted down the lane.

"Where's he going?" Clay asked, nervous. He touched Juan's arm. "Who's Don Ramon?"

"A shaman in the pueblo," Juan said. "He can help with your friend's leg until you get him to a doctor in Merida."

"But does he have medicine? Something for the pain?"

"He has herbs and knows about bones. Even we Maya

sometimes break an arm or leg."

Clay's face reddened. He hadn't meant to offend Juan but the way it came out made him sound like a first-world idiot. Layla looked at Clay. He, too, was clearly holding it together by a narrow margin.

"Can I sit down somewhere?" Donavon asked.

Everyone's attention shifted back to the pilot. His eyes had a feverish cast and his face looked drained.

"Por supuesto," Juan said. He offered the vet his arm and led him through the open gate towards the house. With Clay's help, Juan steered Donavon towards a sapling chair that sat on the low front porch, under a palapa extension that jutted out over the threshold.

Layla found an overturned log and took a seat, glad to be out of the dense forest and away from the insects, the jungle sounds, and the odd feeling of being imprisoned by all that foliage. Clay crouched close to Donavon and spoke in a low voice while Juan set down his firewood. All waited for the shaman to arrive.

🜨🜨🜨

Don Ramon proved to be everything a doctor would have ordered. He cleaned and set Donavon's fractured leg, put him in a hammock in a corner of Manuel's simple main room, and then stepped outside to stoke the fire on an outback hearth to brew herbal tea.

"The tea will calm his nerves and help him sleep. He is very tired," the shaman said.

Layla nodded. She was worn out, too—they all were, after the highly charged emotional nightmare they'd been through. Ten minutes later Don Ramon brought in a pot, poured hot liquid into three cups, and took one to Donavon who reclined in the hammock, his bad leg extended over the top.

"Drink, my friend," he said. "Slowly."

Donavon raised his head, and at first turned away from the hot liquid.

"No, you must drink," the shaman said this time with conviction. "It will be good for you."

Manuel gave the other cups to Layla and Clay, who gladly accepted the offering. After a few sips, Clay was ready to break the silence. He cleared his throat. "Juan, we all want to thank you for saving our lives. Now me and Layla have to figure out what we're gonna do. We don't mean to trouble you. You've already done so much for us."

"Stop," Manuel said. "Say nothing more. We're all human. You would've helped us."

"But we'd be dead or near dead if your uncle hadn't been cutting wood today," Clay said.

"But he was. Your friend already looks better," Manuel said. "With Don Ramon's help."

The shaman looked up when his name was spoken. Donavon's eyes had closed and Don Ramon released the cup from the pilot's grasp. "He needs rest, for a few days."

"He can stay here. In my bedroom," Manuel said. "We'll move him before we go to sleep."

Clay sighed like a weight had been lifted. "That would be so helpful. Thank you, again."

"What are we going to do, Clay?" Layla asked in English, to keep their conversation private.

Neither Juan nor Manuel knew why their plane had crashed in the jungle nor what cargo they were carrying. They couldn't talk freely in front of the Maya men for plenty of reasons.

"Layla, let's step onto the porch for a minute," Clay said.

"Excuse us, please."

All eyes save Donavon's, whose were now tightly shut, locked on the two survivors as they moved onto the porch, the wooden screen door slapping shut behind them.

Layla caught a whiff of the evening air. A tropical flower, perhaps night blooming jasmine or orange blossom, was in bloom.

She walked to the edge of the palapa and peered up at the night sky. Venus hung close to a crescent moon. Tilting her head back, she spotted the familiar smudge of the Milky Way spilling across the heavens.

"What are we going to do?" Moving back to the center of the porch she reluctantly focused her mind on the unanswered questions at hand.

"Your guess is as good as mine," Clay said. "First off, we can scratch the shipment, that's for sure. It's lucky we own it and aren't beholden to anyone, if you catch my drift."

Layla crossed her arms over her chest. "We always own our loads."

"I know, I know," Clay said. Her body language indicated he'd said the wrong thing. He was dealing with the Culiacan Cartel, not some two-bit neighborhood gang. "I was trying to think of something that in some way could be positive. This all really sucks."

Ignoring his disclaimer, Layla shifted gears. "Who wouldn't let us land?"

"Beats me. My gut says Guillermo had no part in it. Maybe the Gulf Cartel."

"The Gulf Cartel because you're working with me? Do they have that much pull in Cancun?"

"Christ, you know that better than me. How much pull *do* cartels have with civil aviation?"

"Well, we make demands on air traffickers and airport

managers. Cancun's the gateway for the south, but Toluca in CDMX is the biggie. It's la linea, the line. You know—army, federales, police, lawyers, governors, judges. We buy off everyone we can reach."

Clay nodded in the darkness. He almost said "Is there anyone you don't own?" but held his tongue. How well he knew the impact of la linea. It was the reason so few crimes in Mexico even got investigated. Everyone was paid off.

"We'll go to Cancun, find out where and why the detour took place. It may take more than a few days."

"What about Donavon?" Layla asked.

"He seems stable right now. We'll run it by him in the morning, see if he's willing to hang out at Manuel's for a bit while we catch a bus to Cancun and check around," Clay said. "Try to figure out who's out to get us. That way we'll know how to proceed."

"Okay. Let's run this by the guys," Layla said.

🖼️🖼️🖼️

The next morning Donavon was awake when Clay walked into the room. "How you feeling, buddy?"

"Still tuckered out," Donavon said as he pulled his body up to a sitting position.

"You had a bad fracture, but the shaman fixed you up pretty good." Clay looked at the pilot and tried to gauge how alert he was. "Got some options and wanted to run them by you—depending on how you're feeling." Donavon nodded, so Clay went on. "We need to find out who denied us landing rights, number one."

"I'm with you there. I'd like to kick that sorry son of a bitch's ass, once I'm better."

"And we gotta stay out of harm's way," Clay said. "Find

out what happens now with the plane taking a dive. Will it pose problems with your license, all that stuff. See if you're listed on any Mexican warrants since you were the pilot. The federales or someone will no doubt find the wreck soon, but I think you'll be safe here at Manuel's."

"I'm pilot on record but they have no clue what I look like. They won't know I lived through the crash. Most cocaine cowboys fly solo and they'll find Jake's body. Maybe I should assume Jake's identity," Donavon said.

"That might not be a bad idea." Clay nodded, as he pondered the idea. He walked over to his backpack and unzipped the side compartment. "I've got your passports."

He opened the navy blue three-and-a-half by six-inch universal tickets to anywhere and glanced at them before handing them over to Donavon.

"Since you both have mustaches and dark hair, you could pass for Jake, to get out of the country. Immigration won't have a death certificate on him right away. This is Mexico after all."

"But how long will I have to stay here?" Donavon asked.

Clay gave Donavon a thorough once over. "How does the leg feel?"

"Not as bad as yesterday," the pilot said with a rueful smile, "but not a hundred percent. Don't even ask me about the rest of my body."

"I hear ya. A crash like that, it's like being run over by a Mack truck," Clay said. "I ache all over. You could say I was shaken, but not stirred."

Donavon laughed, a good sign.

"But seriously, Donavon, I think you need some decent rest before we get you outta here. Take it easy. We don't know how tough it's going to be to figure out this whole mess. At this point it could be anyone."

"So how do we find out?" the pilot asked.

"Go to Cancun, snoop around. Layla and I could travel faster and less conspicuously than the three of us. I have a friend on the coast with a place where we can lay low for a couple days while we're trying to get things in order. What'll happen with the plane?"

"I've never lost one before," the pilot said. He laid his head back on the pillow, looked away from Clay and gazed at something far off in the distance. "So, I'm not totally sure, but with the way they set up paperwork, I'm not implicated in the least. Accidents happen. Plus I have—er, had—an impeccable record. Till now."

"That's what I thought." Clay rubbed the back of his head. "Are you good with waiting for us here?"

"I think it's the only way," Donavon said.

"I agree. I'm going to talk to Manuel, ask him to keep your being here quiet, and ask him to extend that request to Juan and Don Ramon. We'll pay Manuel and ask him to feed you and attend to you for the next few days. I'll give him my cell number so he can call me if he needs to and I'll have him buy you a throw-away phone so you can reach me if needed."

"When will you leave?" Donavon asked.

"The sooner the better. I know Layla's up. She's showered and ready to go. She'll be in to talk to you in a minute."

Clay paused as he reappraised the pilot. "You're good?"

"Yeah, man. It's gotta happen like this." The pilot reached out his hand. Clay grasped it and Donavon pulled the Canadian in to his chest. "It's all good."

133

Chapter 24

Manuel dropped Clay and Layla at the bus depot in Tixkokob, a thirty-minute drive from Motul. He assured them the bus would arrive by one and they'd be in Cancun by nightfall. Second-class Mexican buses were notoriously slow going. Known as the milk run, they made as many unplanned stops as planned ones, so as to drop locals near their homes or milpas, the traditional cornfields they worked year in, year out.

These buses traveled on the libre or non-pay road versus the cuota or pay highway. In an effort to encourage locals to cough up their pesos and use the pay highway, the state, manipulated by whichever former politician owned the private throughway, erected countless topes or speed bumps, thus slowing highway drive time considerably. Rather than four hours to Cancun, including stops at every pueblo, the topes slowed the non-air-conditioned vehicle down to a crawl that took twice as long.

But the silver bullet each Mexican, or Maya for that matter, has in his or her arsenal is the gift of patience. The people of Mexico are unflappable. In spite of the state competing with the federal government to grind the average Mexican's lifespan to considerably less than the world average, they handle everything thrown at them. Their ability to endure difficulty exceeds Job's.

Before they boarded, Clay asked Manuel to take him to a tienda where he could buy two cell phones along with TelMex phone cards, so both he and Donavon would have pre-paid calling time, should they need to connect.

Clay bought a Cancun t-shirt (One tequila, Two tequila, Three tequila, Floor) along with dark glasses. Layla bought a Panama hat with a wide brim and a loose, Maya-style cotton blouse. She found an inconspicuous woven bag with plastic handles to carry her designer valise in. Clay's back-pack looked like it had been born in a Mexican jungle so it needed no camouflage.

After pulling his shaggy hair into a short ponytail, Clay opted for a black baseball hat with "Tulum" stitched on the brim. Their disguises in place they bid Manuel goodbye and boarded the bus. They found two seats together in the back. Layla placed her bag on the luggage rack up top and Clay nestled his backpack next to hers. Both settled into the hard plastic seats, well aware that this portion of their journey would be long, slow, and hot.

But the lengthy trip would give them time to think and freely discuss their next moves, something they hadn't yet been able to do.

Layla hoped they could get to the bottom of the no-landing debacle, but when all was said and done, she was less than certain how it would unfold, and what mysteries would be exposed.

In the narco world, once an airport manager allowed unauthorized landings or departures, the cartel was in the sweet spot. Unless something had gone terribly amiss, those coveted landing rights for planes carrying product never wavered. That made her wonder who would've alerted the authorities. That was the nagging question and from that person she wanted full disclosure.

"Clay," she said softly, ten minutes into the ride as random thoughts bombarded her mind. "Where do we begin? I'm feeling lost."

"We'll start with the safe house. I think once we get a place where we're comfortable, we can rent a car and figure out what's happening."

"I still have to tell Patrón," Layla said, even more softly, in a near whisper.

"Well, telling Patrón is going to be nearly impossible with him in prison."

She twirled a strand of long dark hair around her index finger and thought for a minute. "True. But all I can think about is that pendejo Zoyo. I wonder if he's heard about the dinner."

"He must be mad as hell with what you brought up at Guillermo's, about trafficking."

After so much happening—the crash, losing Carlos—Layla had temporarily ignored the elephant in the room: Guillermo and Zoyo's private enterprise.

"Hijole! Of course he and Guillermo are in it together! He admitted it! How could I ignore that for the past twenty-four hours? I'm losing it! Do you know what this means?" she asked.

Clay lightly touched Layla's elbow, and she took a deep breath. Freaking out on a hot, crowded bus in the middle of nowhere would accomplish absolutely zero.

"Of course they're in it together," Clay said, "and yes, I have a good idea what that means."

"You think he's told Zoyo yet?" she asked. A light bulb the size of a halogen went on in her brain. "Chinga! It feels so long ago and it's not even two days. That little jungle walk must have made me loco. Zoyo knows I'll tell Patrón about him and Guillermo. This could get very bad very fast!"

Clay pushed back his baseball cap. "It hasn't been *bad* so far? Maybe we live on different planets but this has been one helluva bad time. The worst!"

"No, no, no," Layla said, shaking her index finger back and forth in a scolding gesture. "You don't understand."

The wheels were churning so fast inside Layla's head she felt like her mind was smoking. Time to play catch up. "We have a major problem on our hands with Zoyo and Guillermo. Major. If the DEA or someone else stopped our landing at Cancun, then we're fighting on two fronts." Layla shook her head, slowly and deliberately. "We're totally screwed."

"Didn't anyone ever tell you to think positive?" Clay said. "Maybe you should learn to meditate. I'll teach you. If Tony Soprano can have a shrink, why can't you have a guru?"

"Shut up! I'm not kidding!" Layla said, louder than she'd intended. They were, after all, on a crowded bus. Mexicans rarely raised their voices, especially in public. A cultural no-no. Even children picked up on it; they didn't even whimper. A Maya woman three rows up turned to look at them, swiveled back around and settled into her seat, too tired to care, her arms wound around a basket overflowing with stacks of tortillas wrapped in brown paper.

"Okay, okay, I hear ya," Clay said, still irritated but willing to listen. He adjusted himself in the uncomfortable seat to give her his full attention. "Go on."

"Zoyo's going to be out to get me. Once Guillermo lets on that I know about the trafficking, he'll want to find me and silence me before I can tell Patrón."

"Wait, I thought he was on your side, El Zoyo." Clay now whispered the name.

"Not any more," Layla said as her mind began to focus. "There's too much at stake. When Patrón finds out El Zoyo is double dealing, and in a business we wanted no part of, there will be blood."

"Good choice of words, Layla." Clay said in a sarcastic voice. "How can you be so sure?"

"Clay, don't sound like a child. This is the real world, our world, and it's mano á mano. Zoyo and I don't get along on a good day, but after I expose his dealings with Guillermo to Patrón? Do you have any idea what this means?"

"Apparently not," Clay said. He removed his cap and scratched the back of his neck. "No disrespect, but I thought you were the new head of the cartel."

"I'm family. Of *course* I'm next in line. But no one believes I can handle it. Hijole! They didn't think I could handle my bodyguard." She crossed herself before continuing. "God rest his soul. They're just waiting for me to fail and they didn't have to wait long."

"What are you saying? You're a puppet?" Clay asked.

"They think I'm a pretender to the throne, plus I'm a woman. God rest *my* soul!" she said. "They all expect Zoyo to run the show and for me to play like I'm doing something while he's in charge. No one expected me to do more than keep track of the accounts and shipments. It's okay that Patrón let me tip-toe outside the box and do a deal like this one, but run the cartel?"

Clay was getting a crash course in cartel politics. "They played you?"

"Yep, so the other cartels would believe Patrón's family was still in control, a direct line to el jefe. But inside the organization? They withhold stuff and treat me with, how do you say it in English? Kid gloves. Sometimes info gets to Zoyo before me. They don't even think I can shoot a gun. That shows you how stupid they are!"

"Can you?" Clay asked. "Shoot a gun?"

She gave him a withering look. "Of course! Carlos taught me. He took me to the mountains for target practice. I learned from the best."

Suddenly the power left her voice and she deflated in front of Clay's eyes. "Oh Carlos, Carlos," she said, turning away from Clay to stare out the window. She covered her face with her hands, but a minute later her head jerked upright. In a throaty whisper she said, "You puta de madre. How could you die on me?"

She'd gone from sad to mad in a heartbeat. Meanwhile Clay pretended to be busy examining the stitching on his cap.

"Layla," he began in the softest tone possible, "no disrespect, about Carlos and all, but are you telling me there are two factions inside your organization? You and your uncle and… this Zoyo guy?"

She nodded, composing herself for the serious conversation about to come. "Yes, and since Guatemala, the separation's wider than ever, because I'm the only one who knows about the trafficking."

Clay chewed on that for a moment. "Will he be coming for you?"

"When he hears about Guillermo's dinner and the plane crash, he will be coming for me." She paused and looked at the Canadian. "And whoever is with me."

"I'm a target?" Clay asked.

She gave him a no-nonsense stare. "If you're with me, yes, especially since you were at the dinner. Guillermo will tell Zoyo everything. Once he hears Carlos is dead, he'll figure I'm easy to get to. Carlos did his job well; they were careful around him. Good at his work they always said."

Clay stayed quiet again for a minute as he tried to make sense of the bomb Layla had just dropped—the startling disclosure that the cartel's closet was crammed with skeletons. He felt weak in the knees. With a contract out on them, why even bother about the crash, Jake and Carlos' death, Donavon's leg, the loss of product? Why bother about anything?

Two days earlier he couldn't have imagined he'd be riding to Cancun on a death trap of a bus with forty tired Mexicans, sitting next to the figurehead of the largest drug cartel in the world. Now he had a price on his head. What next?

Stay or go. But what good would it do to desert Layla? He was as much a target as she was. And to get out of this mess, two heads were better than one. They still had time on their side as far as he could figure. The crash might not yet be public. Juan Balam didn't seem anxious to tell anyone about it other than Don Ramon.

Well, he'd been in tight spots before. He'd already thrown his lot in with Layla from that first meeting in Ensenada. What other options did he have? Going it alone? Leaving her hung out to dry?

He pondered his next move, finding it hard to ignore Layla's resolute presence. The answer came to him: strength in numbers—if two could be called a force. He cradled his arm on top of the seat behind the narca in a protective manner. "Layla, darlin'," he said. "Here's all I got to say to Zoyo: Catch us if you can."

CHAPTER 25

Cancun, Quintana Roo, Mexico

Cancun bore little resemblance to what Layla remembered from her last visit. Driving through the sprawling barrios into the heart of the city it was obvious that the popular tourist destination, population now over a million, had experienced exponential growth. Intentionally located in an older city barrio, the bus terminal was miles from the hotel zone's luxurious mega resorts and worlds away from where tourists roamed. By the time their bus got to the end of the line, most of the passengers had disembarked.

After the slow-motion crawl over Yucatán back roads, it was dark when they arrived in Cancun. Clay stood and stretched, glad to finally be upright. Layla stood and reached for her bag but Clay had already found it.

They were ready for the next step. Out of the jungle. Off the bus. In Cancun.

"What now?" Layla asked. They stood in the teeming parking arena adjacent to the modern glass terminal. She marveled at the number of buses and people waiting to board for points unknown.

"First I'm gonna call a friend, Barry, and see if he can put us up. He lives south of here in a little fishing village. It's off the radar, real low key. He's a grower, too, but from Washington."

"What if he's not around?" Layla asked, less than impressed with his friend's credentials.

"We'll stay here in Cancun, rent a car. Start our work. Come on." He started walking.

"I've had time to think, Clay, and I can't let this lie—this thing with Zoyo and Guillermo. I've got to strike first, take the initiative."

"Whoa, hold on a minute. What does that mean?" Clay stopped in mid-stride to look at her.

"I've thought it through. I have to get to Zoyo before he gets to me. To us." She gave him a look that bordered on guilt.

"That's a lot easier said than done. The way I see it we're two people versus someone with unlimited resources. You don't even have a bodyguard," Clay said.

"I know, but because there's only you and me doesn't mean we have to stand down. Zoyo is so cocksure he wouldn't dream I'd make a move on him."

"He has an army behind him, Layla. What do you got?"

"For starters? Moral high ground! Christ! Trafficking children and killing them?"

"Well, last time I checked, you were part of the biggest drug cartel in the world. Cartels are known for murder and torture. Doesn't seem like high ground to me."

Layla shrugged off his words.

"Clay, he killed a twelve-year old girl in his house two nights ago. There's standing your ground and holding your turf. That means anything goes. Think of it like this: When villages were invaded in war time, there were no rules for those being attacked.

"That's me now, with what Guillermo's done, and Zoyo. They've double crossed the head of the cartel—my uncle and my jefe. And apparently it's gone on for a while. The gloves are off. Tell me, how long can a leader survive if he allows his lieutenants to steal from him, or double cross him?"

"Not long," Clay said, shaking his head.

She knew that as head of his own organization in Canada, he perfectly understood. A leader cannot pardon dissension—it shows weakness. And once weakness is detected, it cannot be reversed. It needed to be addressed head on.

"You know what I'm saying. Yes, I'm aware of the murders and bribes, the torture. It's a fucked up business. But within our cartel, there's a sense of order because of Patrón.

"With my uncle behind bars, Zoyo is itching for top spot and he's already started by scheming with Guillermo. What else is he doing to damage my uncle's authority? Once that begins, a trampa—you know, a trap—could follow."

"So what do you propose to do?"

"I have trustworthy lieutenants, not just Carlos. I can call out my own army."

He scoffed.

"What? You don't believe I have connections?" she asked, sizing him up. He had no clue how much power lay at her fingertips. North Americans were so naïve. Had they no idea how the world worked?

He didn't really know her—not yet. Guillermo had the resources to find willing soldiers of fortune anywhere on the planet, but so did she. And though she was thought of as the niece with accounting skills, because of her uncle's guidance she was not your average protégé. If help was needed she could call out her own commandos and make it rain bullets on any son of a bitch stupid enough to cross her.

Clay held up his hands in a surrendering gesture. "Okay, I get it. Listen, let me try to get hold of Barry. See if we're welcome. If so, we'll catch a cab and head south. If not, we'll get a hotel and rent a car tomorrow. We can continue this conversation once we settle in somewhere for the night."

ⴽⵍⵎⵍⵎⵍⵎ

Puerto Simpatico, Quintana Roo, Mexico

Forty minutes later, after a rough ride on a potholed road, a cab dropped Clay and Layla in front of a walled compound bearing the name Casa Playa. An amber light positioned under the sculpted head of a Maya god glowed dimly above the massive wooden gate's center. There was little else to illuminate the night.

"Is this it?" Layla asked. She grabbed her bag from the floor and climbed out of the back seat onto the sascab road while Clay paid the driver. The backpack had never left his shoulder. She thought she saw him nod, but couldn't be sure, so black was the night.

"Yes, this is Puerto Simpatico."

She walked towards the walled enclave, taking careful steps. No streetlights, as was so common in Mexico. It was a miracle everyone didn't have permanently broken ankles. On receipt of his fare, the cabbie gunned the motor and took off. Clay watched him speed away.

"Just a minute," he said, moving in the opposite direction. "This way."

Layla stopped in the middle of the road. "What? Where are you going?"

"That's not it, it's over here," Clay said, pointing to the right and walking into the darkness.

Following him, she spotted a high adjoining wall. "But there's no name on it. How do you know it's the right house?"

144

"I've been here before, and that was a decoy for the driver. I don't want a cabbie, any cabbie, to know where we're heading."

"Hmm. Okay. That makes sense," Layla said.

He looked both ways before he pushed the tiny dot of illumination above a round buzzer. That was the only light to be found in front of the nameless compound. There was a soft buzzing sound as wires carried their message inside the imposing walls. They waited.

Moments later they were buzzed in through an ornate wooden gate with metal casings. A winding rock path led to the front door of a well-lit villa. It was a modern-looking structure with tall glass windows rising high over an arched mahogany door. An array of lights twinkled high above. Layla hoped it would be as safe as it looked inviting.

As they walked, Clay said, "Barry's a little different, but we've always gotten along."

Layla stopped just short of the front door, immediately on edge. "What does that mean? Good timing, Clay!"

"He's loud, a bit arrogant, full of himself. You'll see. But he's managed his grow biz for years with no problems. Whatever he does, he does it well. Not the most likeable guy, but I trust him."

At that, the front door opened. Layla saw a bald gringo in Dockers, a Guayabera shirt, no shoes, and a Dos Equis in hand. He was short for an American but well built and muscular, no doubt an exercise junkie to compensate for the height issue.

"Hola," he said, as he welcomed the two of them. "Clay, I see you've gone gringo on me. Love the shirt, man. And you brought company this time—nice surprise." He gave Layla a charming smile and a sideways look. "And you are?"

"I'm Lety," Layla said in English. She flashed the pot

dealer her own star-worthy smile, glad Clay had the foresight to keep her identity quiet.

"A pleasure," he said, slightly slurring his words as he ushered them in. "I'm Barry." He turned to Clay and asked, "So how's things?"

"Could be better," Clay said. "Lots going on. You'll hear all about it."

"Sure, sure. Say, let me get your things. Lety? Can I take your bag?"

"Oh, yes, thank you."

"How about something to drink? Cerveza, a coke?"

"I'll have a coke," Layla said.

"Clay?"

"Cerveza."

"Sit down and make yourselves comfortable. I'll be right back. Don't have help this week. I'm the lone ranger. Let me take your bag to the guest room, Lety, and I'll grab drinks."

As he moved through the kitchen towards the back of the house, he turned and said to Clay, "You'll be sleeping where?"

"Upstairs like last time?" Clay asked.

A look of surprise crossed Barry's face but he recovered quickly. "Sure thing. Right back."

Barry's look didn't escape Layla's notice and once he left the room she asked, "Will he think that's weird?"

She hadn't thought about sleeping arrangements or what questions her sleeping solo might bring.

"No, don't worry. Anything and everything goes in Barry's world."

She shrugged and settled into a leather chair that faced what would be a stunning view of the Caribbean in the morning.

A few minutes later their host was back with beverages, including another beer for himself.

"So, how come the unexpected visit?" Barry asked as he took a drag on his Dos Equis.

"Business, strictly business. I wish it was different, but gotta keep things moving."

"Yeah, I hear you, man. In fact, I gotta be in Chetumal tomorrow for a few days, but you're welcome to stay. I'll leave keys on the counter next to the coffee pot. Feel free to come and go as you please. I'm outta here early."

"That'd be great. We need to rent a car and do some things in Cancun. But we'll spend the night here for sure, probably a couple nights."

Layla had downed half her Coke when she slid forward in her chair and placed the soda can on a coaster on top of an oversized block of caramel colored onyx that served as a coffee table.

"Barry, thank you so much for your hospitality, but I'm really tired. Would you mind if I said good night?"

"No, fine. Go through the kitchen and straight back. Bathroom's on the left. Had a long day?"

"Yeah, we have," she said, without elaborating. "And thanks again."

Clay stood as Layla got up. "'Night."

"Good night, Clay, Barry."

After she left the living room, Clay walked over to the sliding doors that led onto a partially enclosed patio with hammocks hung on either side. He could smell the ocean and hear waves pounding the shore. A light breeze was just enough to clear off the mosquitoes.

"What's happening, my man?" Barry called from inside. "Another beer for ya?"

"Sure, I could use one," Clay said as he finished his first in a long drag. Moving back into the living room, he closed the sliding door with a soft whoosh.

"You gonna tell me what's up or do I have to guess?" Barry said as he ambled towards the kitchen with a backwards glance at Clay.

"Oh, just product possibilities with a little hitch. You know the story."

"Getting product from Cancun now?" Barry asked, extremely interested. He opened two more beers and took a drink from his Dos Equis as he walked back towards the living room.

"No, no, but contacts are here. Gotta set up those contacts."

"And the girl?" An appreciative smile crossed Barry's face. "One hot chiquita." He gave a low whistle.

"Yeah, she is," Clay accepted a second beer from his host.

"Nothing? You ain't gonna tell me nothing more?" Barry took another swig.

"When you get back from Chetumal you'll hear it all. But she's right. It's been a helluva long day. Do you mind if I call it a night, too?"

"Sure. I can tell when a man wants to keep a secret."

Clay stood, ignoring Barry's attempt at breaking his silence. He sneaked a sideways glance at his fellow dealer. From the looks of things, cocktail hour had started a while ago.

"I guess I'll head upstairs, too. No fun drinking alone," Barry said, his final attempt to keep the party going. When Clay moved towards the kitchen to deposit his beer bottle on the sink, Barry began to turn off lights, following the Canadian's lead.

"And for a cab tomorrow, go over to Hotel Del Sol and catch one at the lobby. It's easier than calling those fucking taxi drivers. They can't ever find the place."

"You don't have an address," Clay said, as he climbed the marble stairs.

"And you wouldn't know anything about that, would you now?" Barry said with a chuckle.

"Same church, different pew," Clay said. "'Night, Barry, and thanks, man."

"Buenas noches. Lock the sliders and the front door and gate before you leave."

"Sure thing," Clay said.

That was always a priority no matter where Clay landed.

CHAPTER 26

Though Clay rose early the next morning, Barry had already departed for Chetumal. Good as his word, he left two keys on the counter, one for the door, one for the gate. Clay looked around the well-appointed living room, always impressed with the bling drug dealing brought in. For those in the trade, the fruits of their labors showed best in high voltage dwellings, maxed out furnishings, and killer views. Since most dealers used their home as an office, living in the lap of luxury was a mere bi-product of the business. In many cases their living quarters were also considered safe houses, far from the prying eyes of the feds, the law, and their enemies. Barry's lack of an address was no accident. His hideaway on the beach was safe—a private fortress.

Clay walked to the patio and slid open the sliding glass door. The stunning Caribbean greeted him full on. The flatness of the turquoise sea was thanks to the Great Meso-American Reef lying half mile off-shore, which absorbed the ocean's initial force. The hotel's dock several hundred yards from the end of Barry's beach sported an oversized palapa which added to the tropical paradise look. It didn't get much better than this. Puerto Simpatico was just the right distance from Cancun—an easy ride to the airport but far enough away so there was no hustle, no bustle.

Except on Sundays. Since the last hurricane, Cancun's "hotel zone" beaches had deteriorated, the sand swept away in one of Mother Nature's random acts. In contrast, Puerto Simpatico's beaches, just thirty kilometers south, had grown wider and longer. The downside for Simpatico locals was the influx of Cancunese invading their seaside pueblo every weekend. Parking was impossible. Local vendors and restaurants didn't mind. Weekend grosses bumped up revenues after ho-hum weekdays.

Clay was on his second cup of coffee when Layla walked into the kitchen with red eyes and a frumpy look.

"Buenos dias. Sleep well?" he asked.

"Yeah," she said, shrugging, giving him a cool look.

"So what's up?"

"Today's the day. What's our plan?" Layla asked.

"I think we should get the car and since we'll be at the airport, we should ask around, if you have any connections there, that is."

"Of course we have connections in Cancun," she said, hand on her hip. She gave him a dark stare, daring him to contradict her. It wasn't yet 8 a.m. and her hackles were up.

"I don't mean the airport manager," Clay said.

"Christ, I know! I'm not dumb."

"Of course not. Layla, what's wrong?"

"It's all wrong. Everything. Losing Carlos, Jake, the girl, the load. Even the plane. Hijole! What could be right about any of this?"

"Well, we're alive."

"Yeah, yeah," she said, looking like she wasn't sure if she really wanted to be. "Next you'll tell me this is the first day of the rest of my fucking life. Chinga! I don't need a goddamn lecture."

"No lecture intended."

"You were going to start. I'll take my Buddhist lesson later. Time for a shower. Be down in twenty minutes. We'll see what we can find out at the airport."

🔲🔲🔲

Cancun Airport, Cancun, Mexico

The taxi dropped them in front of Hertz at the airport, no questions asked. Just two tourists in need of a car once they realized how big the Riviera Maya was. Lots to explore in the Yucatán.

For March, the line at the rental desk wasn't long. Once spring breakers arrived it would be a sea of tourists. Clay registered since his name was less likely to be followed up than a Spanish surname. Using Layla's would be foolhardy, another dropped pin denoting the triangulation of her whereabouts. If Google could locate her, so could everyone else.

As they departed the rental offices, Layla noticed a folded Cancun newspaper on a plastic chair in the waiting room. She grabbed it, planning to see if there was any news of the downed plane three days after the crash.

The previous night at Barry's, she'd watched what could laughingly be called Cancun news. In a Mexican tourist resort with fabulous beaches, no one watched the news or even cared if there was any to report. The attractive Latina anchor wore a low-cut sheath and looked as if she'd just stepped out of a Miss Universe pageant.

Clay did the walk around the rental car while Layla sulked. She wouldn't rush him, she knew all too well the car rental game. If one wasn't vigilant, the rental companies tried to dupe their clients. You had to carefully ID all

152

scratches and dents up front or an enormous bill would be presented on returning the vehicle, and not just for use of the car. When she'd returned a rental car in Mexico City a few months earlier, the jack was missing, and the agency accused her of stealing it. Christ, their balls were enormous.

"Ready?" Clay asked, using his "handle with care" voice, treating her like she was a bomb ready to explode.

She nodded.

First stop would be the airport terminal where they'd do some fact checking. Now with two runways, Cancun International was wall-to-wall people, filled at all hours with porters, touts, reservation clerks, and tourists. Layla remembered there was a group of offices behind the airline counters for airport personnel. It was down a narrow hallway in the old terminal.

"This way," she said, motioning behind the counters.

"You sure?"

Her "fuck you" look made words unnecessary. But as they neared the corridor she stopped.

"Yellow tape? What's this?" she asked a security cop who stood alongside the barrier.

"Crime scene," he said.

"What happened?" Clay asked, right behind her.

"Investigating these offices."

"For what? Did someone get hurt?"

"Not here. They're looking for clues."

"Why?" she asked.

"The airport manager was shot, at his house in Playa."

"Shot? Is he dead?" Layla asked.

The man looked at her as if she hadn't heard him. "Yes."

"Who would do that?" Layla demanded.

The man shrugged. "No sé," he said, avoiding her eyes. In Mexico only a fool answered those questions. If you wanted to see sunrise tomorrow, you kept your head down and your mouth shut.

"Oh, God. That's terrible," Layla said. She sidestepped and then steadied herself before spitting out, "When did it happen?"

"Yesterday. His day off."

She turned quickly, nearly pushing Clay over as she sped into the open terminal, away from the cloistered corridor they had just tried to enter. Feeling her throat constrict, she gasped, unable to breathe. Time slowed to a crawl.

Clay was right behind her, as if ready to pick up the pieces. He watched her begin to unravel. "Layla, Layla."

She stopped in the middle of the reception area. People streamed by on either side, rushing towards departure gates or the waiting arms of relatives. She looked ready to collapse.

He put an arm around her waist and started to walk her towards the automatic doors.

"We'll get you some air."

But Layla had no desire to be coddled. "Leave me alone!" she hissed and pushed him away. "Don't you think I can walk on my own? I'm not helpless!"

People stared. They were making a scene. He removed his arm from her waist and quietly followed her to the exit. The door whooshed open and they moved onto the sidewalk leaving the cool air conditioning behind. Outside, the heat was stifling.

Clay caught up with her and touched her arm. "Layla, look at me."

"What?" She snarled at him and pulled away. Her face looked ashen, drained of color, but her body language showed fight, not flight. Fists clenched, she looked ready to pounce.

"Listen, we gotta go someplace and talk. Not here in front of the whole world."

"The car," she said. She started to move quickly across the one-way street filled with Range Rovers, Escalades, taxis, tour vans, and Kombis.

In the parking lot they found their new ride. Clay beeped the key and opened the doors. They got inside. He turned on the ignition and A/C in a single move then rolled down his window to wait for the chilled air to take over.

"Talk to me," he said.

"They killed him because he wouldn't let us land. How did they find out so soon?"

In the short walk from the terminal to the car in near triple digit heat Layla had regained her composure. Clay was having trouble keeping up with not only her mood swings but her stamina.

"Some snitch in the tower or someone he works with?" Clay asked.

"That means it's us, Culiacan Cartel…Zoyo, or Guillermo." She paused to think it over. "Or both."

"But if a plane doesn't land, dozens of people know. It's very obvious there's trouble."

"But he was killed," Layla said. "That means Culiacan knows he didn't allow the plane to land—it either crashed somewhere in the jungle or made it to Merida. Both Guillermo and Zoyo knew we were flying in a load. All they needed to verify our flight never made it past Cancun was a call to Merida. Guillermo was well aware we were flying on fumes."

"So the airport manager took the blame for the change in landing procedures?"

"He probably got a warning from the DEA or the feds," Layla said. "No other reason to turn away a cartel plane. He knew the stakes were high, that he'd pay with his life. Oh God," a sob tried to escape, but she shut it down, fast. "We lost the trail. Dead men don't talk.

"Wait, wait." She pulled the newspaper out from under her seat and unfolded it. At the bottom of the front page was a grainy photo of a man's face. The headline read, "Cancun Aviation Director Murdered."

"That's him! Let me read this. 'The body of José Chan Canul, Civil Aviation Director of Cancun International Airport, was found in a ditch outside Cancun on the Merida libre road west of the city at five p.m. yesterday. He was forty-three.

His wife reported Canul was at his home in Playa del Carmen yesterday morning when he received a call requesting that he step outside. With cell phone in hand, he walked out of the house. His wife heard shouts, a slammed door, then a car speeding away. She ran outside. Her husband was gone.

Señora Canul called the Playa del Carmen Police. She shared all the details she could remember. The abduction car was blue, a four-door sedan, either a Toyota or a Tsuru. Later that afternoon Playa Police received a call displaying Canul's cell number. The caller, however, was not Canul but the killers, taunting police. They disclosed where the body was.

Cancun and Playa police drove to the designated location and discovered Canul's body with seven shots to the head at close range. He appeared to have been tortured.'"

Layla set the paper down in her lap. "He was tortured and murdered for not letting us land," Layla said, subdued by what she'd read. "And they're playing games with the police."

Clay sniffed. "Playa del Carmen Police? Layla, it's a beach town. And everyone knows only one or two per cent of crimes gets investigated here."

"Like that's news to me?" she asked in a derisive tone as she refolded the paper. The stakes had just risen. "It's only a matter of time before they find the plane and the coke."

"What will come down?" Clay asked.

"Chinga! They'll search the entire area. They may even arrest everyone in the vicinity to try and get information. They've done it before. It's fucked up but common procedure: Arrest first, ask questions, and release those not involved later. What about Donavon?"

"I'm gonna call him. Maybe we should pick him up and bring him to Barry's," Clay said, "He'll be safer with us."

Clay reached for his pack on the back seat and unzipped the side compartment, looking for the cell phone Manuel had bought him. "Think I'll call Manuel first."

He retrieved the contacts on his phone and scrolled down to the number. Layla, overwhelmed, silently watched him dial. All of a sudden time had speeded up.

"No answer. Let me try Donavon," Clay said.

Again the Canadian scrolled and dialed. "No answer there, either. Christ."

Layla nibbled on a fingernail. "Maybe you're not getting a signal. Chinga!"

"How long to Tixkokob?" Clay asked.

"On the pay highway, probably three hours."

"Let's drive and dial. We have to get Donavon. Now," Clay said as he threw his pack in the back and simultaneously put the car in reverse. He put on his seatbelt, jammed the car into drive, and squealed the short distance to the end of the parking row. In ten minutes they were on Highway 307 looking for the Merida turnoff and pay highway.

Time to collect all their chickens before someone beat them to the roost.

CHAPTER 27

Motul, Yucatán, Mexico

Manuel wove Panama hats from sisal, what locals called the "green gold" of the Yucatán, so plentiful was the demand for it. In the small town of Motul, weaving sisal was lucrative employment. Twice a month he drove to Tixkokob with finished product, passing his hats on to Pedro, a fellow Maya who wove hammocks. Pedro took the merchandise to Cancun and sold to wholesalers.

It was a fact: Every tourist who came to Cancun wanted a hammock or a Panama hat, sometimes both. For a Maya living in the Yucatán with an eighth-grade education—standard schooling in Mexico—Manuel was doing well. He owned his adobe house and had a pickup truck.

Manuel didn't mind having the gringo pilot with him for a few days. He spoke passable Spanish and after Don Ramon fixed his leg, he was in good spirits. Donavon lavished praise on Manuel's Yucatán recipes, had a healthy appetite and an easygoing attitude. To sweeten the deal, the tall Canadian had given Manuel a stack of pesos to look after his friend and he even gave Manuel a new cell phone, complete with pre-paid TelMex minutes, simply for his hospitality.

"Donavón," Manuel had said earlier that morning, emphasizing the accent on the last syllable to give the pilot's name Spanish enunciation, "I must take my hats to

Tixkokob. I put almuerzo, lunch, in the refrigerator. I'll be home later, mas tarde. Is there anything you need?"

Donavon had finished off the powder in the jungle and was hankering for some mind-bending anything. "Cerveza?" He asked.

"Claro. Will you be all right alone?" the Maya asked, showing concern for his new friend's recovering health.

"Me? Never better."

A half hour later Manuel had packed the time-worn pickup with a two-week inventory of hats and was ready to go. His regular trips to Tixkokob included a little shopping, seeing friends, and eating a big bowl of lime soup with lots of tortillas at Maria's, a local restaurant. The cook was an old Maya woman and Miguel told her it tasted just like the soup his mother used to make.

卐卐卐

Donavon heard a truck pull up outside and figured he must have dozed off longer than expected. Since the bedroom was in the back, he couldn't see who arrived, but assumed Manuel was home earlier than planned. He pushed himself up on his pillow and reached for the carved wooden cane that Don Ramon had given him. He heard footsteps on the porch and decided to meet Manuel at the door. Plus he knew his Maya friend was bringing provisions, beer to be exact, and that was a luxury he was anxiously awaiting. Donavon had been straight ever since he got out of that scary jungle a couple days earlier. The herbal tea sure didn't cut it.

Odd, he heard two voices. He didn't think Manuel would be bringing anyone with him unless it was Juan. That was it! Juan Balam. The voices got louder.

"Hola? Hola? Quien esta?"

He struggled to make his way to the door and was surprised by two men in army fatigues.

The older of the two men was a thirty-something sergeant, stocky with a meaningful black mustache. The skinny guy with him was eighteen at best. A kid.

The sergeant stared at Donavon. "Who are you?"

"Amigo," Donavon answered.

"From where?"

"Estados Unidos," the pilot replied. United States.

"What are you doing here?" the sergeant asked.

"Visiting the Yucatán with friends. Had an accident at the pyramids. Broke my leg," Donavon answered in the best Spanish he could muster, touching his splint for emphasis.

"Why are you here?"

"My friend knows medicine, and helped me before I could get to a doctor in Merida," he said, trying to stick to the party line.

"How did you get here?" asked the sergeant.

"Drove from Cancun. My friends are at the pyramids."

"You didn't come in by plane, in the jungle?" the sergeant asked, a nasty smile curling his lips. "A broken plane?"

Donavon shook his head. "No, no, we drove."

"You must come with us."

"Have to wait for my friends. Just woke up, siesta." He rubbed his eyes to feign sleepiness. Though he may have been down for the count five minutes earlier now he was as alert as a startled rabbit.

"Where is your friend?" the sergeant asked.

"Merida. Business. He'll be back tomorrow." He hoped they wouldn't be back to check on Manuel at any time, ever.

"Well, you come with us. Passport!"

Donavon walked over to where his old shirt was lying on a chair in the corner. Manuel lent him a clean shirt to wear after he'd showered earlier. Before he left for Cancun, Clay had placed both his and Jake's passports that he'd retrieved from the plane into his old shirt pocket. Safe a place as any—the only place, actually, since he owned nothing else. Unnerved by the unexpected wake-up call and the insidious fact that the army was probing him about the plane, Donavon quickly decided to use his own passport, not Jake's.

While they waited, the two military men spoke rapidly back and forth. They kept an eye on him but moved into the main area of the house. With his back to them, Donavon realized he had time to ditch his brother's passport. He pulled both passports from his shirt and stuffed Jake's in between the chair's worn pillow and the chair seat. At least he wouldn't be found with two passports, one belonging to a dead man whose body was in a plane filled with two tons of coke.

"Listo?" Ready?

"Si," Donavon said, resigning himself to an unhappy encounter. He kept his phone, sliding it into his pocket. "Momento," he said. "I need to write a note."

"Hurry!" the younger one insisted. Just then another vehicle pulled up.

Donavon looked around for a pencil, not a common item in a Maya house. He found one on the table in the main room with Manuel's sisal material. He scribbled one word—Army.

He grabbed his cane and was ready just as a soldier walked in gesturing at the two soldiers who had been talking to him.

"He wants us. Now!" the new guy shouted in Spanish. "Get moving!"

"Now!" the younger man repeated, as he pushed Donavon ahead and out the door. "Move!"

CHAPTER 28

Merida, Yucatán, Mexico

Donavon wasn't hooded as they drove him into a cordoned off parking lot at an abandoned warehouse inside a walled compound. By the route they took on the libre road, he assumed they were heading towards Merida, far west on the Yucatán Peninsula, the same city he was trying to get to when the plane ran out of fuel.

What a mess, and he hadn't even gotten his beer from Manuel. Now, after being with the army for the past hour and a half, that other life—staying at Manuel's adobe home, eating pibil chicken, drinking Don Ramon's herbal tea—was light years away. And his damn leg ached like a son-of-a-gun on top of it all.

They had hurried him into the back of an army truck with flaps on either side and positioned him next to the younger soldier who'd first entered the house, now armed. No words were spoken. They hadn't frisked him or tied his hands, no doubt assuming he couldn't go far with a broken leg even if he tried to make a run for it.

Neither had they interrogated him again about the plane. But his position was firm: he knew nada, zip, zero. He was just some gringo, his version of the story, who'd gone to Chichen Itza with friends, climbed to the top of the pyramid, and had the bad luck of falling as he came back

162

down. That happened all the time, didn't it? Christ, those steep steps were killer.

After an entry guard opened the well-secured gate, the truck drove in and stopped. His captor, now with a Turquoise Serpent assault rifle slung over his shoulder—the Mexican Army's weapon of choice—indicated he should get out of the vehicle. The driver came around to the back and stood, waiting for him to climb down.

"Dónde?" Donavon asked, the first word he'd spoken since he got into the truck.

The driver waved his hand toward the building. "Adelante." Onward.

The man with the gun motioned him towards a metal door and said, "El dentro." Inside. The near-darkness spooked Donavon when he entered the building. At first he was unsure which way to go. When his eyes adjusted to the dim light he saw a soldier ahead of him and followed slowly along, relying on the cane to make his way across the uneven concrete floor.

From the ceiling height and the ringing sound of footsteps, he could tell the warehouse was massive, not unlike an airport hangar. Oh, bad thought. Best to not even *think* about planes.

They left the initial entry area behind and entered a new room, this one with more dim lights at the opposite end. At the far corner he could see a table with a couple chairs and another man in uniform standing with his back to them. He had a small baton and was poking at something—something big and black. Donavon couldn't make out what it was at first until ... Oh, no. No *way*!

Several garbage bags—large, black and familiar—screamed "Gotcha."

He hesitated before taking another step, but the kid

soldier gave him a push from behind, causing Donavon to stumble over his cane, nearly falling.

"Cuidado," the young dolt snarled. Careful. "Don't mess this up for el comandante."

Donavon regained his footing, looking down as he walked towards the commander. He hesitated to meet the military man's eyes until he'd assessed the situation.

"Cuidado, señor!" the commander called out in a mocking sing-song, taunting him by echoing the sentiments of his minion. "The pleasure is mine!"

With that catty remark, Donavon looked up, taking stock of el comandante. He gauged the ugly glint in his eyes, the uncompromising set to his jaw, the baton he was brandishing—all to compensate for an underwhelming physique. Even army fatigues couldn't disguise how slender the commander was, all sixty inches of him. Did he think he was Patton? Hell, this was just another third-world asshole. Donavon hated the Mexican Army.

The pilot mentally composed himself. Kidnapped in Mexico. He stood taller, his version of attention, while his leg ached and throbbed simultaneously. This was no time to wimp out. He'd been in Nam and he faced the Viet Cong. In Mexico the enemy was "same-same" but different—either army or cartel, depending on whose payroll they were on.

Just as Donavon prepared to give a flip, derisive answer, his cell phone rang. So he did what anyone would do. He answered it.

"Donavon?" Clay asked, relieved to hear the pilot's voice. "What the hell's going on? I couldn't reach you!"

"It's bad! They got me!" Donavon yelled into the phone.

"What?" Clay wasn't sure he heard the vet correctly. "You okay?"

"No! I'm with el comandante, in Merida, I think."

"Halt! Stop talking! Give me that!" The commander went ballistic as the attending guard tried to grab the phone from the pilot's hand.

"Clay! Clay! Don't know what's going to happen!" Donavon shouted at his last link to the life he'd known before entering the warehouse.

Donavon heard Layla shouting from the phone, "Where is he?"

"Merida?" Clay asked Donavon.

Still holding onto his cell but losing ground with the soldier who'd grabbed for it, Donavon said, "They took me from the house. Alone. No one home."

🔃🔃🔃

The line went dead.

"Donavon! Donavon?" Now Clay was going crazy.

Silence. The vet was gone.

"Is he there?" Layla was nearly jumping up and down in the car seat. "Is he there?"

Clay shook his head. Driving at a hundred twenty clicks on a near empty toll way, there was no sound but the hum of rubber on road. Layla broke the silence with another question. "He's gone to Merida? Why?"

Clay gripped the steering wheel so hard Layla thought the veins on the back of his hands would pop. "He was with 'el comandante.' Goddamn it to hell!"

"Chinga, no!" Layla said, covering her eyes. She pounded her right fist on her thigh. "No! No way! No way!"

"I guess they found the plane," Clay said.

"They must have. What was happening?" asked Layla, pursing her lips in a pout.

"He said it was bad. Not sure what that means."

165

"The worst. Do they have Manuel, too?"

"Don't think so. He said he was alone at the house. Now he's with el comandante."

She shook her head for a second before saying, "Some thug."

Clay stared straight ahead, his eyes never straying from the road.

Layla's look had gone from agitated to somber. She rubbed her left hand back and forth across her forehead as though grappling with the answer to an impossible physics question. She shifted her gaze out the window, watching a bucolic landscape of chit palms and brilliant green pasture zoom by.

"He's just a bagman," Clay said. "You know how many years a bagman gets in Colombia? Two."

"Yeah, but he's *our* bagman," Layla said. "And this isn't Colombia."

"They're trying to figure out who's responsible for the coke."

"They'll report it to the DEA and gloat. Chinga!" Layla said. "It literally fell into their laps. Now the army and federales will collect all the bags like they did when this happened two years ago and deny DEA access to the scene until only a bag or two is left."

"Where does it go?" Clay asked.

"Clay …" Layla gave him a humorless look. "It's Mexico."

"This is so screwed! I know I can dial his number, but that might make it worse!"

"We have a connection, but we don't," Layla said. "What about Tixkokob? We still have to check on Manuel. Find out if he's heard anything about where they've taken Donavon."

"We're more than halfway there."

"Just drive," she said.

CHAPTER 29

Merida, Yucatán, Mexico

Donavon was having trouble convincing el comandante that he had no connection to the mangled plane in the jungle and the drug-filled bags that surrounded it. The commander ordered him to sit and he complied, grateful to be off his aching leg.

El comandante got right in his face. "Señor, what is your name?"

"Donavon."

"Do you think I am a mean man?" His eyes were void of emotion, his voice robotic.

"Uh, no," Donavon said.

"Do you think I am a stupid man?"

"No." The pilot said that with more emphasis.

"Do you know why I brought you here?" el comandante asked.

"No."

"Señor Donavon, now it seems you think I am stupid," he said, a patronizing smile plastered on his uncompromising face as he tapped the baton into the palm of his left hand. "When someone thinks I am stupid, I become mean."

The baton continued its rhythmic beat, like the steady drip of water from a tap.

The two soldiers in the room stood guard on either side of the pilot, several meters back. After the inconvenient phone call, one had snatched Donavon's cell. It sat on the table in front of their commander like an offering to the gods.

"Why are your friends calling?" el comandante asked, gazing at the phone.

"They're worried," Donavon said.

That brought a nasty chuckle. "Hmm. Worried about their friend, wondering where he and his bad leg have gone? Maybe to find some of the coca they brought in on the plane?"

"No, I didn't come in by plane. I told you, we drove to the pyramids."

"Señor Donavon, again you are thinking I am stupid," el comandante said. He continued the tap, tap, tap of the baton into the center of his palm, each rap more meaningful than the last, making a dull thud with each hit. The smooth stick, made from dark hardwood, was twelve inches long and round as a sausage.

"We cannot continue to play games all night long. I need to know where that plane started out and who commissioned it, along with the drugs we found and continue to find. What a mess. Whoever flew the plane had no idea what they were doing!" He gave a harsh laugh. "They tried to land in the jungle! The jungle? Can you imagine? Que stupido!"

Donavon assumed the commander was well aware that the plane's pilot, broken leg and all, sat directly across from him in this decrepit Merida warehouse. But Donavon could stonewall better than most. He'd worked freelance in the seamy underworld of drugs for years, a place where lies and half-truths were considered the norm. He was a pro. Lying to el comandante wasn't a stretch. The Mexican army commander would have to try harder than that.

"Señor Donavon, would you like something to drink? Water?" el comandante asked, changing tack. He was going to play good cop, bad cop all rolled into one. Either he had a schizophrenic personality or he was short on staff.

"Yes," Donavon said.

"A bottle of water!" At the commander's order, a soldier dashed off to fulfill his superior's request.

"Now you will have a nice long drink, and maybe, while you are sipping the cold water, you will remember how you got here. And who came with you to el Yucatán. How is your leg?"

"Fine," Donavon lied.

"Glad to hear it. Broken legs can be ever so painful if not handled properly," he said as he gave a forceful tap to Donavon's leg with his baton.

The pilot winced. He hadn't expected the sudden rap with the baton.

The commander moved in closer. "We certainly wouldn't want things to get uncomfortable for you, now would we?" he asked, a sly grin forming on his prissy mouth. "We have a long night ahead and we haven't even asked who this Clay is." He paused. "I certainly hope we find out before our friends from the cartel arrive."

CHAPTER 30

Motul, Yucatán, Mexico

Layla and Clay pulled up to Manuel's door two hours later. It was late afternoon and his pickup was in the front yard. They piled out of the car, walked to the house, and as Layla prepared to knock on the wooden screen door, Manuel appeared.

His eyes were wild as he opened the door. "Que mal! Que mal! When I got home, Donavon was gone!"

"Yes, we know about Donavon," Layla said in as calm a voice as she could manage. "We talked to him, well, Clay did, just for a minute, today."

"Really?" Manuel asked, immediately relieved. "But the army took him, no? He left a note."

"They did, but they didn't take his cell phone," Layla said. "Clay called his number and he picked up. It didn't sound good. He was with an army commander in Merida. Or he thought it was Merida."

"Oh, no, no!" Manuel said, seesawing back to his previous state of despair. "I should have taken him with me to Tixkokob."

Layla gently patted the Maya man on the shoulder. "You couldn't know what would happen, Manuel. No one knew the army would go door to door. Have they checked on you?"

"No, not yet, and I hope they don't," Manuel said, a shadow of fear flickering in his eyes.

"Since they have a gringo, they're probably preoccupied," Clay said.

"What will they do to him?" the Maya asked.

Layla glanced away not wanting to startle Manuel. Maya who lived in small pueblos away from cities were known for their innocence and generosity of spirit—call it an unbearable lightness of being. All things the cartel was not. Now wasn't the time to educate their friend.

Clay picked up on her hesitation. "Not sure. We wanted to come here and see what happened."

"In Tixkokob the army is everywhere, searching for a plane in the jungle. I saw a platoon setting up a checkpoint. They plan to question everyone coming and going to see what they know."

"Have you seen Juan?" Layla asked.

"He's at his milpa, his cornfield, far out in the jungle. I hope their paths don't cross."

"Me, too," Layla said. "This has happened before, hasn't it, Manuel?"

"Yes, another plane crash. They took in a man from town—they thought he had information."

"What happened to him?" Clay asked.

"He was released two weeks later. Oh, I am so worried about Donavon." Manuel placed a hand on his forehead and shook his head from side to side.

"So are we, but I don't know what we can do," Layla said, "without knowing where he is. We have his cell number, but if we call, it might make things worse."

Manuel was quiet for a long moment. "I feel very bad. This isn't right."

Clay and Layla shared a guilty look.

"Would you like some tea?" Manuel asked, sensing he'd touched on an uncomfortable subject. "I have water boiling."

"Yes, yes," Layla said, understanding the man didn't want to burden them with thoughts of what could well be happening to their missing friend at that very moment. "Tea would be good."

Clay had a pinched look on his face as he walked towards the door with Manuel. Layla could read his mind—he was feeling guilty. She hoped the fresh air would clear his head.

◧◧◧

Merida, Yucatán, Mexico

Donavon started to sweat. The cartel? As if the army wasn't bad enough. When they arrived that meant his interrogation would start in earnest. That was el comandante's game.

"Who is Clay?" he asked, no doubt hoping his disclosure would stun the pilot into a confession.

"A friend," Donavon said.

"Why is he calling you?"

"To see if I'm all right."

The baton stopped its infernal tapping and the commander gave Donavon a derisive stare.

"*Are* you all right, Señor Donavon? Do you think you are all right when you tell me nonsense? It seems to me you are a very stupid man."

He looked down at his baton for a moment before he continued. "Do you think the cartel won't be able to get information from you? You think you're strong enough to withhold *anything* from the cartel? I just touched your leg, a little tap. But what they will do? Let me tell you, they have ways to make you talk. And guess what? Everyone talks in the end.

"I have nothing more to say. Even if you told me everything about your friend Clay and how you got here, they would make you tell them again. So I am going to leave and let you think about our guests. They should be arriving soon and are so anxious to meet you. Goodbye for now. Oh, and how do you gringos say it? Oh, yes—have a nice day."

ꔷꔷꔷ

Donavon sat looking at the lone table, empty except for his phone, in the poorly lit warehouse. No water had arrived. Another Mexican lie. Two soldiers stood far behind him at attention. The cartel was coming, or so el comandante said, if he was telling the truth.

There was really nothing to do but prepare himself for the worst. Nothing could be done to avoid it. He tried to steel himself from the panic that was beginning to creep in, the fear he was sure el comandante had planted in his mind to turn the screws a little tighter. He sat pondering it all, vacillating between disbelief and fear. That's when his mind began to focus.

Though he wasn't religious, after spending so much time in Southeast Asia he'd come to respect eastern religions though not a single soul knew this. With the godless crowd he ran with that would qualify as one flew over the cuckoo's nest territory.

Did he believe? Believe in what? God? No. Salvation? No. Heaven? No way. Reincarnation? Maybe. The atoms didn't go away, right? They stayed put and though they might get rearranged, as in totally reshuffled, the molecules never left planet earth. Dust to dust.

Stardust, actually, and now in this final moment of examining his core beliefs, he knew what he was made of and where he came from—he came from the stars, just like Carl Sagan said. He was made of stardust.

CHAPTER 31

Don Guillermo entered the warehouse yard with a full regimen of bowers, scrapers, and bodyguards. By the size of his retinue, one would think he was heir to the Saudi throne. On entering the compound, el comandante met him personally at the gate.

"Is he here?"

"Yes, Don Guillermo," el comandante said. "He's waiting in the warehouse."

"Excellent! Has he said anything?" Guillermo asked.

"No, nothing at all."

"Well, we'll see if we can change that." A malicious smile crossed his plump, sagging face. He glanced at a bodyguard on his immediate right who grinned back.

"Please, after you," el comandante said, waving his hand towards the door.

Within moments, Guillermo and his entourage entered the warehouse and followed the commander down the same path Donavon had walked hours earlier.

From his position at the table facing the opposite wall of the building, Donavon heard footsteps. It sounded like an army. They've brought reinforcements, he thought, of the worst kind. With the exception of Layla, he'd yet to meet a member of the cartel. That was about to change.

He didn't do them the honor of turning to acknowledge them. He knew what he'd see: a handful of hungry killers, thirsty for blood. A moment later a paunchy, well-dressed man stood before him with two henchmen by his side. Unlike the jefe's attire, their garish skintight suits screamed low class. Both however, sported a noticeable fashion accessory—tight leather gloves.

Missing in action was el comandante. He'd either decided to stay in the background or pull a no show for this part of the performance. He was gone. This meeting of the minds—armed forces and cartel—clearly proved the cartel had enough resources to buy off anyone and everyone they needed—army, navy, *and* the marines.

A booming voice said, "So, this is Señor Donavon! So good to meet you. El comandante has told me all about you."

Donavon glanced into the chilling eyes of the man who controlled how long he would continue to breathe. But the pilot showed no deference. He didn't answer. He simply met his gaze.

"I see you've had a little spill and hurt your leg. El comandante said you had an accident at the pyramids? Tsk, tsk. Maybe one shouldn't be so adventurous in el Yucatán. You can't be too cautious, verdad?" the man asked rhetorically, turning and addressing one of the buff bodyguards who now stood directly behind his pompous sack of shit jefe.

"Si, Don Guillermo."

Don Guillermo! The name exploded in Donavon's brain. This was the scumbag who raped and killed girls and ran a human trafficking network in Guatemala. This was the guy who was responsible for the crash—he was sitting in the hot seat because of this one man. Donavon tensed, instantly ready to tear the pig's eyes out.

"Señor Donavon, el comandante tells me your friend Clay called," he said, motioning with his eyes to the cell that sat on the table in front of them. "My my, how odd. We both know Clay, the pot grower from Canada. He recently had dinner at my villa along with a lovely young woman you may also know. Maybe she's your friend, too."

Donavon stared blankly at the huge hulk, saying nothing. Then a thought crossed his mind— if he was quick enough, he could seriously hurt the guy, get in one good blow. Christ, he was going to die anyway, so it was kinda like being a suicide bomber. If you're gonna go, take as many with you as you can. But he'd have to wait for the perfect moment. They'd underestimated him by not cuffing him. And Don Ramon's cane still leaned against his chair.

Pace yourself, my man, he nearly whispered.

"Cat got your tongue?" Guillermo laughed, and his henchmen laughed, too.

What a bunch of suck ups.

"Too bad about that. Now, I want to know where your friends are. I haven't seen them for a couple days and I would love to find them. Tell me, where are they?"

Don Guillermo waited. Donavon said nothing.

"Señor Donavon. It's not wise to keep me waiting." His voice was a whisper as he leaned in close. When he was inches from Donavon's ear, he bellowed in a full baritone, "Give me an answer!"

Donavon nearly jumped but somehow remained calm. His instincts told him to humor the thug. Timing is everything.

"Don't know his whereabouts and I don't know the girl," he mumbled, pretending to appear cowed.

"Oh, stupid, stupid. Of *course* you know the girl. Layla, the niece of Patrón, el jefe de Culiacan. She's quite pleasing on the eyes. That long, dark hair, those big"—he paused meaningfully as he raised cupped hands to chest level—"eyes."

177

His bodyguards guffawed.

"And such lovely legs. A girl like her no one forgets. But Clay called you, here in the warehouse! Does he know where you are?"

"No."

"How do you know?" Guillermo asked.

"I haven't seen him lately," Donavon said.

"Since the plane crash?"

He may as well cop to the crash. Obviously they'd found the plane, or someone had. The black garbage bags were evidence. "Yeah."

"Okay, now we're getting somewhere. Javier!" he commanded. "Bring me a chair, I want to sit down with Señor Donavon while we chat. It's not often I get to talk to a pilot, and an American pilot at that."

A moment later Javier, chief go-fer, brought another chair. In the meantime, Guillermo lit a cigarette, blowing smoke directly in Donavon's direction. As a confirmed non-smoker such behavior would normally irritate him, but now, second-hand smoke was a concern no more. Donavon watched the gray-blue haze curl lazily into the air, the only place to look other than at a no-good gangsta. The smoke spiraled upward—heavenward, if there was such a place.

Taking the chair offered by his sidekick, Guillermo sat down. Donavon tried to gauge how fast the guy could move. He carried a lot of extra weight, the kind that came from years of good eating and drinking and a way-less-than-active lifestyle. Maybe back in the day he was agile, but obviously he'd gotten fat and lazy as he worked his way up through the ranks, leaving the ugly business of defending himself to others who were younger and more suited for the job.

The pilot considered his options. He could get in one

good punch and a well-aimed blow with the stout Maya cane. A parting shot on his way out.

This'll be for Jake and the poor little girl Guillermo killed. How the hell do these guys live with themselves? Killing a twelve-year old? That in itself was reason to believe God didn't exist. No just God would allow such things.

Donavon concentrated his special-forces training on studying the cabrón sitting in front of him, seemingly without a care in the world. His fat unworried face was so near that Donavon could see straggly black hairs poking out from his sweaty, dimpled chin. Guillermo's defenses were down. He was clearly confident the injured vet would sit there and take his medicine.

He thinks I'm a wounded warrior.

But his wounds were the farthest thing from Donavon's mind. He was tracking the fallibility of the fat man and pacing himself.

As Guillermo smoked, he began to blow smoke rings, concentrating with such effort, he seemed more like the village idiot than the captain who ran Culiacan's Guatemala operations. He barely concentrated on Donovan or the conversation. This was routine. He knew what answers would come and knew he wouldn't be getting his hands dirty in this cat and mouse game. The man took pleasure in the initial phase of questioning, enjoying the implied threat, the tension, and the fear it caused in his prey.

"Back to my question, Señor Donavon. Where are Clay and Layla?"

"I don't know."

"When did you last see them?" Guillermo asked.

"At the crash."

"Where did they go?"

Donavon said nothing.

The capo let the question dangle and relaxed into the chair, concentrating on his smoke ring technique; one was so perfectly round, he commented loudly on its flawlessness. To Donavon, it was strangely eerie. It felt like some obscene preliminary, or foreplay, if there was such a thing as foreplay to murder.

Before blowing each smoke ring, Guillermo inhaled in preparation, then looked up towards the ceiling as he watched his creation float away. Donavon noted the guards stood further back than before, with the table conveniently in between. Their jefe's eyes left Donavon each time, and shifted skyward.

Donavon decided to let him go on a minute, feeling comfortable in his interrogator role. Then he'd take his shot.

This wasn't like the Viet Cong and the merciless torture that occurred during those interrogations in Nam. Because it was combat back then, there was always the possibility one could make it out alive. During wartime, prisoners could be kept alive for intelligence, trade, or POW status. Even if you were captured, there was hope.

The cartel was a totally different scenario. If they nabbed you, well, he'd never heard of anyone making it out alive. If a ninety-year old grandmother sat before them, she'd go down like all the rest, and they'd probably rape her before it was over.

Mexico. What a fucked up place to die.

"Where did they go, Señor Donavon?" Guillermo asked again.

Donavon could play for a little more time with the puta de madre before he slugged him.

Just give an answer. Any answer. "Cancun."

"What? Cancun? Now we're getting somewhere!" Guillermo chortled. He paused to put out his first cigarette and light another, carefully tapping it on a silver cigarette case to pack in the tobacco. Donavon noticed he smoked Marlboros but the harsh Mexican knockoffs with funky branding. A real cowboy. Donavon almost laughed. Mexicans couldn't even properly cure tobacco.

Guillermo took a couple long draws and looked at the end, waiting for the ember to burn in earnest. Then he started again with the smoke rings.

"Do you know where they are in Cancun?"

Donavon noticed the bodyguards were getting bored with the conversation. Too slow for their liking. One kept adjusting his leather gloves, anxious for his turn. But he'd speak with his hands, not his words.

"Umm, no," Donavon said.

One more draw on the cigarette, one more set of smoke rings and then—show time.

"Oh, come on, think harder," Guillermo said, tilting his head back, lifting his eyes skyward. As he did so, Donavon sprang into action.

He grabbed the cane, gripped it tight, and slammed it into Guillermo's chubby face before anyone—the capo or his bodyguards—had a clue what was happening. Donavon heard the crack of the cane as it hit his mark, Guillermo's fat nose. Blood splattered everywhere.

"That's for Lupita, you child molester! And for Jake! Fuck you!" he screamed at the top of his lungs, flailing with the cane. He heard Guillermo's howl of anguish.

The capo roared as he came at him, blood spurting from his face. Donavon moved quickly to the side and away from the chair, just as Guillermo's henchman tackled him from behind, pounding his head onto the concrete floor.

"That all ya got?" Donavon managed to gasp.

Once, twice, a third time. It felt like being hit by a sledge hammer, so hard were the knocks. Lights started to dim. Donavon felt brave and weak at the same time. He was losing consciousness. With luck he'd never recover, would miss the dismembering of his body that would happen any second now that he was down. He went limp, his bad leg bent back in a crazy position. It should have hurt but he felt no pain. I avoided my own funeral, he thought, as consciousness faded.

Then something happened—he was floating, floating high above the scene, watching the events unfold below, but somehow oddly removed. It was as though he had two bodies and they were attached by the narrowest of silver strands at his abdomen. His old body lay on the warehouse floor while two vile Mexicans kicked the shit out of it. Meanwhile his new body floated above the melee, observing and drifting.

He saw el comandante run back into the warehouse. Now the soldiers were getting in on the action. His body was being used as a punching bag but he felt nothing. There was total separation from that body, which resembled a tattered, bloody rag doll. Still, no pain. His focus shifted. Something somewhere seemed to be beckoning, trying to get his attention.

He forgot the scene below feeling strangely at peace and began to concentrate on a stream of white light that emanated from a circular tunnel just above him. It looked as good a place as any to drift towards, and that was the last thing he remembered as he reached out to touch the void.

CHAPTER 32

Motul, Yucatán, Mexico

Clay's new cell phone rang.

"Don Guillermo here," a familiar voice said. "You were expecting your friend Donavon? Sorry, but no. No more. If you and Layla are as easy as he was, I'll be through here soon and back to Guate. Oh, and there's a package for you in Merida. Twelve kilometers east on Hacienda Xcanatún road.

Click.

"Christ, he's killed Donavon," Clay said, his voice a monotone. "That fucker, Guillermo."

"What? Oh, no! How do you know?" Layla's face drained of color. She jumped up and paced around the room. Her chest felt tight, constricted. But no sobs came.

"His cocky attitude. He said, 'No more,' about Donavon. There's a package for us near some hacienda. Xcanatún? Fuck! How can Donavon be dead? How?" Clay let out a low moan.

Layla was so drained from the events of the past few days she couldn't even cry. In her heart she knew Donavon was a dead man walking once the army grabbed him. They had to tell Manuel, and they had to make sure the Maya man remained safe and wouldn't become another statistic, thanks to Guillermo or the army.

She stopped pacing. "It's time," she said, as she watched her friend.

"Time for what?" Clay's voice was distracted, powerless.

"Action. Where's Manuel?"

"Out back, making tea," Clay said.

"Get him. We're leaving, all of us. He can go to Juan Balam's milpa and wait things out, until everything dies down and the federales quit storming the jungle. Or he can stay with a friend in Cancun or Valladolid. It doesn't matter where. Anywhere but here."

Clay was out the door in a flash.

"Can't wait," she said to herself, "Have to get to him first," she said. "My phone."

To hell with them tracing her. She punched in her brother's number in Culiacan.

"Martín!"

He picked up on the first ring. "What the hell's going on?"

"I need you. I need your help." A long pause followed. "Hola? Hola!" Layla screamed into the receiver.

"Hey! I'm here. What are you calling *me* for?" her brother asked.

"Faith in you, in your judgment, and hoping you want to see me again—alive," Layla said.

"What happened?"

Layla paused, put her hand to her heart. "Carlos is dead."

"How?"

She took a gulp of air then began. "Plane crash in the jungle. Cancun wouldn't let us land. Long story. I'll catch you up."

While Layla filled her brother in on the past days' events, Clay told Manuel about Donavon and the need for him to depart his house until every trace of the plane crash, along with the federales who were investigating it, was gone.

"Are you okay, Manuel?" Clay asked.

The Maya man nodded. He looked stricken, saddened beyond belief. A single, perfect tear rolled down his cheek. He wiped it away with the back of his hand.

"I'll help you pack your sisal and your hats," he told the Maya. "Either go to Juan Balam's or a friend's house. You can't stay here."

"Can I take my truck?" he asked, avoiding eye contact with Clay.

"Only if you are going far away. Cancun or a place no one will recognize it."

"I think Cancun. Yes, Cancun."

Layla was off the phone, looking expectantly at Clay and Manuel. "Clay told you about Donavon?"

Manuel looked down. "Yes."

"It's very sad. But we have to protect you, and the only way that can happen is if you leave until everything has blown over."

He nodded, wiping his hand underneath his nose, somehow avoiding more tears.

"I will pack my sisal and go to Cancun," Manuel said.

"We'll pay for the cuota highway. Less checkpoints. Who do you know in Cancun?"

"Family."

"Good. Clay, this is what's going to happen. Martín knows a hacker, a techno nerd he went to school with who can locate anyone on the planet—from anywhere—with triangulations generated from a throw-away phone. Sounds impossible, but he swears it's true.

"Guillermo called us. We have his coordinates. Martín will call one of Patrón's first lieutenants and let him know what's happening. I need all intel on that fucker. Guillermo's in Merida and he won't stop till he finds us. We have to locate him and make our move first. We have snitches everywhere, plus he works with us. His whereabouts shouldn't be secret. Even the fucking maid will know where he's at. People talk."

"How will the geek get the phone?" Clay asked.

"DHL, from Merida. They don't take as many precautions as FedEx. I'll send it to Martín. He'll have it tomorrow or the next day. We leave here with Manuel. Make sure he locks up and send him off. You and I head to Merida. Find a secure spot, hunker down. We'll wait for our intel to find out where that puta de madre is staying."

"What about the package near the hacienda?" Clay asked.

"You know how cartels do things. They deposit people's bodies as though they're deliveries from parcel post. Just like with Canul, the airport manager." She considered the unethical practices used by her cronies. Send a message— loud and clear. Same as it ever was.

Do. Not. Fuck. With. Me.

"You're saying it's Donavon?"

"Donavon's body for sure. But near a hacienda. Hmm. That seems odd he'd mention it. He's not the type to slip up. Or maybe he's so sure of himself, he thinks he has us on the run.

"The one good thing about traveling light, as in you and me, we can outmaneuver his huge operation. He travels with an entourage," Layla said.

"What'll we do for heat?"

"Martín. Gotta figure out where we'll be staying. He can DHL us a couple of pieces, or he'll provide a name in Merida."

"I thought Merida stayed pretty quiet," Clay said.

"It does, or it has. Only that one incident—ugly—twelve beheaded bodies about five years ago, again, sending a message. They elected a woman governor, a do-gooder, to run the cartel families out of town. You've heard it before.

"Well, the cartel killed twelve innocents—some not so innocent, actually—and they told the media Merida would be under curfew until they decided to end it. Everyone had to be off the streets by eight or they'd kill a person a night," Layla said.

Clay shook his head. "That's sending a message all right."

"A friend was in a restaurant when that came down—every cell phone went off at the same time—she said you never saw Mexicans move so fast!" Layla smirked. Speed was not what her countrymen were known for, in spite of the silly cartoon with a mouse in a sombrero. "They cleared out in a heartbeat! Merida's home to lots of cartel families. They like to keep business far from where they live. Manuel! How you doing?" Layla asked.

"Bien. Listo." He picked up a duffel bag with one hand and slung a large backpack with his sisal products over his shoulder. He took a last wistful look around his home.

Layla didn't miss it. "Manuel, I know this is hard. I'm so very sorry. Your life has been turned upside down because of the kindness you've shown to strangers."

"It's like the saying, no good deed goes unpunished," Clay said, muttering.

"What?" Layla demanded, turning sharply and glaring at Clay. "What did you say?"

"You heard me. They saved our lives and we've done nothing but threaten theirs."

"Christ, Clay! Don't you think I know it?" Her hands went to her hips and she felt both rage and guilt. Her face was flushed as she spit out, "I'm not proud of this, any of this, and we both know it really *is* my fault. Chinga! I am so pissed about Donavon! It's like a stack of bodies is trailing me around—an endless stack of bodies! I'm trying to do damage control, and I will repay Manuel and Juan, somehow, some time. But now, Clay, I need to focus."

Layla turned and headed for the door, letting the screen slap noisily shut behind her. Manuel had stayed quiet, busily adjusting his backpack, pretending the two weren't having a moment. Clay watched Layla's stormy departure before he walked to the door himself. He opened it wide for Manuel and grabbed the heavy duffel to help lighten the Maya's load. It was the least he could do after displacing the very man who'd given them shelter from the storm.

CHAPTER 33

"Do you know Merida?" Clay asked Layla, as they raced along the toll highway heading to the westernmost part of the Yucatán Peninsula and its largest city.

"I've been there a few times. You?"

"Yeah. I like the place. It feels real—so different from Cancun."

"Cancun's a showpiece—Mexico for gringos," Layla said matter of factly as she readjusted her seatbelt, settling in for the drive.

"True, but you can't beat the water and those white sand beaches."

"You're right. I love Sinaloa, but Cancun is gorgeous," she said.

"What about hotels?"

"I only know the big ones. But on the back streets Merida has a ton of posadas, small hotels with eight or ten rooms. We'll find one of those, off the radar."

"What about Donavon's body?" Clay asked, turning to look at Layla.

"It's not wise, Clay. I'm sorry. Guillermo's people hope we'll do something sentimental. Did he have his passport?"

"Yeah, I gave him both his and Jake's a couple days ago, before we split for Cancun."

"Orale, it's only been two days," Layla said, shaking her head. She tried to grasp all that had happened in that short amount of time. "Poor Donavon. I really liked him."

She let out a sigh as she leaned back on the headrest and closed her eyes, hoping to block out not only the sunlight but the sudden surge of emotions that tore through her body.

"Me, too," Clay said, "Me, too."

🔯🔯🔯

Merida, Yucatán, Mexico

Merida was bursting at the seams with daily life. Women in huipiles hawked fresh fruit and nuts. School kids toted backpacks filled with books. People streamed in and out of countless tiendas. The streets were jam-packed due to narrow sidewalks and an overflow of humanity. The city's population was a million strong and growing.

"Keep driving," Layla said, as they continued down Calle 61, the main road into the city, past a jumble of auto parts and tire stores, mechanics, rotisserias, hardware and paint shops strung along the thoroughfare.

Eventually this centuries-old street would run into the main plaza that also served as an unofficial line of demarcation—tourists and expats on one side, local neighborhoods and businesses on the other.

"Wow, I forgot how big Merida is," Clay said. "The streets are crazy!"

"You have to remember, Mexicans who live in cities share extremely small apartments with generations of family, so streets and parks double as their living rooms. Streets can offer more privacy than their homes, because everyone lives virtually on top of each other. It's an anonymous privacy.

"Take a right on 60 at the main plaza then a left on Calle 57," Layla said.

As they passed Parque Hidalgo, where the city's oldest hotel, El Gran, sat beneath a towering almendron, kissing lovers could be seen entwined in each other's arms on a quaint park bench.

Layla nodded at the lovebirds as they drove by. "I've never been to Paris, but there's probably more PDA in Mexican cities than in the city of love."

"Well, I have been to Paris," Clay said, "and I think you're right. I guess in Merida the world's a stage."

After circumnavigating the bustling main plaza that included the stately Governor's Palace, the ancient cathedral, and the city founder's mansion, Palacio de Montejo, they drove up and down each street, looking for a quiet, private spot, with enclosed parking.

Clay liked Hotel Montejo at Calle 62, but it was too close to the heart of the tourist center for Layla's taste. They went further afield, going far up Calle 53 between 70 and 72 on the extreme outskirts of the tourist zone. There, they found an out of the way spot called Hotel Casa Zamna.

"This looks more like it," Layla said. "A quiet posada. Let's see if they have rooms."

They parked the car on the street and walked back to the entrance of the nondescript hotel where a British innkeeper greeted them. He had a large suite with two bedrooms and sitting room available at the far end of the complex next to the garden. For parking, they could pull the car into his private gated lot.

"We'll take it," Clay said. "Can we pay now for three nights and let you know our schedule?"

"Certainly," the owner said. "Going to do some sightseeing?"

Layla looked at Clay. "Yes. I want to show my friend your city. He's had enough of Cancun."

"Right. Cancun can get old after a while," the man said with a chuckle. "Everyone likes to come here for a few days and see the real Yucatán. Need any help with your luggage?"

"We're fine for now," Clay said, adjusting his backpack. He pulled a stack of pesos from a side pocket. "We'll pull the car inside the lot. Do you have an extra room key?"

"Of course," the man said as he turned around and pulled another key off room twelve's ring.

Layla took the key and stooped to get her bag. "Can you point the way?"

"Down the path to the left of the entrance, all the way to the back, behind the koi pond."

"Thank you, señor," Layla said, flashing one of her killer smiles. "You've been most kind."

🔁🔁🔁

"First I'll call the Merida Police and tell them where they can find Donavon's body." Layla settled into an easy chair after she checked out the humble two-room suite. "Do you have your secure phone?"

"Here ya go," Clay said. He handed her his Nokia 8210, a drug dealer's treasure. Due to its age, it had no tracking device.

The Merida Police Department put her on hold for several minutes but after Layla relayed her tip to the lieutenant on duty, her work was done. She hung up.

"That's it," she told Clay. "We check the papers tomorrow and see if it's reported."

"What now?"

"It may not be too late to send your new cell to Martín.

Let's catch a cab and drive by the DHL office, see if they're open and grab a bite. I can't believe it but I'm famished."

"Okay," Clay said.

"Hopefully we can get it out tonight, then I'll buy another phone, call Martín, and let him know when to expect it."

Ten minutes later they were taxiing to a DHL office in the tourist zone right off Merida's main plaza. Layla sent her package and found a nearby corner tienda selling TelMex phones.

"Put it in your name, Clay," Layla instructed when the clerk asked for identification.

He whipped out his passport, filled in the form and bought a couple of pre-paid calling cards.

"Dinner?" Layla asked as they left the shop.

Clay nodded. "Now I'm hungry."

Not wanting to dine right on the zocalo, they wandered a few blocks away from the center, all the while gazing at Merida mansions, many remodeled and owned by foreigners. Though the towering exteriors looked bland, Layla explained, the interiors were often showpieces. Merida's architecture copied that of old Spain, their windowless facades mushrooming into haute couture interiors with cascading gardens and sometimes pools. These central courtyards were surprisingly cool and quiet, surrounded by smoothed walls of cinder block that acted as a blockade to the Yucatán sun and even the most audacious street noise.

Clay and Layla came across Alberto's Continental Cuisine, a whitewashed mansion turned restaurant. After a quick nod of acceptance from Layla, the couple entered. Inside they discovered an oasis filled with antiques and art.

The back wall displayed Madonna art, all in wood and brass, next to an ethereal painting of a floating Guadalupe. They walked up polished marble stairs to where an older gentleman in a tired business suit stood next to a mostra-dore. Layla couldn't take her eyes off the high-ceilinged dining room where oil paintings covered every wall. A long center table with linen tablecloths, all in white, sat dead center, complete with silver candelabra and ornate place settings.

The maitre d' greeted them. "Two for dinner? The garden?" He motioned to his left.

Clay and Layla's eyes followed his gesture. At the garden's center stood a giant banyan. Three-meter-high walls, smooth and whitewashed, were covered with more art, mostly religious icons in every possible medium. In fact, the entire place teemed with mystical artifacts. It was a shrine, a holy grail, to spirituality and art.

"I'm Alberto," the elderly gentleman said as he led them down a wide set of stairs into the sunken garden. A well-lit bar sat at one end.

"A quiet night out?" he asked, leaning in as he made a lavish gesture of opening the menu for Layla. "May I have the waiter bring you a cocktail? Margarita?"

"Si, por supuesto," Layla said in Spanish. It had been a long, over the top day—another friend lost, another wrinkle in their plans. She should make it a double. Maybe it was time to try a little therapy—the kind that could be found inside a bottle.

She could think of no better way to relax than with drink in hand. She'd been avoiding alcohol ever since she discovered Lupita. It was her unspoken penance to Guadalupe or Mal Verde, Mexico's dueling patron saints—like she would cut a deal with some supreme deity and give up drinking if somehow the girl was allowed to escape and live. But that hadn't happened, and Carlos had died, too. Not to mention Jake, and now Donavon.

Enough of that—time to shift gears. Bottoms up! Arriba, abajo, el centro, el dentro! Up, down, center, inside. She loved that silly Mexican toast.

Time to numb the pain.

CHAPTER 34

Before catching a cab back to the hotel, they stopped at an OXXO convenience store to buy a six-pack. Twenty minutes later, back at the posada, Clay handed Layla a beer and she plunked down in the suite's one easy chair and punched in Martín's number. She seriously needed to take the edge off—the tension was still building even after three margaritas and a relaxing dinner, and the pressure was not going to lighten up anytime soon.

Her call to Martín was a revelation. He'd been working overtime trying to discover anything and everything about Guillermo's whereabouts since they last talked.

"He's staying at a hacienda between Merida and Progreso. There'll be a grand fiesta for Semana Santa. This guy, Emilio Vargas, throws it every year, a masquerade ball for Pascua, at Hacienda Xcanatún. Guillermo never misses. Vargas owns the place and they have a lot in common. This guy makes wine, so does Guillermo. They both own cattle."

"Is he connected?" Layla asked.

"No, apparently just a rancher. Cattle and henequen. Did you send the phone?" Martín asked.

"It went out tonight, DHL. They said late tomorrow, maybe. What about the other thing?"

"The heat? I'll send you a pair. Need an address, phone number."

Layla read the hotel information off the key chain.

"I'll be looking for the package, Martín. We'll stay here until further notice. I'll use this cell for a couple days, then burn it."

"What's your plan?"

"He killed the pilot. Threw his body out near some hacienda. We're not going to claim it for obvious reasons. I left a tip with the police. They'll make a statement when they find the body."

"You think it's the same hacienda his friend owns?" Martín asked.

"My exact thoughts." She rubbed her palm over her forehead as she pictured their friend, the pilot. Dead. Poor Donavon.

"So you're gonna do what?" asked Martín.

"Kill him."

Silence. "There will be repercussions, especially if he's tight with Zoyo."

"Oh, he's tight with Zoyo. It's way beyond a conflict of interests," she said, getting steamed all over again. "You want me to do nothing? It's total insubordination. Patrón would be pissed enough about the double-dealing and the sex trafficking, and now Guillermo's out to get me."

Martín sighed. "You do what you gotta do. How you handling it?"

"Okay. I'm ready."

"Too bad about Carlos," Martín said.

"Thanks. It's been hard. My new friend has helped a lot." She shot a small smile at Clay.

"Pace yourself. When you get my package, you'll feel better, then take care of business." There was a brief pause. "But remember, cuidado. You're opening yourself up for a world of hurt."

She closed her eyes. Why was revenge so hard? Why did

every reaction create a Richter scale of grief? "I hear you. And Martín? Thank you."

She disconnected the call and sat in silence for a few moments.

"What's the buzz?" Clay finally asked.

"Guillermo's staying at a hacienda between here and Progreso, owned by one of his pals. We'll know for sure when Martín gets the phone, but I'm positive it's where they dumped Donavon's body. Apparently, he comes here every year for a masquerade ball during Semana Santa, you know, Easter week."

"That's when we do it?" Clay asked.

"It's the perfect ambush," Layla said, nearly salivating as she put it all together. "He's so arrogant, he expects nothing from us and believes he's perfectly safe. This is our chance, Clay. I'm taking that puta de madre out."

"For Donavon!" Clay said. He raised his beer high.

"For Donavon!" Layla responded.

They clinked bottles, each uttering a silent oath.

⊡⊡⊡

Martín stayed in Culiacan so he could focus on his end of the bargain. He'd made a promise to his sister. Amazing how trouble could stretch or mend family feuds. With the Culiacan Cartel, strife was a strengthening bond.

DHL performed beautifully and Clay's phone had been delivered to Martín the next day. The day after that, the innkeeper told Layla she had a package at the front desk. Martín had sent two nine millimeters and a lot of ammo—a Glock 30, presumably for Clay, and a small Beretta 950 for Layla.

"Have you used these before?" Layla asked Clay.

198

"All nine millimeters are good. My gun of choice."

"I had a Beretta 92FS, an old service gun. Should we find a quiet spot and practice today?"

"Good idea," Clay said.

Before heading out, Layla called Martín to advise him that she'd received the package and also to see what information the encryption revealed.

"You were right on the hacienda," he told her.

"Great. Now we can start planning. When's the party?"

"Saturday night, Holy Week. Right after Good Friday. You have a week. How you gonna get on the grounds?"

"I already know," Layla said. "Every fiesta has mariachis and singers, no?"

"Si, si," her brother replied.

"Well, I need to find out what mariachi band will perform, and convince them to hire me."

"I didn't know you could sing."

"Martín," she said. "Once they see me, do you really think they'll care?"

Martín gave a sharp laugh. "Layla, you never change."

"So how do we find the group?" Layla asked.

"I'll see who I know in Merida and check around. We'll talk soon, hermana. Ciao."

🔯🔯🔯

Layla directed Clay to Paseo de Montejo, the grand boulevard lined with stately mansions built at the turn of the twentieth century, thanks to profits from the lucrative henequen trade. With demand for Panama hats growing worldwide, Merida enjoyed a long-lasting boom economy from their "green gold." Elegant Paseo de Montejo ran directly into the Progreso highway heading north.

Clay and Layla needed a spot for target practice. If they drove far enough out of the city, they'd find what they were looking for on Merida's rural outskirts.

Layla hadn't used a gun in a while. With Carlos constantly by her side, the need simply did not exist. But when he taught her the basics, he taught her well. It seemed strange that a guy with such a penchant for dragging her down could be good at teaching her, well, anything. But he was. Just another one of life's little mysteries.

Back in Culiacan, Martín labored over how to give his sister an edge up on her adversaries. The only thing he could think of was equal parts muscle and back up. She was sorely lacking a bodyguard, and though he knew she could handle a gun, Layla and the Canadian could not match the forces Zoyo and Guillermo could pull together.

Her mariachi idea appealed to the macabre in him. Seed the group with assassins. The hard part: finding a group of gunmen who could perform. But even if he couldn't find any who could carry a tune, the group that did perform would be accompanied by at least one gun-toting member of the Culiacan Cartel.

🔲🔲🔲

Before turning off the Progreso highway they stopped at a roadside tienda, grabbed a twelve-pack of Coronas along with several fresh salbutes from a woman serving lunch to a long line of workers from the back of her car. Three Igloo coolers sat in the trunk along with a stack of plastic plates and she tirelessly passed out platefuls of finger-size corn tortillas piled high with pulled chicken, finely chopped cabbage, and pickled red onions. The crowd was hungry and business was brisk.

Sitting in their car in the parking lot, Clay and Layla started in on the steaming food.

"Oooh," Clay said, as he dug into his second salbute, slowly pulling the tortilla apart in his mouth as he savored the flavor, red juice from the onions dripping down his chin. "This is one of the things I love about Mexico."

"No napkins?" Layla said, laughing, as she watched him try to discreetly wipe away the dribble with the back of his hand. Eating Mexican finger food without looking like a complete barbarian was an art form she'd perfected long ago.

"No! The food! But a napkin would be nice."

"True, our food's the best," Layla said, nodding between bites. "Especially in Yucatán."

They cracked cervezas to wash down lunch. The day was warm, their stomachs full, thirst quenched. Life was good.

Back on the highway, they spotted a side road that looked like a ticket to nowhere.

Several kilometers off the main highway they came upon another side road. They hadn't seen a soul since the taco lady at the tienda, but they kept on driving. It was easy to get to back country in Mexico, even outside large cities, and Merida was no exception.

Another turn found them facing an area with a generous berm. Clay pulled over and told Layla to wait while he checked to see if this was their spot. In five minutes he was back.

"It's perfect. Behind those chit and chaka plants," he said, pointing at the bushy shrubbery, "there's a field. Wide open." He opened the back door and grabbed his pack.

She piled out of the car, bringing with her the cold Coronas and a bag of empty bottles they'd gone through at the hotel.

At their makeshift shooting range, Clay unzipped his backpack and pulled out the DHL box sent by Martín, gently removing the two guns. He'd placed the ammo in one of his zippered side pockets along with the silencers. Layla stood by, watching him unpack it all.

"Here you go, Layla. We're coming to the last leg of our journey," he said. A somber look came over his face. He loaded a clip into the Beretta and handed it to her.

She felt the conviction and emotion he conveyed in his simple yet profound statement. "For now, Clay, for now."

She knew what he said bore truth. It could be the ultimate last leg of their journey. The outcome, that in due course would work itself out through a manner of timing, trickery and skill, was the big unknown.

But Layla well understood the need to remain positive and she believed it was also Clay's core philosophy. Thrown together by fate, they'd come to see eye to eye on most things, and now they were teaming up in what could be a fight for their lives.

CHAPTER 35

"You're good!" Clay said, amazed at the accuracy of Layla's shots and how easily she handled the firearm. "I don't know if I'm any better than you."

"Of course you are. Don't patronize me," Layla said. She gave him her cut-the-crap look. She expected that kind of flattery from the cartel guys but not from Clay. "Let's make a new rule: complete honesty."

He laughed. "I think we've established that I couldn't lie to you if I tried. Your bullshit detector is firmly in place."

"Now it's your turn," Layla said. "Let me see you beat my record." She gave him a sassy grin.

Clay walked to the fallen tree trunk they were using as a base and set up a few more. "You're putting pressure on me, Layla," he said. "I don't know if I can handle this."

"Remember, if a woman beats you in Mexico, you will die a slow and painful death. It's not allowed! Your friends would cut off your cojones!"

He laughed in spite of her perceptive truth. In Mexico women were abused for a lot less than outshining their men in a game or sport. Mexico had invented machismo. Clay was sure of it.

They traded jokes and retorts as well as trading off shooting for another thirty minutes. Clay tested Layla again and again, making sure she could easily load clips into the Beretta, and finally showed her how to fire the Glock.

"Just in case something happens," he said, his smile gone, looking at her with new meaning. "Let me see you load it now. Always good to have backup."

She understood what he meant. Exactly what Carlos would have said. Cover your bases. Take no chances. Chinga! She'd already taken enough to last a lifetime. And as Carlos always said, "Live another day."

After they destroyed the beer bottles they stacked stones on the tree trunk and used them for targets. Both felt like they were accomplishing something as the day grew steadily hotter.

Clay watched her finish the clip. "We've done a good job here."

"Time to go back?" she asked. The heat was beginning to wear on her.

"I think so. Let's load up this mess and get back to town."

It didn't take long to toss the remaining pieces of leftover glass into plastic bags before heading back down the path to the car.

"That was good," Layla said as she opened the car door, fanning herself with her hand. "I feel confident about shooting the guns. Both of them." She slipped into the passenger seat.

"Me, too. You did good," he said, as he backed the car onto the narrow road, and put it into forward gear.

Ten minutes later, just before the Merida highway, a black car fishtailed in front of them on the dusty sascab as it barreled around a curve onto their side of the road. Two determined-looking men were in it. One held a gun.

It was aimed straight at them.

CHAPTER 36

"Layla! Get the Glock! Hurry!"

She had already grabbed the backpack from the rear seat and ripped open Martín's package. Thank God, the gun was still loaded. Clay swerved as the sedan tried to crowd them off the road. The driver overcorrected and slid onto the shoulder, wheels sliding and screeching as the vehicle attempted to regain traction.

"Hold on! Can you take aim?" Clay cried, revving the engine.

Her window was already down. "Chinga! I'm aiming!"

The woman could perform under pressure. She had the Glock in hand. In spite of Clay's dare-devil driving, Layla steadied it on her forearm, aiming back at their pursuers' car.

"How the fuck'd they find us?" Clay asked. He stepped on it, ratcheting the rental up to breakneck velocity.

Layla's head jerked towards Clay. "Oh, no! My cell!"

"What?"

"He tracked me on my cell, same way Martín tracked Guillermo. I called him from Guatemala. Fuck! Now his goons have us in their crosshairs."

"Not for long!" Clay said, maintaining control as he pushed the vehicle faster yet. Their car lurched drunkenly from side to side. He heard a lone shot ring out. And another.

One of Layla's bullets connected with the black car's windshield, shattering it. The vehicle slid further off the shoulder, wobbled, and lodged at a precarious angle. It shuddered and smoke steamed from its engine. She wasn't sure if she'd hit either of the thugs, but damage had been done.

"Ditch that phone, Layla! Every second you hold onto it, they have a line on us!"

"What about all the data?" Layla demanded, a petulant tone to her voice.

"Fuck the data!"

She grabbed for her purse, dug in, and retrieved the phone. *Was I born without a brain?* One more mistake like this and there would be no showdown with Guillermo—only their lifeless bodies discovered in some anonymous ditch, as dead as Donavon's.

She disabled the locator app, amazed she could do it at high velocity, took a last look at her iPhone and smacked it hard against the dash. The glass screen splintered and cracked. She flung it out the window into the roadside's low-lying growth.

"Happy now?"

"Damn! I'm not the enemy!" Clay's face was an unrecognizable mask of anger.

"I know! I know!" she said, unnerved by what an imbecile she'd become and embarrassed by her futile attempt at smashing the phone before throwing out the tracking device that had given the enemy full disclosure on their whereabouts. Maybe she deserved to die.

How could she even hope to take out Guillermo, or Zoyo, or both? Leader of the cartel? How about president of a women's garden club? Her level of self-esteem was near rock bottom as Clay powered the rental onto the main highway and away from their near-death experience, the closest call they'd had since the plane crash. She shuddered. What would have happened if they'd stayed ten minutes longer and the gunmen surprised them in the open field?

"Now what?" she asked.

Clay snorted, still riled. "Back to the hotel, get our stuff, and split."

"Where to?" Layla asked.

"I don't know!"

"Gotta ditch the car. Park it on the street somewhere. Take a taxi to a car rental. There's one in town near the tourist zone; a Canadian owns it. At least it was there a few years ago."

"How's your internal GPS? Can you find it?" he asked without glancing her way.

"Think so. First the car."

Although the conversation slowed down, the velocity of the rental retained its speed. They were twenty kilometers outside of Merida. On the main drag of the city they would still be a target. Time to get lost in one of the city's sprawling, anonymous barrios.

"How about Muna?" Layla asked.

"Where the hell's that?"

"South of Merida, sixty kilometers, enroute to the Uxmal pyramids."

"Not a bad idea," Clay said, this response less of a growl.

In twenty minutes they were back on Paseo de Montejo, but the stately mansions that bordered the grand boulevard no longer held any charm.

"The northern barrios are better," Layla said, "More working class but people have cars."

"Involve no one." Clay gave her a hard look. "We don't need more bodies piling up."

She winced. She counted four out of four, thanks to her inability to gauge the barometer of human tolerance, not only for herself but for those she should have been protecting: Carlos, Lupita, Jake, Donavon. She read Clay loud and clear. He'd sided with her, and if she didn't up her game, he, too, could become part of the body count.

Best to get to the hotel and free James, the British innkeeper, of any links to them or their whereabouts. He was just a hotelier. No need for his torture or murder simply because they laid their heads on his pillows for a few nights.

"Turn right," she said.

Clay maneuvered the car onto a side street.

"Keep going, past the tracks."

After driving up and down residential streets they found a spot next to a deserted park with overfilled garbage cans, a few scruffy trees, and a partially destroyed wall. No one around, just a handful of parked cars around the perimeter. They grabbed their belongings from the car along with the bag of broken bottles.

"Leave the doors unlocked," Clay said. "In a few days I'll call Hertz and tell them it's been stolen. I always pay for total liability, bumper to bumper."

He walked over to the park, deposited the bag of broken glass into the over-flowing dumpster, and met Layla back on the sidewalk.

"Let's go," he said. "Eventually we'll find a taxi. It's a cinch there isn't Uber in Merida. We'll stick to the back streets though. Walking down Paseo is too obvious."

She nodded. His instincts were good. Time to rely on someone else for a change, someone whose head was still screwed on in the right direction.

CHAPTER 37

Merida, Yucatán, Mexico

Clay flagged down a taxi three blocks away and they jumped in.

"Drop us at Hotel Casa Zamna," Layla said to the driver.

"Por supuesto."

"So what else do you know about that place you mentioned?" Clay asked. Even with a nondescript cabbie he refused to mention the name of their next lodging spot.

"Small. Off the grid. No tourists."

Clay nodded as he digested the info. "Okay."

After a hasty retreat at the hotel with a promise to return the following year, Clay and Layla waved goodbye to James, the accommodating hotelier.

"I'm glad he didn't ask where the car was," Clay said, as they walked away from the hotel.

"You think he's in danger?" Layla asked.

"Let's hope not. I think if they'd figured out our GPS sooner, they would have shown up at the hotel. So where's this car rental?"

They caught another cab and Layla directed the driver to a hole-in-the-wall car rental agency off Calle 64. "It's here. Oh, no, he's closed for siesta."

"Who still does that?" Clay asked. "This is the twenty-first century! I thought you said he was Canadian."

"It's Merida, Clay. Different time zone, different century, okay?"

"Wait, he's removing the "cerrado" sign."

They jumped out of the cab and walked into the agency. "We want your fastest ride," Clay said. "Got anything with a little power?"

"Chevy's the best I can do. Four-door."

"We'll take it."

"It's parked in a lot around the corner. After you sign the contract I'll walk you over."

In twenty minutes they were in a new rental car, heading south out of Merida towards the Uxmal pyramids. Next stop, Muna.

🔁🔁🔁

"Time for some damage control," Clay said as they drove south on Highway 180 following signs for Uxmal.

"Yeah, yeah," Layla said. "What do we do?"

"Call your brother and let him know about our close call with Guillermo's men. See if he has any idea who they could be, what's up with our Guatemala pal. The phone's in my pack."

She searched Clay's backpack until she found it. "Martín, change of plans. We're on the move."

"Que paso?" What's up?

"They tracked us. Through my cell!"

"Ohhhh, no!" Martín shouted. "What the hell, Layla? You're as bad as Little Beto's wife now, forgetting to change her cell number? That could land you in jail just like Beto!"

"Or in a ditch. I know, I know. Totally stupid." She felt her face reddening. "I forgot to throw it out, even after we sent you Clay's."

"Layla, Layla." His patronizing tone reminded her of their long ago teen years when he and Reynoldo constantly taunted her.

"Estupido!" Layla said, embarrassed by her mistake.

"Tell me what happened?" Martín asked.

"We were shooting—target practice—in a deserted field thirty kilometers from Merida. Just as we were getting back on the main highway two goons came straight at us."

"Where are they now?" Martín asked.

"I took out their windshield and the car's off the road. Clay was driving. We didn't stick around. We got our stuff from the hotel, ditched the other rental, got a new one. On the move."

"How you doing?"

"Okay, but I guess I blew our cover," she said.

There was a second of silence. "Now it's all out in the open. Look at it that way. You knew he was coming for you, anyway. My guess they were just a couple hired guns. No doubt Guillermo figures you'll be coming for him. But we won't make it easy. We'll be sneaky as shit. Don't worry, hermana. I'll cover your ass."

This was a side of Martín Layla had never witnessed. It was down to the two of them and Patrón now. The rest of the clan was dead and gone. Maybe that meant something, even to him.

"Get settled, then call me. I have information that will cheer you up!"

CHAPTER 38

Muna, Yucatán, Mexico

"Martín!" Layla nearly shouted into the phone. "We found a place, a safe place. In Muna."

"Where?" her brother asked.

"On the road to Uxmal. It's a tiny pueblo five kilometers out of town. This artist has a posada and rents rooms. We're here for at least three days. Have you found out anything?"

"A lot. First off I found the mariachi group."

"Great! When can I meet them?" Layla asked.

"Soon. I talked with the bandleader. Told him you were a mariachi singer extraordinaire from Guadalajara with family in Yucatán. Lety Domingo. You're singing for free this time, sort of an audition, but he's also making good on a favor. You know how it goes."

"Uh-huh." She found an easy chair and settled into it, removing her sandals as she spoke.

"Before we finish I'll give you his name and number. If he has any doubts, we'll put pressure in all the right places. You have to meet him though. I told him you have your own outfits. He wants to do a rehearsal this week. That way he can see how to work you into their songs. He said they might rehearse at the hacienda."

"Perfecto!"

"If you can see the hacienda first it'll give you a leg up."

He paused. "That'll be important." They both knew what he meant, there was no need to state it aloud.

"What about Clay?" Layla asked.

"I've been thinking about that. What color's his hair?"

"Brownish blond."

"Can you get some dye? He can't look like a gringo. Does he have a tan?" Martín asked.

Layla gazed skeptically at Clay, who was well into his second beer. "You could say so."

"What are you talking about?" Clay asked.

"How you'll look as a Mexican. But he's so tall!"

"He doesn't have to be in the group, Layla," Martín said. "He can be your manager."

"Better," Layla said, nodding. "He'd stand out too much up on stage."

"Good, then Clay's your manager. Oh, and here's more news, the fiesta is costumes required for everyone. It's a masquerade ball."

"Okay. I'll call tomorrow and we'll shop for costumes in Merida," Layla said.

"One for Clay, too. The name of the guy who's in charge of Los Mariachis de Yucatán is Alfredo Cortez. All he knows is that he has to hire you, at least once. I insisted it be soon and stressed your stage presence. I told him you're a real prima donna with a following, but from Guadalajara, not yet known in Yucatán. He suggested the Semana Santa fiesta."

Layla grabbed a pen and he gave her Alfredo's number.

"Call him tomorrow and say you'll be at rehearsal. And throw in something about music to sound like you know your stuff."

"No hay problema."

"Go shopping, lay low. Your pueblo sounds good. Oh,

and I'm sending you backup guys. I'll arrange when and where later. They'll have a getaway car, changes of clothes. Be prepared for a fast exit. I've been thinking and it's too tough to get anyone else up on stage with you. It's all gonna come down to you. You'll have one good shot. Maybe, just maybe, two."

"What if Zoyo's there?"

"Chinga, Layla! I don't want a bloodbath on my hands. Go for Guillermo. We'll sort the rest out with Patrón afterwards. He doesn't know about the stuff going down in Guatemala yet. And he has no clue about Zoyo's tricks. We have to take out Guillermo first, then make our case."

Layla was silent. "But what if I could get them both?" Layla asked.

"We don't even know if Zoyo will be there," Martín said with emphasis. Though Layla could fixate on a topic and not let up, Martín was a logical, practical thinker. Even getting a clean shot at Guillermo could prove iffy, he explained patiently. In the end it would all come down to luck. The possibility of getting Guillermo *and* Zoyo in the crosshairs? Same odds as winning the Mexican loteria, twice.

Layla grunted then reluctantly made sounds of agreement.

"We'll talk again soon, hermana. Take it as it comes. One more thing, I'm making you a new passport. You're Lety Santiago, from Guadalajara. Different surname than the one I gave the mariachi guy. If you hit your mark, the policia will question him. Oh, and you'll like this. You're five years younger. I'm working stuff out on my end. You get organized on yours. Gotta run. Ciao."

"Ciao." Layla put the phone down and addressed Clay. "This is the deal. I'll call the manager of the group and let him know I'll be at rehearsal. I'll tell him my manager is coming with me. Martín told him I'm a real prima donna so I'll pretend I'm high strung."

Clay suppressed a smile.

"What?" she demanded, noticing his attempt to not laugh out loud.

"Now Layla, we've been getting along so well. Let's not ruin a perfectly laid-back night."

"Clay! What? I'm not that bad!" she said in protest.

"Darlin', you have your moments. Don't we all? But seriously, how's it gonna play out?"

She brought him up to speed and relayed Martín's apprehension—there would be one opportune moment only to do the deed.

She was quiet for a moment. Too quiet for Clay's liking.

"What's wrong?" he asked.

"I'm afraid once Zoyo knows Guillermo's been hit, he'll make a play on Patrón."

Clay mulled that over before answering. "What about the prison? Your uncle must have paid guards for protection on the inside—staff or other prisoners—or both."

"I'm sure he does," Layla said in a flip manner.

"Does he or doesn't he?" Clay's eyes bored into hers.

"We never talked about it." She couldn't meet his eyes any longer and looked down.

Clay let out a puff of air. The learning curve was too high. If Layla had been male heir apparent they'd have clued her in down to a gnat's behind. But she was a female stand-in facing a unique set of circumstances. They never bothered with details because no one believed this day would ever come. Hell, it was as far flung a possibility— her at the helm—as Helen leading the army at Troy. The cartel and Patrón had simply not been prepared for the totally unexpected.

Treason, betrayal, possible murder from within—all the elements of a Shakespearean tragedy lay right in their laps. Layla and her sidekick brother, the underdog who'd been passed over in favor of a younger sister, were dealing with the very basis of what a cartel boiled down to: pure power at the most dangerous level, the tipping point where only one victor walked away. How quickly had it unraveled? Probably long before Patrón landed in prison the second time.

But none of that was important. All that really mattered was they were here now, facing a turning point.

CHAPTER 39

The drive to Merida was uneventful and Clay followed signs for el centro and the main plaza where he assumed they'd find clothing shops. After exiting the main highway he spied a parking lot and pulled through a gated entry.

"We can walk back to the plaza," he told Layla as he handed the keys to the attendant. "We'll look for dress shops for your costumes."

Layla nodded absentmindedly, clearly preoccupied; she hadn't said much all morning.

"Do you want anything?" he asked as they navigated Merida's narrow sidewalks. "Say, there's a nice cafe with tables on the street. Let's grab some java." He steered her towards a table and called over a waiter. "Dos café negro," he said, taking a seat and watching their server walk inside the restaurant. "Layla, what is it?"

She hung her purse over the back of the chair and sat down. Finally she spoke. "I'm blowing it again."

"Now what?" he asked.

"Come on. I'm in over my head. You know it."

Layla had read his mind. "Well, things *are* happening fast," he said in a nonchalant manner. No need to make her edgier than she already was.

"I could hold Patrón's life in my hands, by what happens this weekend."

A shadow crossed Clay's face. "You're right, but hold on.

I thought you needed to do this, not only to prove a point, but to take back control. You said Guillermo and Zoyo have been double-dealing your uncle, the whole organization. You're the one that told me a cartel can't last long if those at the top are being duped."

"That's true," Layla said.

"What else can you do, Layla? Crawl in a hole? This is your life. You were born and bred for this."

"No, no. Not me," she said, looking down as she shook her head. She picked up a spoon and examined it, avoiding his eyes. "It was supposed to be Reynoldo. He could have handled it. If he was alive all this stuff with Zoyo and Guillermo would never have happened."

"Listen," Clay said. He reached across the table and took her hand in a firm grip. "Look at me. Reynoldo's dead. Did you get dealt a bad hand because you're a woman in Mexico? Maybe. But you're here and you're tough. I haven't seen you shirk or back down. You think well on your feet and you're a straight shooter, in both senses. You reacted with rage at Zoyo's double-dealing since your uncle isn't able to deal with it. Now it falls to you."

He paused another moment and willed her to look into his eyes, to gauge if he was getting through. "Your brother's proving to be a standup guy and he's sending reinforcements. Plus don't forget, they tried to kill us, so they're not innocent and they're not taking this lying down."

While he talked she adjusted her posture, sat a bit straighter. She began to see herself from an outsider's perspective, as though a window had opened onto her inner world. The slump disappeared from her shoulders.

When the waiter returned with two coffees, he placed them on the table and asked, "Todo bien?" Everything okay?

"Por supuesto." Of course, she said, answering the

question as though it held double meaning, as did so many statements in Mexico, land of the double entendre. She drained her cup in a couple of sips. Looking at Clay, she said with conviction, "A strong cup of coffee was just what I needed."

Clay smiled. The old Layla was back. "Did I see a dress shop around the corner?"

"I think you did. It will be fun to shop for my mariachi clothes—and your costume, too!"

Clay saw that she was going to fake it until she made it. From cartel accountant to mariachi singer to assassin, she was all in and ready for whatever was thrown at her next.

⊡ ⊡ ⊡

A few hours later Clay and Layla struggled with several bags of dresses, ruffles peeking out at the top in various shades of red and pink, along with two black velvet sombreros.

Layla looked at her watch. "It's time for a break. I could really use one."

A block off the main plaza they found a posada with a garden café and artsy outdoor bar.

"I gotta call the mariachi guy."

"Go ahead," Clay said. "I'll get us something to drink. Michelada?"

"Por favor." Layla loved the spicy beer, tomato, and lime juice drink mixed with ice and a dose of hot sauce.

Layla dialed the number. "Bueno. Señor Cortez? This is Lety Domingo. Como esta? My friend tells me I'll be working with you this Saturday, at a hacienda in Merida."

"Yes, yes, we're happy to have you," Cortez said. "You perform in Guadalajara?"

"For years, in my uncle's group. We gig every weekend. Singing is my passion," she said.

"Do you have any favorites songs?" Cortez asked.

"*Guadalajara*, of course. But I know them all—*Volver, Jalisco, Ella, Tres Años, Todo Una Vida*. Whatever you like. When can I meet the group for practice?"

"I'm glad Martín told you about rehearsal. It's tomorrow."

"He mentioned a hacienda?"

"Si. Hacienda Xcanatún. Twelve kilometers northeast just off the old Merida highway. Do you want to come around one? I'll introduce you to the others and we can rehearse the play list."

"Por supuesto. I hope you don't mind, but could I bring my manager with me?"

"That's fine, dear. I'll have gate security put you both on the list. What's his name?"

"Felipe Hernandez," Layla said.

"I'll tell security you'll both be there for rehearsal. Tell them you're with Los Mariachis de Yucatán. Ciao."

"Ciao." Layla put down her phone. Settled. Clay wandered back with two drinks.

"Hola, Felipe," Layla said. Her lips curved into a grin. "You are now Felipe Hernandez. And I'm Lety. We've got to get to work on your hair color. You'll be tall, dark, and handsome."

"It's all set?" he asked.

"We're both on the list for tomorrow's rehearsal. We have clearance at the gate."

"Perfect," Clay said. "The plot thickens."

CHAPTER 40

Muna, Yucatán, Mexico

Back at the Muna posada, Layla removed her dresses from the bags and spread them around the room. Green, pink, and red ruffles spilled everywhere, a cacophony of color and gauze.

"Maybe I should have been a singer, you know?" she said to Clay as he opened the small fridge for a couple of cervezas.

"Well, no offense, but maybe you should brush up on your tunes. Rehearsal is gonna come real fast, and your new pal's gonna wanna see what you can do," Clay said. He handed her a beer and walked to the French doors that led onto a small deck.

"Don't worry. We went to the Mariachi Festival in Guadalajara every year. I loved it as a kid and I memorized all the songs. I wasn't lying to Cortez. My voice isn't bad, either."

"That's good because he'll expect something from you," he called from the deck. He breathed in the warm night air and sat down in a deck chair.

"I'm going to call Martín, see when the guys from Culiacan will be here."

"Martín!" she said a moment later. "We have costumes and I'm lined up for rehearsal. Now what's happening with our guys?"

"José Calabra and Alfonso Sanchez are enroute to Merida. You'll meet them tomorrow. They'll be at the Inter-Continental just off Paseo Montejo. You know, that big old mansion they converted into a hotel? It's inconspicuous because it's large and always crowded. I got them a suite on the top floor. Check in and let them know what's happening. We'll still talk, but José will be your main contact."

"He's good?"

"Hermana, don't you remember? He used to work with Carlos, before you became Carlos's job. I wouldn't be sending him if he wasn't the best."

Carlos. The mention of his name stopped her cold. Attempting to sound normal, she cleared her throat and said, "I've been devising a plan, since we talked."

"No need to go into it with me. Explain it to the boys. They'll be fully loaded. You know what I mean. Whatever you want, you got it. Think things through, sleep on it, dream on it, and make sure they understand down to the last detail. They'll do whatever you ask. Oh, and they're bringing your new passport. Gotta run, talk later."

"Good, and thanks," Layla said, realizing the plan was in motion. "Ciao." She was in capable hands. Clay was right. Martín had proved himself. He was organized, thought two steps ahead, and was the perfect confidante.

She stood humming a serenade, and walked over to the couch where she'd draped layers of ruffled dresses. She picked one up, holding it against her slim figure as she gazed into a narrow mirror above the room's lone bureau. The delicate material that made up the brightly colored bodice felt soft to the touch while the ruffled petticoats were stiff and starched. She admired the fine threadwork and guessed the dress had been sewn by an accomplished seamstress who created one of a kind gowns to feed her family. How many days or weeks had been spent working on the finished product?

As she hummed, she realized she'd be rehearsing not only for her stage debut but also for the getaway. The next forty-eight hours were going to get real interesting.

🔁🔁🔁

Merida, Yucatán

The five-story Inter-Continental Hotel bustled with intensity and radiated old world charm. Layla glanced at Clay as they walked through the grand foyer.

"Nice place," he said.

They arrived at a bank of elevators located in the side hall next to a marble staircase. "I'll call José. Her contact picked up on the first ring. "José! What room?"

"Five oh nine." He answered in Spanish.

"Pronto," Layla said.

A few moments later they knocked at the door. It was opened by Josê. Behind him stood his fellow accomplice, Alfonso.

"Adelante," José said. He pulled the door wide open and stood aside.

"José, Alfonso." Layla grasped each man's hand for a moment. Their paths hadn't crossed in years. No need as Carlos had protected her well. She'd nearly forgotten about these guys. "This is Clay. No doubt Martín has told you about him. Clay, José and Alfonso."

"Mucho gusto," Clay said.

José, a stocky, dark-haired man in his late thirties with Aztec features did a short bow at the waist, then shot his cuffs. He was dressed in tan slacks and a light linen jacket. Alfonso, the taller of the two, also had dark hair. He was more low-key, in jeans and a navy blue Guayabera shirt. He stepped up to Clay and stuck out his hand for a handshake.

"We've got a lot to talk about," Layla said. "You know Carlos is dead."

José looked down. His face became a mask. "So sorry, Señorita Layla."

Alfonso nodded in unison. "Lo siento."

"Gracias," she said, trying to shake the grief that washed over her like a tsunami. As acting head of the cartel, there was no room for emotion now, especially in front of the crew.

They were watching her closely, alert for any sign of weakness. She stiffened first her spine then her resolve and gave each an icy stare. José looked away first and Alfonso followed suit. That ended the reunion.

"Let's have a seat, gentlemen," she said as she walked across the floor to a modern ultra suede sofa, sat down and stretched out her shapely legs while draping an arm on the back of the couch, just another lioness at the watering hole.

Clay sat off to the side, giving her room to conduct business.

"Martín no doubt told you we're having problems, on the inside. You're here, both of you, because you are Patrón's most trusted men. We have an issue with Guillermo, our Guatemala captain. I discovered a sex slave, a twelve-year old niña, in his villa when we were there for dinner six nights ago."

José and Alfonso exchanged glances, not missed by Layla.

"You knew about that? The trafficking?" she demanded in a dangerous tone. Her body language shifted into fighter

224

pose, her hands instantly perched on the edge of the couch. "No!" José said quickly, unprepared for her dramatic change of mood. "I am just shocked."

Layla assessed him—were his intentions pure?—and continued. "That's not all. He's running these young girls, a lot of them, through the cartel, and not documenting it. After my discovery, we were denied a landing in Cancun and our plane went down. We lost Carlos," she paused for effect, now thankfully composed, "and the co-pilot in the crash. And our friend, the pilot, was killed by Guillermo's death squad two days later."

She let them mull that over a moment. "Guillermo is not acting alone. Two of his men tried to kill us," she nodded in Clay's direction, "a couple days ago, on a side road north of here. It's war, plain and simple. Him or me. I'm taking him out at the fiesta Saturday night."

Both men nodded and José asked, "What can we do?"

"You, as Martín explained, will drive the getaway car. Clay and I will get into the hacienda with the mariachis. I've been hired as their singer for the fiesta. It's at Hacienda Xcanatún. We'll do a drive by later so you understand the layout. There may be a way to get you on the premises, but after I've killed Guillermo, getting off the premises will be tricky—I know there's at least one guard gate. That's where our planning comes in."

"How will you get to him?" Alfonso asked. It was the first time he'd opened his mouth since they'd sat down. He was a large man with expansive shoulders and a lot of bulk—a person no one would mess with. But his dark sorrowful eyes were large and expressive, seemingly unfit for the profession he'd chosen. He looked as if he could cry on cue.

"I'll be performing on stage with the mariachi group in full costume. The dress has enough material to hide my nine millimeter. They'll probably do thorough security checks for the partygoers, but so far, it sounds like the mariachi group isn't closely watched. I'll find that out at rehearsal."

Clay shifted in his seat.

"Clay," Layla said, looking his way, "do you have anything to add?"

"We'll have a diagram of the hacienda and the security gates and figure out where you can wait while Layla's performing, before the hit takes place."

"Do you know the time?" José asked.

"They'll tell me tomorrow at rehearsal. I think the fiesta starts at six outdoors, and from what Martín said, it will move indoors around nine, when dinner is served. We'll let the guests get toasted along with Guillermo and play it by ear. Clay will have a phone and call you when it's finished." She paused and added, "Only if there's time, of course."

"How will you get off stage?" José asked.

"I'll worry about that, but it's going to be fast. Once shots are fired, even with a silencer, the place will go into full lockdown. I'll know more after we see the hacienda."

"Does anyone know who you are?"

She gave a rare smile. "That's the only blessing. I'm anonymous here because it's so far from Sinaloa. And on stage I'll be wearing a sombrero that'll cover my face."

"Where will we take you?" This time Alfonso asked the question.

"Maybe near, maybe far. We're still making arrangements."

The less these two knew the better. She trusted them—she had to, what other option was there? Though Martín swore by them, as far as Layla was concerned, three could keep a secret only if two of them were dead. How many times had she heard Patrón utter those very words?

"So, I'll be in touch tomorrow after rehearsal. We'll drop

off my bag, a change of clothes, and little else. We've been traveling light since the crash."

She rose from the couch and Clay did the same.

"I think we've covered it. Well, hasta mañana," she said, walking towards the door.

"Oh, momentito!" José said, and hastily rose from his seat. "I almost forgot, your passport, from Martín."

He hurried over to an easy chair where a well-worn leather bag lay open, rummaged in a side pocket, and pulled out the gray document. He strode back to Layla and presented it with another short bow.

"Gracias," she said, deigning to bestow a magnetic smile on the minion who would forever serve her.

José stepped back, his work at present finished. He moved quickly towards the threshold, undid the deadbolt, and swung the door open.

"'Dios, Señorita Layla," he said. He gave another stiff little bow.

By this time Alfonso was on the move, not to be outdone by his partner. He stood at attention as their jefe made her exit.

"Ciao," Layla said, looking back at the two men as Clay headed for the elevator. She lifted her chin in a quick upward movement, a habit she'd picked up from Patrón, and then she was gone.

CHAPTER 41

Hacienda Xcanatún, Yucatán

Guillermo's nerves had been raw since his arrival in Merida. It started before that when he heard about the plane crash, not knowing if Patrón's niece was dead or alive, then finding and interrogating the American pilot and killing him.

The fucker—after breaking his nose, he deserved to die!

Not only did it still hurt like hell, it looked like hell. A private doctor from Merida tended to him as he convalesced at his friend's luxurious hacienda, but even the prescribed Oxycodone couldn't touch the pain. Chinga! He was three days into it and couldn't shake the throbbing. He doubled up on painkillers hoping to get some relief. In vain. Besides that, his face looked like a tequila sunrise, resplendent in various shades of reds and purples, not to mention two black eyes.

So instead of enjoying himself at Xcanatún over Semana Santa like every other year—riding horses, wine tasting with his friend, taking the occasional stroll around the hacienda grounds—he holed up alone in his room, nursing an excruciatingly sore face.

Granted, it was lavishly furnished, but how could he enjoy himself? He ached all over and his nose now listed to the left. He could be a stand in for a zombie out of *Tales from the Crypt*.

There'd been a brief moment of joy when he discovered he had Layla's GPS coordinates, but she and the Canadian had outfoxed the hit men he sent to kill them. Never send a boy to do a man's job. Chinga! He should have done the deed himself.

Those fuckers couldn't even finish the task. And they ruined the car—the entire front end crushed in when they went over a berm. Well, they were history. Why had they bothered to call after failing to deliver? It was well known that he took no prisoners, and had zero tolerance for incompetence.

Most troublesome of all was the big unknown: Had Layla told anyone about the trafficking? Did Patrón know? And what about Zoyo? Christ, he hoped that son of a bitch hadn't heard the news. He'd do more than break his nose.

So here he sat in a deluxe room in a Yucatán hacienda, practically bedridden during Semana Santa. Thank goodness the fiesta was a masquerade ball, and it was still a day and a half away. He could hide his hideous face behind a mask and no one would have the slightest idea that he looked like death warmed over.

Two o'clock. Time for another round of painkillers. Maybe he'd chase them with a little wine, to take the edge off.

Layla and Clay drove up to the entrance of Hacienda Xcanatún, the lone security gate permitting entry onto the hacienda's extensive grounds. Since Emilio Vargas, the owner, was a rancher and in no way connected to the narco mafia, the paranoia level so common to Layla and her crew was significantly lower. And they were in the Yucatán, not

Sinaloa, home to cartels and drug lords. El Yucatán, a breath of fresh air. Still in throwback mode.

"Buenas tardes," Clay said when they cruised to a stop at an elaborate hand-carved gate with wrought-iron flowers woven top and bottom. A uniformed gate attendant smiled and asked their names and business.

"Felipe Hernandez y Lety Domingo. Los Mariachis de Yucatán," he said, in his best Spanish accent.

"Claro," the young man said as he checked the list and located their names. He stepped back from the car to jot down the license plate and went on to explain they must take the first turn to the left which would put them by the stables. After parking, a stone path would lead to the back entrance of the hacienda and a doorman would specify where the rehearsal would take place. He waved them through.

"Not even a second glance," Layla said.

"Yeah, guess the hair dye worked," he said. "And my stash grew out pretty well."

"I like your dark mustache—such an *exotic* look," Layla said. She gave Clay a reassuring pat on the arm. "Tranquilo, Felipe."

They drove down a manicured drive, bordered by stately Queen palms on either side. Production facilities for the still-working henequen plant could be seen in the distance, where puffy clouds rose from impressive smoke stacks.

Alongside the stables, they pulled into a wide parking area where a number of older cars and trucks were parked. These vehicles belonged to workers who pampered the gentleman rancher's extensive list of friends and relatives, those lucky enough to regularly frequent his comfortable hacienda. By the looks of it, the Semana Santa fiesta required an enormous crew to prepare for the splendid highlight of the week-long Easter vacation.

"Pop the trunk, Clay." Layla got out of the car. "Whew, hot today."

"Yeah, I'm still not used to the Yucatán sun." He walked around to the trunk. "I'll carry the clothes. You handle the hats and shoes, okay?"

Layla nodded. "Plus my make-up." She grabbed a small valise she'd bought in Merida now filled with makeup and hairpieces. Clay handed her a bag with the sombreros and shoes. As they prepared to head up the stone path, another young man in uniform approached.

"Por favor, señor," he said with a shy smile. "Allow me to assist."

"Gracias." Clay handed him the costumes and grabbed the sombreros and shoes from Layla.

They marched up the path to the rear of the sprawling hacienda. At the back entrance, as promised, stood a doorman. He, too, had a clipboard.

"Lety Domingo y Felipe Hernandez, Los Mariachis de Yucatán," Lety said in a soft voice, flipping her long hair over one shoulder, turning on the charm.

Clay watched the effect on the young man and had to smile. This woman had no trouble opening doors wherever she went. The attendant appeared a bit flustered as he looked over the multi-page list, going back and forth a few times before he finally found their names.

"Of course. Señor Alfredo said you should meet him in the ballroom."

As if on cue, a maid arrived. "Señorita, por favor," she said, indicating she'd lead the way.

Layla alias Lety handed the valise to the maid, and drew herself up to full position, that of the prima donna mariachi singer she now portrayed. The maid motioned to the man with the costumes to follow them and walked through the small back entrance and into a dark hallway. Clay trailed discreetly behind the entourage, trying to blend in, if a guy well over six feet could.

They zig-zagged through the sprawling hacienda. "A GPS would be handy," Lalya said in a whisper.

Clay frowned. He was having trouble committing the route to memory. After passing through countless rooms and yet another hallway they arrived at the grand ballroom, entering as guests would, through one of two sets of double doors. The maid waved them towards the stage, handed the valise to Layla, and left.

The opulent room radiated warmth, uncommon for such an enormous space. Maybe it was the deep mustard color of the walls, so typical in Mexican interiors, with gold leaf trim on high cornices. From the vaulted ceiling hung ornate cut-glass chandeliers; the one hanging dead center was the largest Layla had ever seen. At the opposite end of the oblong hall the band members stood on stage talking.

Layla's leather heels clicked as she glided along the parquet floor, her presence emanating an undeniable glow. As if by radar, the men's faces turned in unison to watch la Mexicana saunter across the room, swinging her valise as she made her way towards them. One man in particular, obviously Alfredo Cortez, perched a hand atop his brow to zoom in on her, the other on his hip.

"Buenas tardes!" Layla sang out in a perky sing-song, well aware all eyes were on her. She was glad she'd bought a new outfit in Merida when she picked out her costumes.

"Señorita Lety?" Alfredo asked. Though no stranger to mariachi performers he'd never seen one so striking.

"Claro!"

"Bueno! Que *bueno!*" he said, nearly fainting in gratitude.

Clay and Layla walked five steps up to the stage, and Clay immediately fell back to an invisible position, distancing himself not only from center stage but from the woman he just walked in with. They didn't want to see him anyway, and the less conspicuous he was, the better. All eyes were on Señorita Lety.

Alfredo rushed to greet her, grasping her hand in an obsequious manner. Now that her entrance was made and her place in their hearts was secure, she played the role of demure ingenue.

She touched Alfredo with her right hand, placing it over his, and gave a little squeeze. "Señor Cortez," she said, in a low purr. "How wonderful to meet you. I am so happy to be here." She turned, showing her best profile to the seven men that made up the band. "Caballeros! How kind of you to allow me to sing with you."

She gave a curtsy, and ended it by placing her hands together in a *namaste* pose that would have looked ridiculous if anyone else had attempted it. Layla knew how to play to, and manipulate, a crowd. She possessed a trait few were born with and countless others aspired to: charisma. This was a side of Layla that Clay had not yet seen. He was impressed. She should have gone into show business. Longer shelf life. She might have had to dodge a ripe tomato now and again, but never a bullet.

Her throaty laughter echoed softly through the vast room as she mixed and mingled her way through an array of greetings and salutations. While working the crowd of bandmates, she paused momentarily as if she'd just remembered something in the far recesses of her mind. She extended her hand back towards Clay in a fetching wave-like motion. Once she had everyone's attention, she made an announcement like a ringleader at a circus, "My manager, Felipe Hernandez," she said in Spanish.

He gave a slight wave and faded back into oblivion, right where they wanted him. Alfredo Cortez smiled at the beauty who'd joined their ranks and asked the men if they would take their places so rehearsal could begin.

With the band occupied it was the perfect time for Clay to do some snooping. First and foremost, he had to determine the best path for a quick exit. While the group tuned up, Clay looked around the area beside the stage. The maid who accompanied them had long ago disappeared, along with the guy carrying their wardrobe and shoes.

Clay located both exit doors. One side appeared dark, and from the other, light peeked in. Natural instinct drew him towards it. He assumed this would be where he and Layla would make their exit in a mere forty-eight hours. He glanced at the costumes and decided that finding a dressing room would be a prudent ploy. He grabbed the clothes and Layla's running shoes and gave a nod to Alfredo who clearly understood his mission when he saw what Clay carried.

From behind center stage Clay heard the trumpet give several sharp blasts and the marimbas resonate; then he heard a voice. Holy Mackerel! Was it Layla? The girl could actually sing!

She may have been on a steep learning curve for cartel business, but her natural talent and ability to charm those around her she had firmly under control.

Costumes in hand, he made a show of searching for the dressing rooms while venturing into the cavernous back stage area. He hoped to discover how to wind his way back to the rear entrance of the hacienda through the labyrinthine hallways. Perhaps he could find another exit in the process, which would serve them very well indeed.

CHAPTER 42

While Layla rehearsed with her new group, Clay located a dressing room, hung costumes, and found a closet for her "getaway" running shoes.

Layla planned to hide the nine millimeter Beretta in one of the sturdy stitched inside pockets she'd sewn into her long, ruffled skirt. In the other pocket would be a silencer. Putting the two together would happen when she did a wardrobe and shoe change, right after the first set. She'd also carry a folded fan, and would practice with everything that evening after rehearsal. Clay prayed the crowd wouldn't focus too much on the entertainment after pre-dinner cocktails and dinner in the grand ballroom. With wine and spirits freely flowing along with what would surely be exquisite food, he hoped the band would be a mere sidebar to a gala fiesta.

From the dressing room, a dark hallway extended along a corridor. Muffled metallic sounds reverberated in the distance. The closer Clay got to the noise, the more distinct became the rattle of pots and pans—definitely the kitchen. A large staff was already on the premises to prepare the feast that would soon feed hundreds of guests. With a restaurant-sized kitchen, he assumed there would be an outside entrance for delivery trucks to drop off wares and produce.

Clay stroked his dyed mustache and patted his darkened hair, hoping it didn't look too phony. But kitchen workers wouldn't be interested in somebody wandering around like a lost puppy in the hacienda's back rooms or hallways. They'd all be working full tilt, preparing for the big banquet. If this hacienda's preparation for the fiesta had anything in common with other Mexican events it would be far behind on what should have already been accomplished. He'd yet to see the day when anything in this country ended up being early—or on time, for that matter. Workers would be too concerned about keeping their cushy inside jobs rather than worrying about some fool bumbling around in the kitchen.

He walked down the corridor, LED lights beaming the way, pulled a pen and paper from his pocket and began to draw a diagram of where he'd been. He leaned against the wall under a light and started with the stage, the dressing room, the turn he'd just taken, and finally, the hallway. He sketched the long corridor where the kitchen was located. José and Alfonso probably wouldn't need the drawing, but he planned to make them a copy just in case.

He had just stuffed the diagram in his pocket when the swinging kitchen doors flew open and a man in a white server coat bolted out pushing a room service cart. It was draped in a spotless white tablecloth, and on it a silver tray held a full ice bucket along with a bottle of red wine.

A second later the door swung open again and another guy rushed out, asking the first, "Are you taking that? Don Guillermo's been asking where it is."

Guillermo! The name exploded in Clay's brain. What the hell? But of course the fucker was already here. It was his friend's hacienda and this was fiesta week.

"Who puts ice in red wine?" the first guy asked with a snicker, ignoring Clay.

"It's not to drink, estupido. It's for his face. Have you seen it? He looks like a tequila sunrise!"

They both laughed.

"How 'bout those black eyes!"

"Wonder how he got 'em," the other said. "Beat up by a little señorita?"

They both cracked up. "Little for sure," the first guy said knowingly.

The laughter stopped.

"Better hurry," the other guy said, "He says he needs the ice right now."

"Tell him to put a cork in it," the first one said. "I'm double-timing here. He's right near the stables. I won't be long."

He shoved off at a full run, the cart creaking noisily as it careened recklessly from side to side.

Clay exchanged a complicit smile with the second guy, who ducked back into the kitchen. Clay discreetly followed the room service attendant to see where Guillermo had been keeping himself these past few days.

Who or what could the Guatemalan strongman have had a run in with? A cupboard, a door, a person? It sounded like he was in hiding, using ice to tone down an injury. Clay tried to keep up with the room service attendant and also take notes on where the guy was going. He prayed he could remember how to get there, this was too choice. If they knew what room Guillermo was in, maybe Layla wouldn't have to take the chance of shooting him while on stage and making a run for it from a very public venue.

Ahead, he saw the attendant round a gentle curve and stop abruptly in front of a door. Just before the curve was an exit door on the right. Not wanting the room service attendant to see him, Clay slowed down and waited until he knocked. The door swung open but Clay couldn't make out who answered. After the waiter entered, Clay rushed to the exit to check if it was locked and if not, to see what it opened onto.

In luck! No lock on the inside. He pushed the door open and looked at a terraced garden, not far from the stables. The stables were on the other side of the parking lot and very close to where they'd entered the grounds a short while earlier—a perfect position for their getaway.

But he didn't want to ditch the car by leaving it on the premises. Even though the rental was in his name, not Layla's, why leave a paper trail? Best to take a taxi to the hacienda and drop the rental off in Merida before the fiesta. Once they got to the parking area, they'd have to hoof it to where José and Alfonso would be waiting, in a spot that was still to be determined.

Clay realized he'd been mired in thought too long. Best if room service didn't see him lurking around. In spite of his black hair and mustache, a guy his size was noticeable in Mexico.

He hurried back down the corridor, hoping he could duck somewhere should the attendant come out of Guillermo's room.

Guillermo's room. What an amazing revelation. He couldn't wait to tell Layla.

If they could take out the fucker in his suite, it would place them closer to the getaway car. If Layla shot Guillermo in the grand ballroom, silencer or not, the hacienda's security gates would slam shut. Clay knew their safe getaway would be a toss-up. It would all come down to one big throw of the dice. Seven come eleven—give me some sugar, baby.

CHAPTER 43

I t had been nearly an hour since the rehearsal began. Clay had finally checked out the kitchen, finding another exit door much closer to the stage. When Layla's practice was over, they'd do a slow walk-about and he'd share what he knew, assuming her band mates didn't want to tag along and chat.

Clay was fixated on a kitchen escape. Once outside, they would need to race to the road to catch the getaway car. Layla planned to wear a camisole and leggings under her ruffled gown, ditching the break-away skirt for easy movement.

After the outdoor portion of the fiesta she'd change from heels into running shoes before going on stage. With a long skirt no one would notice, and in one of the skirt's deep pockets she'd carry a short-haired curly wig.

Another major issue to ponder was what action to take once they were out of the hacienda and on the other side of security. Within fifteen minutes the road would be crawling with, well, everyone, especially if one of the dinner guests, a friend of Vargas's, had been murdered.

But the biggest problem came down to the logistics of the first few minutes right after the hit. Layla would be center stage doing the deed and afterwards, every single second would count.

"How was practice?" Clay asked, back at the stage. The performers had begun putting away their instruments as they prepared to leave.

"Oh, fine," Layla said, smiling as she turned and gave a little wave to the trumpet player. "Nice guys, and really good, too."

Alfredo Cortez came up to her. "Lety, that was incredible. You did a good job with the songs. Thank you."

"A pleasure, Alfredo," she said, giving him her full attention.

Cortez looked away, a little embarrassed, and said, "Saturday back stage at six?"

"Por supuesto. Do we come in like we did today?"

"Either that or you can come in the back way, through the kitchen."

"Oh, I know where that is," Clay said, interrupting. "We can go out that way?"

"Yes," Cortez said. "Me and the boys usually go through the main entrance after rehearsal, but if you're familiar with it, go ahead and leave that way, and come in that way for the fiesta."

"I put the costumes in the dressing room so Layla'll be ready for Saturday," Clay said.

"Excellent. Well then, hasta luego."

"Thanks again, Alfredo. Ciao."

Layla grabbed her make-up valise and started walking back stage with Clay. "Any luck?"

"Guillermo's here," Clay said in a whisper. "I know where his room is."

Layla stopped short. "Where? Show me."

"Not now. Too dangerous. I just thought it through. You know he has bodyguards. We have to do this by the book, like we've been planning."

Clay ran through his discovery list and went over the possibilities of a surprise visit to Guillermo's room, versus killing him at the ball.

"Chinga! If I had the gun now, I could just ice him. He'd never expect it!" Layla said.

"But you don't. You do it at the end of the first set, assuming he's within range, as planned. You face the left rear exit. The band is set up more to the center and stage right. You pull out the gun and you do it."

Layla sulked a moment, but recovered quickly, after realizing her prey was in sight. "If we're lucky he won't be at a crowded table."

"It's all gonna come down to luck. Then we exit, this way. Follow me." He led her down the corridor to the kitchen.

He entered the bustling kitchen for the second time in a matter of thirty minutes. Earlier he'd played the go-fer with an errand to run, filling a glass with ice water for his client. Now he pretended to show her how to exit the hacienda.

They smiled at the workers as they ambled past walk-in freezers, rows of pots on commercial stoves, pans of simmering sauces. Layla tried to take in every imaginable scenario as her nose appreciated the tantalizing aromas coming from all directions.

"See that exit over there?" Clay asked, moving his head ever so slightly towards the door. "I'm going to move real quick, then pretend I made a mistake."

She nodded and followed along behind. He pushed open the door, and from there they spied the parking lot.

"No, no!" said a man in white, a sous chef, shaking his head as he hurried towards them. "Use the other exit."

"Oh, sorry," Layla said, looking appropriately flustered. "Isn't it a shortcut to my car?"

"Si, the parking lot is there, but you know, security ..." he said, as he looked at her. "You are with the mariachi group?"

"Yes, Saturday I sing!" she said, and let out a melodic laugh.

He smiled, nodded, and went back to work.

"Wow," Layla said as they traversed the wide room, bustling with food workers. "It's close."

"Yes, but we can't use the car. Security will be in lock down. Once we're in the lot, we'll dart out the back way to the road. I figure it's a quarter kilometer."

Layla nodded, glad she kept up her normal exercise routine, no matter where she was. "Let's nose around back there when we get the car, before we leave the grounds today."

"Yep. We'll find the best pick-up spot for the boys. I'll have them park as close to the front of the line as possible," Clay said.

"Did you actually see Guillermo?" she asked.

"No, but it sounds like his face is bashed in pretty good. Room service was taking ice along with a bottle of wine. The ice was for his face!"

"How do you know?"

"I overheard room service talking. They said lots of bruising."

"What happened?" Layla asked.

"No idea. But apparently he's not up to par. Maybe we'll luck out."

"We have to," she said. A little frown furrowed her brow. She couldn't stop going over everything in her head. "What about Zoyo?"

"What about him, Layla?"

"Will he be here?"

"Christ," Clay said in a whisper as they walked the back corridors. "How would I know?"

"Well, why not two for the price of one?"

"Layla! We've discussed this. First of all, we don't know if he's even here. We'll get Guillermo, and you'll deal with Zoyo later. Listen, for one minute remain in the moment. Please. Be here now."

When he started spouting Buddhist philosophy she knew he was concerned. Clay didn't want to complicate things more than they already were. And this was shaping up to be a complicated plan. Muy complicado.

CHAPTER 44

Back at the Muna posada, Layla flopped down on a chair, mired in thought. The hour-long drive had been unusually quiet as both she and Clay considered their plan, how to implement it, and—most important of all—how to survive it.

The Hacienda Xcanatún road was twelve kilometers from the main highway and the property itself was fifty minutes from Merida. Once Vargas called police, it would take them at least thirty minutes to arrive at the hacienda turnoff. With luck, by that time José, Alfonso, and the getaway duo would be passing federale sirens on the six-lane super highway, heading the other way.

"Clay, we have to assume Guillermo has bodyguards. Martín said he travels with an entourage."

"They'll be our real threat. Not the police or federales."

"But would Vargas allow a swarm of guards on his property? Maybe one or two, but no more. It's Semana Santa after all—Pascua, the holiest day in the Mexican year," Layla said.

"Does Vargas know Guillermo's connected?"

"Good question. We know he has vineyards and cattle. I assume Vargas thinks he's another gentleman rancher, like himself."

"Regardless, there will be bodyguards," Clay said. "He knows we're close. He sent those goons for us."

"Maybe he thinks we split. And how in the hell did he get

his ugly face beat in?" Layla switched gears. "Clay, are you confident the boys can get us to the main highway before the police arrive?"

"As long as we hotfoot it outta there. I'll take them on a drive-by tomorrow. We'll leave Muna, get a room at the Inter-Continental. You practice with the silencer and gun in your pockets, in your skirt," he said, pointing to a duplicate of the dress she'd wear at the fiesta.

He was pacing slowly back and forth in front of her. "I can't stop thinking about the bodyguards."

"What? Chasing us?" Layla asked.

"Yeah. I'm hoping they won't be allowed in the ballroom."

"He probably leaves most of his thugs in his suite, so as not to mess with the ambiance at his friend's fancy hacienda."

"But he may have talked Vargas into allowing one or two to join him. We've got to be ready for that. That'll be our main worry. Beating them to the getaway car and giving them the slip," Clay said. "It could be difficult."

Layla was fit, as was he. But bodyguards? He remembered Carlos's taut body and the way the man measured his movements. Being a professional bodyguard was an art. Their bodies were finely tuned instruments, as were their minds. There was method in their unwavering natures.

"Seems odd one wasn't hanging around his room. Maybe they're not allowed on the property?"

"No, that's wishful thinking. Possibly they were in the room with him. We have to assume he's guarded and they'll have guns and plenty of ammo—something we have very little of. What have we got? Surprise and a burning desire to see that asshole dead," Clay said.

Layla nodded. She'd sleep better once Guillermo was six feet under. Killing the scum would bring not only closure, but avenge the deaths of Carlos and Lupita, Donavon, and Jake, and signal that the Culiacan Cartel was alpha dog and took no prisoners. "It's Culiacan rules now."

"Culiacan rules? What?" Clay asked, holding his palms up in a quizzical manner.

"You never heard about them? The rules..." she let the word roll off her tongue, "... include collecting debts from someone who owes you. Guillermo owes me. Big time. He tried to kill me. He killed my friends, and he killed Lupita. He stole from my uncle. He must pay."

Clay mulled that over. "No second chances..."

"Never. It's what we talked about in Cancun. Those that wrong you have to get their due. *Everyone* in Culiacan knows the rules." She stared at him until he looked away.

"So where should the guys park? There were already a lot of cars on the side of the road when we left today. One more car on the roadside won't shake anyone up."

Layla allowed the previous subject to fade away. "I agree. Tomorrow you'll show them where?"

"Yup. You got that right," Clay said, "It's my job."

🔲🔲🔲

Clay and Layla left the Muna posada at noon and an hour later they pulled into the underground garage at the Inter-Continental. They parked and went up the basement elevator to the top floor where José had booked them a suite not far from his and Alfonso's. They knocked and a few moments later Alfonso ushered them in.

"Buenas tardes, gentlemen. We need our room key." Layla plunked down on the couch. Clay remained standing. Alfonso hastened to locate the key on the secretary desk in the corner and handed it to his jefe.

"Gracias, Alfonso," Layla said. "Now, our plan. Tomorrow morning Clay will take you out to the hacienda so you'll know where to wait for us. We have an overall picture of the backstage area and how to make a quick exit, through the kitchen."

"I want you to see this," Clay said, motioning to the men. He pulled the sketch from his pocket. "This is both the interior of the hacienda and the grounds."

He walked over to the dining table with the map of the stage and corridors he and Layla had walked just a day earlier. Both José and Alfonso followed and watched intently as Clay pressed the sketch out onto the mahogany table and walked them through the drawing, from the ballroom to the corridors, and out the kitchen exit.

"From there, we drop onto the parking lot and it's gonna be a race to meet up with you guys up here." He pointed to the road that ran parallel to Vargas's property. "We'll run it."

José looked at Clay, then at Layla.

Layla glared at him. "What? You think I can't run to the road? I saw that look!"

"No, Senorita Layla," José said, flustered. "Of course I know you can run that far."

"I'll keep up. Don't worry about me!" she said, tossing her hair back. Layla was clearly tired of the macho bullshit and wanted no one questioning her abilities. Especially a getaway guy.

Clay knew her heightened agitation was simply pre-game jitters. This was a risky undertaking where failure would reflect on Layla's ability to run the cartel, while her success would merely reinforce that Culiacan Cartel was still top dog, no matter who ran the show.

"Then where?" Alfonso asked. He was busy looking over Clay's map, undisturbed by the turbulence swirling around him. The man maintained the calm of a Buddha. In fact, he looked like the Buddha—big, rounded body, moon face, calm demeanor.

"We hightail it to the road, and once we get on the highway, we'll give you directions which way to go. But we gotta get to the Merida highway."

"Tell them about Guillermo," Layla chimed in from her spot on the couch. She had kicked off her shoes and tucked her long legs underneath her. She looked more like a tired teenager than a Mexicana narca, her flash of anger now behind her.

"Oh yeah," Clay said. "Guillermo's already there. I know where his room is."

"Where?" José asked. The new bodyguard adjusted his cuffs and stood a little straighter, waiting for an answer. Even low-key Alfonso perked up.

Pointing back to the map, Clay said, "His room is right here. He's not in great shape apparently. Something about getting his face punched in."

José asked, "Que paso?"

"Not sure, but he was using ice for the bruises and black eyes."

José and Alfonso exchanged looks, trying not to smirk. Bosses never got involved in anything physical. Bodyguards shielded their jefes with their lives and if by some outside chance a bruise or injury occurred, it would be to them, not to those they protected.

"Someone got the better of him. The fucker," Layla said from her position on the couch.

"That's only the beginning of his troubles." Clay shot a conspiratorial smile at José and sat down at the table. "Got a pen?"

José pulled a pen from his jacket. "Here, Señor Clay."

"Call me Clay," the Canadian said as he reached for the hotel stationery. "Gonna draw you a copy of this map." He set about copying the diagram of the hacienda and grounds. "I don't think you'll need it, but you never know. And I want to warn you: We know he'll have bodyguards. Probably two. They'll be our main problem." He paused and looked directly at both of them. They well understood his meaning.

"If you can get us to the highway, we'll be—hopefully—passing the Merida Police, going the other way. The hacienda's fifty minutes from Merida, thirty minutes to the cutoff and roughly another twenty to the property. You'll see tomorrow."

"Do you have any cerveza?" Layla leaned back on the couch.

"Si, Señorita Layla," Alfonso said. He jumped to do her bidding. "Es bueno, Corona?"

"Seguro!" Layla called back. "Mi favorita!"

"One for me, too?" Clay asked.

"Por supuesto!" Alfonso said. He grabbed two cold ones from the mini-fridge and opened them.

Clay was beginning to like the bodyguards, who were more like getaway guys. They knew their place in the cartel hierarchy and obviously respected Layla in spite of her high-handed behavior. They'd probably known her since Carlos began guarding her. The Culiacan Cartel had a very family-oriented vibe for a business bent on hell and destruction. Tomorrow would be the day they proved themselves to their new boss.

And Clay and Layla would prove something too: No one fucked with them and theirs. Their tiny band of four was ready to wreak havoc on a double-dealing tyrant who'd killed their people, murdered young girls, and diced their load.

Anything short of total revenge indicated cowardice, which ultimately led to failure. And failure was not a word that would ever be uttered. That, too, was a Culiacan rule.

CHAPTER 45

Layla woke in her bedroom at the Inter-Continental with sunlight streaming in through the window. It couldn't be that late. She listened for noise outside her bedroom door but heard nothing. She checked her watch, nine. She'd slept in. Probably just as well. Today was going to be a biggie, and tonight—tonight could go on forever.

She did a luxurious body stretch, like a cat, before slipping out of bed to find her t-shirt that served as a nightgown. She put it on and walked to the door.

"Clay?" No reply.

He said he'd be gone early with the men, and apparently was as good as his word. She walked into the suite's living room, admiring the Maya décor. On a granite counter in the kitchen she spotted a pot of coffee. She walked over to find a cup, and next to it Clay's note: *Back about noon.*

Good. They were preparing for the night's activity. She had total confidence in Clay as well as José and Alfonso. Getting Guillermo had become a shared mission of vengeance.

To José and Alfonso, Carlos was one of their own. They'd come up together in the ranks back in the early days. Carlos's path had taken a different direction when he became the protector of young Layla. No doubt, they now figured they were responsible for her.

Of course she hadn't disclosed her misgivings about Zoyo to the two getaway men. It was not their place to know

251

what went down in the upper circles. That was something she'd hold close to her chest until she met with Patrón, after the present task was over and done with.

She poured herself a steaming cup, taking in the pleasant aroma of Mexican coffee. She needed caffeine. And after a shower, while the guys were gone, she'd practice again with the Beretta and the silencer, pulling it quickly from the pocket of her skirt. She decided when she changed gowns, she would put the gun with silencer already attached into her pocket. Easier than fiddling with it on stage.

Even though she'd rehearsed numerous times last night—over and over again—she knew practice could well determine success or failure. It was time to call Martín, find out where to head after their mission ended. She'd also let him know José and Alfonso were good people. Amazing that, in one week's time, old wounds from a decade ago had been erased; she and her brother were cooperating for a common cause.

Layla began to search for her phone. She wanted to hear her brother's voice.

🔁🔁🔁

Martín had resented Layla ever since Patrón chose her over him years ago. How long was it—ten years? Twelve?

It wasn't his fault that Patrón hadn't chosen him. He simply wasn't Reynoldo. Where Reynoldo was outspoken, Martín was pensive, silent. Reynoldo showed no fear while Martín played it safe. Martín was Meyer Lansky to Reynoldo's Al Capone.

After Zoyo's son Beto was nailed by the US feds, Reynoldo hit his stride. Then came the ambush. Reynoldo died, Patrón went to prison, Zoyo took over.

Martín didn't mind playing second fiddle to his older brother. The guy was a whiz at everything he did. His death came as a blow to them all, especially Patrón, who'd been grooming him as his successor. The jefe went into a deep funk while in prison and would barely speak. He accepted few callers, the exception being Layla, as he fell into a state of self-imposed exile.

While Layla made frequent trips to the prison at Alicante Grande, Martín found himself stuck in inventory supply, a polite term for warehousing, and a very safe place. By the time Martín was involved, Culiacan was top dog. No one would dare short them on a load or withhold profits.

With his brother gone, the game plan changed. There was a void—an actual hole—in the family where Reynoldo had been. Though Patrón leaned heavily on Zoyo, he came to resent his partner's son, Little Beto, who by all accounts was a savvier version of the nephew he'd lost. As long as Patrón and Zoyo were alive, pecking order wasn't questioned. But El Patrón knew his family's destiny relied on who fell next in line should he be taken out.

Patrón had laid the groundwork for the cartel and wanted his bloodline at the top, Reynoldo or no Reynoldo. If he wasn't careful, Zoyo's clan could one day rule a dynasty he'd built from the bottom up.

Patrón began to rely on Layla, carefully grooming her as his backup and successor. Martín watched from the sidelines while she played cartel ingénue and basked in the glow of their uncle's praise.

So now, Martín was in Sinaloa, and Layla was there, in Merida, waiting to avenge their uncle. In one short week, they had rebuilt not only a friendship and a family but a dynasty—their dynasty.

Martín doubted Zoyo would be at Hacienda Xcanatún,

and was cautiously hopeful that Layla and the Canadian could dice Guillermo. He knew the Guatemalan traveled with plenty of force, but he'd learned Hacienda Xcanatún would never allow so much muscle on the property. He doubted Vargas knew his Guatemalan friend was a card-carrying cartel capo; he wouldn't even think about bodyguards. There was the kidnapping issue, of course—everyone worried about that in Mexico these days—but not so much in Yucatán, the land that time forgot.

Martín's phone rang. "Bueno," he said, before checking the number.

"Hola Martín!" Layla spoke passionately into the phone.

"Hermana." His voice softened. "I've been thinking of you. Que paso?"

"All good. Tonight's the night. José and Alfonso have gone with Clay for a drive-by of the hacienda. When I was at rehearsal the other day Clay found the closest exits. We're set."

"You seem sure," he said, relaxing.

"I feel ready. I have my Beretta, the silencer, and big pockets in my mariachi gown."

"Any sightings of Guillermo?" he asked.

"Clay didn't see him but he knows which room is his. If I had a gun yesterday I could've done it."

Martín sighed. "Que lastima." Pity. The disappointment in his tone was obvious.

Layla sighed in unison. "I know. But the good news is that he's not feeling well. Someone beat his face in. Clay overheard room service talking. They were taking him ice for his bruises and black eyes."

"Well, you're gonna luck out, hermana. Oye, I've got you reservations on a flight from Cancun to CDMX. Tonight, for two. One a.m."

"Mexico City?"

"Si, the anonymous city. Better than here in Sinaloa. They'll come for you, Zoyo's boys, once Guillermo goes down, because they will know that you know."

"Unless Zoyo shows up here, and I ice him, too."

Martín laughed. "My pretty, hopeful sister." Her Pollyanna attitude had never changed; he and Reynoldo had always kidded her about it. "*Who* Layla, in this business, thinks positive?"

"Loco, I know. But we don't know till it happens, right?"

Martín had given the Zoyo issue some thought. "But really, listen." He cleared his throat. "We don't know if Zoyo's involved with trafficking. It's Guillermo's word against Zoyo's."

"Why would he lie?" Layla asked.

He could hear in her voice that she was ready for blood—Zoyo's along with Guillermo's.

"Once Guillermo is dead, Zoyo can say what he wants, hermana. We can't take out a sitting cartel head on hearsay. And our own guy! We have to clear this with Patrón."

Her brooding anger simmered on the other end of the line.

"Damnit, Martín! A dead dog can't give you rabies—I'll be in danger till Zoyo's finished!"

"I know, I know. That worries me, of course, but we can't make a life and death decision on Patrón's oldest partner without his say-so. Trust me, it has to wait—for now."

"I hope it's not too late by that time." She spat it out, trying to guilt-trip him.

"It will work out, believe me. And the truth will all come out, too, if he's truly involved. Now, tell me your plans."

There was a pause, then Layla let out a noisy huff of air. "Hmmph. The outdoor fiesta starts at six. We're taking a cab. The guys have their instructions where to wait for us on the road."

"How far from the hacienda?"

"A quarter kilometer. We have to avoid his bodyguards—he's sure to have at least two."

"I've heard he has two. What about the rental car?"

"Clay's getting rid of it today."

"Good. Now once you're in Mexico City, go to Hotel Excelencia. The room is booked in Lety's name. Lay low for a while. I'll see Patrón, tell him what happened."

No reply from his sister except a sigh.

"How are you doing? You okay?"

"It's coming fast now, Martín. Tonight I will be on a flight, away from here."

"Good riddance to el Yucatán, hermana. It hasn't done you any favors..." his voice drifted off as he spoke. He was thinking of Carlos and knew she was, too. "Listen, what do you think of José and Alfonso? Could you work with them?"

"They're very respectful, kind of old school. It's nice. I like them."

"We'll shift them over to you after tonight, okay?"

"Right, Martín." She sighed again. She felt a hole in her heart, in the spot Carlos had occupied all those years. She tried taking a deep breath but even that didn't steady her. She felt raw inside. Her voice trembled when she spoke, blurting, "Why did he have to die?"

As a cynic and realist, Martín was short on 'what if's.' Sympathy was not his strong suit. But just this once he would honor the man his sister had fought with and loved. "Hermana, he loved you. He honestly lived for you." He paused before adding, "Though sometimes he may have shown it in strange ways..."

Layla laughed first, then Martín joined in. Gallows humor.

There was sadness in his tone as he continued, "Ahh, Carlos, poor Carlos. I don't know what to say to you, Layla, except you are one of the lucky ones. You know why, don't you, hermana?" He paused for effect before saying, "At least you have known love. With all its ups and downs."

Her brother's kind words started the tears Layla had been fighting back for days since she lost Carlos in the crash. A surge of emotion poured from her.

"I miss him. I miss him so much," she said, weeping softly. She walked over to the counter to grab a handful of tissues.

"Si, mi amor, si," her brother empathized as he listened to her sobs. "Love is very special. But you're also lucky in another way: You can avenge the death of the one you loved."

She pondered his sly segue. He had switched tables on her, to get her back on task. A weepy assassin? No such thing existed.

She rubbed her runny nose with a tissue, then two more. Breathed another shaky sigh. "Okay, I'm listening."

"As you were Carlos's job, avenging Carlos's death is now your job."

She nodded. "I know, I know." Martín could always speak in a way others understood. He had a knack for reading people's emotions, maybe he even felt their needs. Not that he much acted on it—she knew he was an insular being, a loner. But the fact of the matter was simple: Carlos was family, the closest thing Martín had to another brother.

She sniffed and walked over to the mirror to assess the damage she'd done after her crying jag. "I won't keep this up too much longer, hermano. I just needed a good cry."

"Well, a cry's okay now, but *tough* is what's needed later."

"Okay, point taken. So, I'll talk to you tonight from either the car, the airport or CDMX, whatever's easiest. I love you, Martín. Thank you, for everything."

"De nada, Layla. We're in this together."

"Claro," she nodded absently. "Claro, mi hermano. Ciao."

CHAPTER 46

A s Layla dressed for the gig, a knock came at the door.
"Layla?" Clay asked. "It's nearly five."

"Si, almost ready."

She walked over to the full-length mirror and took a
long look. Her slender body was resplendent in a mariachi
costume of reds and whites, with ruffles on top of starched
ruffles. A narrow row of silver buttons, bordered on either
side by finely stitched embroidery, extended down to the
waist of the silky bodice. Sweeping back her hair, she put
on the sombrero, tilting it to see how much of her face it
covered. She was glad she'd bought a narrow black mask to
more fully disguise herself.

Layla opened her make-up valise and took a look at the
Beretta and the silencer. She placed a white scarf on top of
the hardware and closed the valise. She took off the sombrero, walked up close to the mirror and simply stood there.
She stared directly into her own eyes, taking stock of the
person reflected back at her.

"The woman is coming," she said softly, almost a whisper.

A bit louder, more serious. "The woman is coming."

And then a third time, with total conviction. "The
woman is coming!"

Her mantra complete, she strode to the door.

After stopping first at the security gate to check in, the taxi cruised up to the parking lot and dropped them off. Clay paid the cabbie while Layla grabbed her make-up valise and the sombreros.

They shared a look. "It's show time," Clay said, taking his hat.

The back entrance was bustling with an army of people. In the distance Layla heard canned ranchero music coming from the courtyard.

She cocked her head. She'd forgotten how much sound a good audio system could put out. The sound of mariachi music blaring through powerful speakers could well hide the distracting noise of a gunshot in the soon-to-be-crowded ballroom.

Once inside, they walked towards the kitchen. Layla and Clay had come dressed in costume, and others had chosen to do the same. There were pirates, giant chickens, a Zorro, musketeers, fancy señoritas. The two conspirators moved gingerly through the bustling kitchen sidestepping the motivated staff, hoping to get another peek at the exit door.

That's when Layla spotted a buff, intense guy in a dark suit lecturing a food service employee who was gripping a silver ice bucket.

"He needs it now!" the suited man said in a hiss, waving his arms energetically at the server.

Layla's first instinct was to hide. She knew the look, could feel the vibe. Hijole, she could almost taste it. He was cartel, plain and simple. She gave Clay a sideways glance and he gave the slightest of nods. He'd also ID'd the enemy.

"Don Guillermo needs the ice now!" the cartel honcho said in a louder voice, lifting his head high to look around, praying someone would challenge his authority.

The timid server quaked in fear. He knew he was dealing with a made man. He didn't want to lose his head over a meaningless bucket of ice.

"Señor," he said beseechingly. "I promise you. The room service attendant will be right back."

"He's in pain *now*!" This time it was a yell.

Everyone's head turned, even those pretending they hadn't overheard the ruckus.

Layla tried to scoot past him as quickly as possible, but not before the bodyguard caught a glimpse of her shining locks, flared skirt, and low-cut bodice.

"Oh, mariachis tonight?" he asked, lowering his voice several decibel levels to a seductive tone as he reached out and caught Layla by the left wrist. She whirled around, full skirt fanning out, ready to give the performance of a lifetime.

"Si, señor! What song may I sing for you?" With her seductive smile she could have lit up the entire electrical grid for the city of Merida. She detached herself from his grip, but stepped closer to the brute so Clay could pass behind her and move farther from the fray.

"Oh! *Solo Una Vida*?" he asked, dazzled by her presence.

"Only One Life!" she repeated in Spanish. "Yes, it is yours! But excuse me, I'm running late for our performance. They can't start without me. And we don't want to keep the party waiting."

"Maybe I'll see you after the fiesta?" he asked, a hopeful glint in his eye.

"Possiblemente," she said with an infectious tinkle of laughter, playing the saucy señorita to his dominating macho. "Ciao."

And she was off, trailing after Clay who had moved steadily towards the door. As they exited into the hallway,

Layla slid against the comfort of the wall. Her heart was racing. She rubbed her wrist where the bodyguard had grabbed her. "Gotta catch my breath."

"Christ almighty," Clay whispered. "Well, we know he has *one* man in tow."

Layla recovered quickly. A little hiccup like that couldn't put her off her game. In fact, it energized her. She was unknown here!

"Clay, they don't know us!" Her voice came out in a nervous squeal. "We're invisible to them, only mariachi singers. Hijole! That was a good omen."

"I'd say. You were magnificent. I gotta remember to travel with you more often," he said in a light tone. "My life keeps getting more and more exciting."

"Did you hear him?" she whispered as they moved quickly down the hallway to the back stage entrance. "His jefe is not feeling well."

"That will be an understatement by the end of the night."

A nasty laugh escaped. "True!"

They hurried into the stage area, anxious to get the show on the road.

CHAPTER 47

A lfredo Cortez looked relieved when they arrived on stage, breathless. "We're nearly ready to go outside. So glad you're here." He took her hand and gave it a light squeeze.

"I have to put my valise in the dressing room," Layla said.

"I'll take it," Clay said. "You go with the performers."

Her bandmates were chatting and tuning up, a mixture of nervous energy and excitement. She could feel it, too. Her skin felt alive, nearly on fire.

"No, I need to check something. Come with me," she said to Clay.

They headed to the dressing room. On a hook on the back wall hung her new gown, very similar to the one she was wearing, but two-piece.

"Where are my running shoes?"

"In there," Clay said, pointing to a small closet in the corner.

She walked over, opened the closet and started rifling around. "Are you sure you put them in here?" Layla asked.

"Of course!" he said, though a touch of worry crept into his tone.

She started to rummage with a vengeance. "They're not here! They aren't here!"

He ran over and tore everything out of the closet. The shoes were gone. "Fuck!"

"Oh God! No! What am I going to do?" Layla wailed, but softly. "What am I going to do?"

"What happened to them? Were they stolen?" Clay asked.

"Who would steal them? And why?"

A grim look came over his face. "You'll have to do without."

She twirled around and faced him with a devastating glare. "What?"

"You heard me. Wear your heels on stage, then off they go, either before we split through the kitchen or in the parking lot. Or wear them. It's grass, not gravel."

"Chinga! Are you fucking kidding?" Her look turned harder and more intense.

"It'll work out."

"Easy for *you* to say!" She screamed, then caught herself as reality sunk in. "Oh God, I don't know if I can do it." Her persona went from larger than life to the size of a Maya woman's embroidered handkerchief.

Clay walked to the door and closed it. When he turned around he was all business.

"Listen, you're doing this. Whatever way it comes down. We are not changing a thing. Nothing. Got it?" There was not even a glimmer of the old Clay she thought she knew.

Layla trembled for a second, reviewing options—none good. She turned away, put a hand on her hip, the other to her forehead. She stood like that a few long moments, her shoulders slowly heaving up and down as she breathed deeply. Finally she turned and confronted him, her face contorted in anger. "Jesus y Maria! Have it your way."

He gave her shoulder a quick squeeze. "We're gonna get through this. I mean it."

"Don't touch me!" She jerked away from him as though

he were a leper. "I gotta go—get the door—now! They'll wonder where I am."

He opened it for her: show time.

🔁🔁🔁

Two hours later, the trumpets gave a final blast, ending the first part of the fiesta. Layla and her bandmates wore satisfied expressions and Señor Cortez looked particularly pleased.

"We have forty minutes to prepare before the ballroom," he said when he came over to thank her. "Get something to drink, sit down, try to rest. It could be a long night."

Layla smiled blandly at the bandleader. *If you only knew,* she thought.

She flounced her skirts and began to walk back towards the dressing room, all the while keeping an eye out for Clay. As she entered the garden's back entrance, she spotted him. They made eye contact at the same time, a look of complicity with a touch of complacency. Just business, as it were. *What a fucked up way to make a living.*

Clay came over. "That was amazing," he said, as others streamed by on both sides.

"Hmmph." She was wound tight, still chapped about the shoes and unwilling to let it go.

"Would you like water, juice?" he asked.

She grimaced. "Coke."

"Right. Let's go this way."

They wandered through the partygoers to get to the service bar. It was knee-deep in waiters and fellow revelers. Somehow everyone had discovered it.

"Wait here," Clay instructed. "I'll get a couple cokes."

"Yeah."

She looked for a spot that wasn't a throughway, a place to take a load off, both mental and physical. With her heightened sense of awareness, she couldn't ignore the stylish décor everywhere she looked. The lighting was superb. Sparkly amber LED teardrops illuminated the trees high over the bar like tiny stars, and the courtyard they'd just finished performing in could have been a garden at the Alhambra. If she hadn't just discovered she was undertaking the biggest mission of her life barefoot, she might have been able to enjoy it.

Her thoughts returned to the present and she glanced at the bar. Clay was edging his way towards the counter. When he returned with their drinks they'd find a place to sit for a few minutes before her costume change.

She hadn't seen Guillermo in the courtyard—a good thing, she figured. It would be dark in the ballroom and he'd be farther away than the audience had been outside. When she'd peeked in before the performance she'd counted at least fifty big tables. At ten people per table that meant a group of five hundred. Vargas had quite a party on his hands.

Suddenly panic set in. What if Guillermo wasn't well enough to make the fiesta? Chinga! What would she do? She'd have to go to his room and take her chances, bodyguards or not.

As she pictured yet another unforeseen possibility someone touched her on the arm. She swung around, startled.

"Oh. It's you." Her voice was heavy with disappointment. The cabrón had found her.

The bodyguard was so full of himself he didn't catch her disdain.

"Señorita! Look at you! What can I get you? Tequila? Margarita?" he asked.

"Oh," Layla said again. "No, no. I never drink when I'm performing."

"You save it for later, si?" He chuckled. An ambitious smile crossed his face, hoping for corroboration on his goal—her.

"Not really," she said, trying to sound confident, flip, and elusive, all at the same time. She flung her head back, forgetting she still had her sombrero on and nearly decked him.

"Hey, watch it!" he grunted harshly. It didn't take much for his loutish self to rise to the surface.

Acting appropriately flustered, she smiled demurely, touching his arm. "Oh, señor! So sorry. This silly sombrero! How clumsy of me. Are you okay?"

He recovered quickly after her apology, murmuring, "Sure, no problem."

"My manager is getting me a drink," she explained while backing away. "What are you doing here?"

"Oh, my jefe. He wants something to drink, pronto. I told him I'd check the service bar, so he didn't have to wait so long. He's not feeling well and wanted to get a buzz going fast."

"Well, he sounds like a smart man," she said, dishing out another smile. "But if you'll excuse me, I must see my bandleader before we begin, and here comes my refresco."

Clay spotted her with the bodyguard and hesitated. She cocked her head towards the dressing room.

"Is that him?" the bodyguard asked, when he saw Clay with two cokes.

"Si. Will you be having dinner?" she asked. "I still want to sing that song for you. Try and get a table up close to the stage, so I can see where you are."

Now it was his turn to return the megawatt smile. "Of course, señorita."

"Don't forget." She distanced herself from Guillermo's hired muscle. "Put a reserved sign on the table. Close to the stage!"

She gave a little wave then floated off toward her dressing room with renewed stamina. She was going to get up close and personal with him. The clock was ticking.

CHAPTER 48

They headed quickly towards the dressing room, side-stepping partygoers, service employees, and waiters. Layla needed to change clothes, get the Beretta and silencer, stick the flashlight and wig into her skirt pocket, and not forget to breathe.

"I think we lucked out," she told Clay, her anger now behind her, as they hurried towards the dressing room. "I asked the bodyguard to sit close to the stage so I could sing to him."

"That's priceless, Layla."

They entered the backstage area and were surprised to see a guy hanging around the dressing room. He looked like another bodyguard!

"Excuse me, coming through," Layla said in a haughty tone, all pomp, flouncing her skirts and trying for the very busy "Don't bother me" look.

"Are you the mariachi singer?" the fellow asked.

"What do you think?" she asked in a condescending tone. "Now if you'll excuse me and let me through, I have to prepare for my performance."

"I have a message for you," the interloper said. "From Javier."

"Who?" Layla asked, riled by his persistence. "Really, I don't have time for this."

"He's the one you're singing to—you know—the song."

She exchanged a perturbed glance with Clay.

He took over. "Hey man, she's busy, didn't you hear her?"

"Was I talking to you?" the nuisance asked, a foul mood surfacing after being rebuffed. He dismissed Clay, then stepped in so close that his lips nearly touched Layla's ear. "He just wants you to know he'd like to see you afterwards."

Layla swatted him off like a fly. "I'm sorry but I have another commitment. Now if you'll excuse me, I need to change. Please." She placed her hand on the doorknob.

"Out of the way, my man," Clay said, standing tall at his full six feet two, towering over the new bodyguard who was well built but had no height. "You heard the lady."

Not about to be snubbed, the apparent bodyguard ignored Clay and spoke again to Layla, this time in a rougher tone. "He doesn't like it when people say no to him."

Hands on her hips, she nearly shouted, "Well, sorry, but I have to get ready. Now leave me alone!" She couldn't afford to lose her composure.

"He's not going to be happy."

"I'm singing him a song, for Christ's sake. What more does he want?" Layla asked.

The man sneered. "More, chica. A *lot* more. He'll see you after the show."

Bodyguard number two gave her a withering look and strode off with a determined swagger.

"Chinga!" Layla said as she pushed open the dressing room door and collapsed onto the small folding chair inside. "Now I've got a fucking stalker from the cartel! Of all the screwed up things. And meanwhile all I want to do is kill his boss."

Clay looked at her and they burst into pressure-relieving laughter.

"Well, he's definitely gotten mixed up with the wrong girl,"

Clay said, snickering. "He should have done a Google search on mariachi singers before he fell head over heels. Even I could have told him you're trouble."

The ludicrous situation took the edge off the running shoe problem. Layla grabbed the new gown and walked behind the changing screen to dress. Clay settled into her chair and turned the other way, offering a bit more privacy for the newly minted prima donna.

"They'll be up close for sure. I wonder if Guillermo will recognize me," Layla said from behind the dressing screen.

"With all the excitement and noise, I don't think so. I bet he's probably on pain pills, at the very least neo-percodan if not something stronger. And the red wine. He won't be expecting jack shit, much less a killer mariachi singer."

A moment later Layla emerged from behind the screen in her second costume. A cummerbund united the bodice with the breakaway skirt, making it look like a dress. She opened her valise and grabbed first the wig, then the flashlight, and stuffed them into her left pocket. She reached to the bottom of the case and brought out the gun and silencer.

"Clay, check the door," she said.

"It's locked."

"Humor me. Check again." Her tone demanded obedience.

He got up to confirm the door was locked. "Done. How are the shoes?"

"Hmmph."

"Think you'll wear them?"

She ignored the question while she put the gun in her skirt pocket and pulled it out. Staring at the weapon, she answered, "Don't know, maybe."

She did the move again and again until it felt like her practice sessions.

271

"Okay. Now I just have to wait for that fat pendejo to sit down at the table with his over-sexed body guard."

"You feeling good about this?" Clay asked.

"Feeling fine."

"Can I get you anything?" Clay asked.

"An invisibility cloak? A steady hand?"

Clay smiled. Good old Layla of the unswerving nature was back.

"Let me sit for a few minutes." She requisitioned the dressing room's only chair. Clay leaned beside the door, hands behind his back. "I'm just going to close my eyes for a minute. Think about tonight.

"Sure thing."

Layla shifted the folding chair towards the closet and sat down. She could feel the true weight of the gun and silencer from where it hung in her pocket. Heavy. She closed her eyes, settling into a deep breathing regimen she'd learned eons ago. Long steady breaths. She felt the calm descend.

She imagined Guillermo in his dining room in Antigua. His fat body filled her mind. Next she pictured herself, gun in hand as though it belonged there, and shifted his form to the ballroom at Hacienda Xcanatún at a table with a white tablecloth near the stage. In her mind's eye, Javier, the horny bodyguard, sat next to him. Her song finished, she turned, pulled out the gun, stuck it between the folds of her skirt, and faced the audience.

She caught Guillermo in her cross hairs, and then she pulled the trigger.

CHAPTER 49

Ever since the pilot broke his nose, Guillermo felt like shit. Maybe he shouldn't have come to Vargas's ranch for Semana Santa after all. Due to the unexpected situation with El Patrón's niece one problem had snowballed after another.

And where was Javier? Always running off. Too bad he was such a useful motherfucker or he'd replace him. No denying he was good with a gun, and loyal as a lap dog.

He walked to the bathroom and rifled through his grip, pushing aside shaving cream, razor, toothpaste. He finally found what he was looking for—the bottle of pain pills prescribed by the Merida doctor. Along with the red wine, it was the only thing that took the edge off. He grabbed a bottle of water sitting on the counter and downed two.

He needed to bolster himself for the evening. Maybe a shot of tequila would work better than wine. Hijole, he still hadn't been out with the partygoers. He'd already missed the first half of the fiesta and now it was nearly time for the dinner buffet and live music—mariachis, his favorite.

He walked to the wet bar next to the mini-fridge. Two tequila bottles sat on a silver tray on the granite counter— Don Julio Real and Herradura Reposado. He grabbed the Don Julio, reached for a shot glass and poured the amber liquid into it. He tipped back his head.

The tequila burned as it went down, but the after-effect

was a warm, soothing sensation that calmed every ache and pain in his battered body. He decided to pour another.

He set the shot glass down and stood with his hands on the wet bar to steady himself. Now to find his Zorro mask, to cover his bruised face. As he straightened up, he noticed he had a real buzz going. This was going to be all right. He was at a party, after all, and it was Semana Santa. Everyone would be a little toasted. He'd join right in.

Where was that Javier? And Antonio? He hadn't seen that pendejo for hours.

ᘁᘁᘁ

Javier gave the triple knock, their signal, two times. No answer. He hadn't been gone that long. He knocked again. Still no answer. Guillermo didn't like being barged in on. And Antonio should be guarding; it was his shift.

Javier set the wine bottle down so he could get the room key out of his pocket. He inserted key in lock and turned the knob. What he saw next was a total surprise. His jefe was lying face down on the floor.

He ran in and struggled to turn the big guy over. The fucker was already wearing his little black mask, like he was actually going somewhere.

"Don Guillermo!" Javier said in a panic, shaking his boss.

Guillermo's shirt had pulled out of his rumpled brown slacks and an impressive roll of lard lay exposed to the world. His fat belly jiggled when the bodyguard shook him.

"Boss! Wake up!"

After another few shakes the Guatemalan captain began to stir.

"Javier?" he said with a pronounced slur. "Where have you been?"

"Don Guillermo, I went to get your red wine, like you asked. Here it is. Where's Antonio?"

"Chinga! I don't know where Antonio is! You tell me! And I don't want wine! I'm doing tequila shots! Help me up. What time is it?" he asked, acting like he hadn't fallen over face first in a heap on the floor.

"Sure, boss, sure," Javier said. "Time? About nine."

"Puta de madre! We can't miss dinner and mariachis! Help me get ready. Grab a clean shirt, hurry."

Though Guillermo was slurring his words, his attitude was the same as ever—impatient and demanding. Javier ran to the closet and pulled out the first shirt he could find, a light beige Guayabera.

"That won't do, you fool!" Guillermo said, nearly bellowing. Apparently he hadn't lost strength in his vocal chords. "The ivory cotton! Now!"

Javier returned to the closet and grabbed a long-sleeved starched shirt from the hanger. "This one?" he asked in a subdued voice.

"Yes, yes. Get over here!"

The bodyguard did as instructed. By this time Guillermo was sitting up on the floor, waiting for help.

"I'll take off my shirt," his jefe said. "Help me put on the new one. And don't wrinkle it. Are these pants okay?"

Not wanting to be yelled at again, Javier nodded.

"Good. Well, help me up! What do I pay you for?"

Cowed by his boss's demanding behavior, Javier did as he was told. The jefe sure had a temper for an old guy.

"Okay now. Get me one more shot."

"Tequila?" Javier asked.

"Chinga! I told you what I'm drinking. Don Julio."

Javier ran to the counter, poured a shot, and walked mincingly back to his boss, careful to not spill a drop. He handed it over. Guillermo grabbed greedily for the shot glass and tilted back his head. He was becoming used to the liquor's slow burn. It was mother's milk.

"Aaah, good. Let me look in the mirror, then we'll go," Guillermo said as he stumbled towards the bathroom and his pill bottle, hanging on to a chair in his path.

A moment later he was back in the suite, adjusting his mask, but in slo-mo. Javier had never seen anyone move with such pronounced precision. "Listo?"

Was he ready? "Yes, boss." That was all Javier could manage to squeak out.

They started towards the door and heard the distinctive signal—three fast knocks, two times. Finally, Antonio was returning to guard the room.

⚅ ⚅ ⚅

In the grand ballroom, the first set was moving along, with just two more songs before the close. Layla was singing with true emotion, trying not to blow it, but she couldn't stop worrying about where Guillermo and the bodyguard were. Would they even show? Granted, there was a reserved sign on a front table to the right of center stage, but what if something had happened to the Guatemalan capo? Or was the bodyguard pissed because she wouldn't commit to an after-hours tryst? Oye, she had a bad case of the jitters.

The partygoers were a lively crowd, up and down in their seats, the tables adrift in a constant sea of movement. There was an ongoing stream of people going back to the spread at the dinner buffet for seconds, plus a slew of latecomers finding seats. The raucous merriment was a perfect backdrop for Layla's task, complete with trumpet blasts from on stage. With so much happening, it could very well not only cover any gunshots, but camouflage the commotion that was sure to follow. If her aim was true, Guillermo's slumping body would prove a "dead" giveaway, but she'd have to deal with that fallout later.

She began singing her second to last song and twirled around to see if she could spy Clay back stage. There he was, eyes on her, a nervous look pasted on his face. He was obviously feeling tense, too. Just as she whirled back to face the crowd, a bit slower than the last time after feeling the weight of the Beretta bearing down on her right pocket, she spotted the unlikely duo coming through the ballroom's main entrance.

Ojala! Glory hallelujah! Guillermo looked tipsy, unsteady on his feet, and she was thankful the second bodyguard wasn't coming along for the ride. Only Javier. She began to sharpen her focus.

The two men slowly walked the gauntlet of dinner tables jammed with guests chatting, eating, some dancing next to their chairs. Guillermo was balancing his overweight body on Javier's steady frame. Should she take out the bodyguard or would that extra shot waste precious getaway time?

If she was lucky, he'd be busy attending to his downed jefe, which would stall his pursuit for a few seconds. Those extra moments could prove vital to the evening's outcome for her and Clay.

They neared their reserved table as the song ended. Seeing Guillermo's condition, she knew there was no way in hell he would have a clue who she was, but Javier spotted her on stage and in spite of the predicament he was in—helping an inebriated old fat man into his seat at a party—he beamed her a smile.

With any luck at all, in a matter of minutes he'd be out of a job.

She did a side turn to coordinate with the guitar player who was the bandleader, and moved farther from center stage. She knew Clay was following her every move. The intro came up, the trumpet blast, and the marimbas started in. Within moments, Layla's voice could be heard above it all, like a minstrel of death—a mourning dove.

Time began to move slowly. The first few bars seemed to drag on for hours. The next several bars picked it up, but then seconds dragged on like minutes.

Layla dared not turn around too soon. She had to time things just right with the Beretta and hoped the other band members wouldn't be looking at her. She sidled to the right again, out of their range of vision. She reached the middle of the song, turned, slowly put her hand into her pocket and felt the cold steel of the gun barrel.

She grasped the gun, pulled it out, slid it into a ruffle of her break-away skirt. Had anyone seen her? In her peripheral vision she could see that the band was merely a backdrop to a scene of revelry. No one was watching her or anyone in the band. They weren't even looking at the stage. Not even Javier. He was busy propping up his gordo jefe.

She felt a burst of confidence, as though she had all the time in the world, and let the gun settle there against her thigh, waiting another second or two before taking off the safety.

Javier was having a conversation with Guillermo, who, though woozy, seemed to be demanding something. The bodyguard looked up at the stage one more time, gave the slightest of smiles and sent a tiny wave her way. Then he did something she could only have prayed for—he turned in his chair, got up, and headed towards the buffet table.

She was well into the last stanza of the song, just before the refrain. Again the trumpets blared. She said a silent prayer and tilted up the ruffle of her skirt to prepare to shoot. She looked first at Guillermo—her mark—darted a glance at the buffet table—wait a minute—who was Javier talking to? What the hell? Zoyo!

Layla nearly dropped the gun. What was he doing here?

She dared not turn around to look for Clay. She would do what she came to do, and as she had promised Martín, she wouldn't shoot Zoyo. Did he have bodyguards? Of course he did. The song was winding down. She sang the last note. Guillermo was there at the table, no one else around. Time to do it. She took aim exactly as she had done in her imagination, waited for the final trumpet blare of the song, and pulled the trigger. This time for real.

She saw the Guatemalan capo clutch his chest, hands over his heart. His head jerked upwards. A look of confusion crossed his face before his substantial upper torso slumped onto the table, scattering utensils and wine glasses into a jumbled mess on the spotless white tablecloth.

She didn't even bother to see if Javier or Zoyo caught what happened. The only thing she noticed was the surprised look on the marimba player's face as she darted off the stage, gun in hand. Then she was backstage, running behind Clay. She pulled the wig from her pocket, tore off her break away skirt. She dropped the flashlight, didn't bother to pick it up, and was instantly on Clay's heels. They ran determinedly down the hall to the kitchen, a path they'd both memorized.

Two men trundled a room service cart ahead of them, turning to identify the ruckus. In that moment of hesitation, Clay darted around them and through the kitchen's swinging entrance door with Layla on his heels. Coming out the kitchen's exit door at that same moment was Antonio, the bodyguard, with another cartel look-alike, surely one of Zoyo's boys, carrying a bottle of red wine each and a silver ice bucket, laughing. The commotion brought them immediately to attention. In their line of work, action meant something.

As they watched two people dash into the kitchen, Antonio must have recognized Layla or spied the gun, and he let out a yell. Since they were already out the one-way exit door they could only re-enter the kitchen through the swinging entrance door, but it was blocked by the servers with the cart, as perfectly choreographed as a slapstick comedy routine.

"Run!" Clay shouted, not looking back to see what was happening.

"Right behind you!"

Clay nearly collided with a sous chef carrying a pot of something huge and red. Layla skirted the potential mayhem and kept moving. Servers darted out of their way, unsure of the cause of the uproar. The two bodyguards nearly hurdled the room service cart, racing back into the kitchen to see where the runners were headed.

Clay hit the kitchen's exterior exit door first, swung it wide, and ran. Layla was on his tail. At first, the parking lot's brightness brought anxiety. They'd hoped for the cover of darkness, not the near-daylight of halogen floodlights. But as they approached the stables the lights were much dimmer. Layla heard the door crash closed, and seconds later slam open.

"They're coming!" Layla said.

"Keep moving!"

"The gun," she managed to gasp. "Heavy." Her sturdy Cuban-heeled dancing shoes were holding up but the gun's weight was slowing her down and they were still far from the horse fence that bordered the property.

"Ditch it!"

"Where?"

She spotted the answer just as Clay yelled it, "The well casing!"

The well casing just past the stables looked defunct, a perfect anonymous spot for a murder weapon. She tossed it in as she passed by. Seconds later she heard a dull splash.

She could hear footsteps in the gravel behind her. "They're coming!"

"Shut up!"

She took Clay's advice and ran with total abandon through the dark, eyes on his back. Clay had turned his flashlight off so as not to alert the pursuers of their location. Layla watched Clay dip in and out of rows of trees as he headed towards the fence. The dewy grass caused Layla's leather soles to slip and had slowed her down from a sprint to a jog.

"The fence!" Clay warned her.

She saw him jump. She wasn't far behind and decided it was time to lose the shoes. She heard a thud. Clay was over.

"Come on, Layla!"

She jumped the fence and her heels sunk into the damp grassy earth. Kicking off her shoes, nearly falling, she stumbled forward. The grass felt cool on her bare feet and she ran with more confidence. Steadily she made her way across the vast expanse of lawn toward the road.

Run, run, was all she could think, glad the Beretta was gone along with her flouncy skirts. Did she see the road? No lights to define it, not in the Yucatán, but they'd driven by the ranch enough times that she had her bearings. She couldn't hear anyone behind her due to her own heavy breathing but that didn't mean they weren't there. Chinga! She heard another thud. One of the bodyguards had jumped the fence!

"Layla, nearly there!"

She was starting to tire and running without shoes scared her. What if she stepped in a hole, tripped on a branch?

Clay kept yelling, "Move it! Almost there!"

A stream of light pulsed behind her. How did they get a flashlight? Ahead she saw a tiny blink, Clay's signal to the getaway car.

"Psssst! Over here! Jump!" He called.

It was another fence blocking them from the road. Clay leapt over as before. Extremely tired and losing energy, she grabbed the top of the fence and somehow pulled herself over it. Then she was on pavement. Asphalt had never felt so good, even on her bare feet.

There were nearly fifty cars lined up along the roadway in front of Hacienda Xcanatún. Chauffeurs and drivers leaned against the vehicles, chatting casually and drinking sodas.

"Where's the fire?" one shouted as they ran by. The others laughed.

Clay and Layla kept running towards the head of the line where Alfonso and José had parked the car. She was panting heavily. She heard a car start.

Clay called in a loud stage whisper, "José?"

It seemed like the bodyguards were tracking their progress, as though they had night-vision goggles. Alfonso was behind the wheel, engine running, car door on the street side open, waiting for her to drop in.

"Tenga prisa!" José called in an urgent voice. Hurry.

"Okay, okay!" Clay shouted back. He reached them first and rounded the car to the curb side saving the open door for Layla. He pulled open his door and barreled in. Within seconds she jumped in from the road side. She collapsed against Clay's body as the car zoomed off, her door still open. She screamed. José, riding shotgun, reached far over the back seat behind driver Alfonso, grabbed the door handle and slammed it shut.

"You're here, Señorita Layla! You are safe!" José said, true relief in his voice.

"Did another car start up?" She struggled for words, between gulping breaths.

"No," Clay said, turning to look behind them. Total darkness. "Nothing so far."

"We were being chased," she spit out.

"By who?" José asked.

"Guillermo's bodyguard and," she paused to get more air, "Zoyo's man."

"Zoyo?" Clay and José spoke at the same time.

"Yes, just before I shot Guillermo, I saw Javier at the buffet table talking to Zoyo."

"So that other bodyguard in the kitchen was Zoyo's?"

"Definitely," she said. "And they'll all be after us."

"Did you kill him?" José asked.

"Guillermo? I got him! He slumped over the table clutching his fucking heart. Who knew he even had one? Call the contact Martín gave you, José. He'll let you know what they're saying at the ranch."

"Layla!" Clay said. "You fucking did it!" He was bouncing on the back seat.

"I got him, Clay."

"Bueno?" José said into his cell phone. "Que paso?"

The car was silent except for Layla's heavy breathing.

"Si, si!" José said excitedly. "Si?"

"What? What?" Layla asked.

Her new bodyguard turned around and gave her the biggest smile she'd ever seen. "Muerto, Señorita Layla. Guillermo es muerto!" Dead.

CHAPTER 50

The cuota pay highway would soon be crawling with police so Alfonso decided to take the libre road towards Cancun, at least as far as Valladolid. It would be safer to pick up the pay highway there because by then they would be far out of Merida and no one would think they could have traveled so far so fast.

Clay had his trusty backpack and Layla's Louis Vuitton tote was in the back seat just as she'd packed it a day earlier, complete with a change of clothes, makeup, purse, and a pair of sandals—not fashionable, but sturdy and comfortable. She had plenty of pesos and a passport in Lety Santiago's name. Who knew if the Merida police would think a mere mariachi singer would take a hit out on a Guatemalan captain with connections to the Culiacan Cartel? Martín had wisely given her a different surname that her bandleader wouldn't recognize if questioned.

Layla swigged bottled water to try to bring down her body temperature. She still felt edgy but the car's A/C helped. Two hours later, when they saw signs for the Cancun airport exit, she breathed a sigh of relief.

"Did anyone see the car?" Clay asked Lalya. "The chauffeurs?"

"I don't know, but ditch it, José. No doubt someone will remember something. After you drop us at the airport, get a hotel in Cancun and tomorrow catch a flight to Sinaloa," Layla said.

"Si, Senorita Layla," José said. "That's what Martín said."

"What about Zoyo?" Clay asked.

"I don't know," Layla said. She stared out the car window into the darkness.

"He'll be after us—you for sure." Clay said. "What the hell was he doing in Merida?"

"He's friends—or he was—with Guillermo. Business partners. He probably knows Vargas."

"What will you tell El Patrón?"

"My brother's handling it. He'll be at the prison tomorrow to tell him everything. Once we get settled in at the airport I'll give Martín a call. Let him know what happened."

Clay checked his watch. "The plane will be loading soon—we won't have long to wait."

"Si, si," Layla said.

Alfonso took the exit for Cancun International. How modern the boulevard was now, four wide lanes with towering palms and billboards on either side, advertising Rolex watches, Cartier diamonds, Palace Resorts, Marriott hotels, all at home in the Riviera Maya. Splendid ads displaying glamorous people having the time of their lives, all lit up with the power of LED.

Alfonso cruised to the departure terminal and pulled up alongside the passenger drop area. Even at that late hour, the curb was jammed with Kombis, tour buses, SUVs, and passenger cars.

"Señorita Layla?" Alfonso asked. "This is okay? Or you want me to park?"

"This is good, Alfonso," she said, a little catch in her voice, feeling a kinship with these men. "I want to thank you, José and Alfonso. You did a great job—a very important job—

for me and the cartel." For a moment Layla dropped the jefe mask and grabbed Alfonso on the back of his shoulders, then she reached over Clay to grab José's outstretched hand in both of hers. "I'll never forget what you did for me. Never." She shook off the emotion before it got ahold of her and grabbed her tote. "Martín will be in touch very soon."

José got out first and came around to open her door as Clay stepped out curbside. She reached into the driver's window and gave another quick pat to Alfonso's bulky shoulder, a lingering reminder of Carlos in some odd way, then squeezed José's arm.

"Thanks again." With valise in hand she walked over to the curb and met Clay.

"José, Alfonso," the Canadian said. José grasped Clay's hand. "Till we meet again." He reached through the car window and patted Alfonso's broad shoulder.

Layla rummaged in her purse for her new passport as they walked into the air-conditioned comfort of the departure terminal. "Aero Mexico," she said to Clay. After they checked in and went through to the boarding gates she'd look for a baño to change into her travel clothes.

Down at the end of the reservation counter they spotted the familiar airline logo. Though the airport wasn't packed, there was a steady stream of travelers despite the late hour.

"You're right," she said. "We actually just made it. Here's your ticket."

He grabbed it and took a look. "First class."

"Only the best for me and my pals," she said.

Half an hour later they were at the gate, seated comfortably next to each other. Neither spoke. Like all other travelers, they were tired.

"Boarding first class passengers," the flight attendant said over the loud speaker. "For Aero Mexico flight 235 to Mexico City."

They rose in unison and headed to the counter, first in line. They walked down the ramp and entered the cool comfort of the first-class cabin. An efficient flight attendant took Layla's valise and placed it in the compartment above her seat. Clay placed his backpack alongside Layla's bag. Layla took the window seat and settled in as the flight attendant brought them bottled water.

Once they were in the air, she was back. "Something more to drink?"

Clay answered first. "Champagne?"

The Aero Mexico flight attendant smiled. "Of course! Do we have something to celebrate?" she asked with a coy smile.

Layla gave a slight nod. "You could say that."

"May I ask the occasion?" She looked at the attractive couple before her. They seemed so cozy together. Engagement? Birthday?

"Wheels up," Layla replied.

The flight attendant gave her a quizzical look but knew her job too well to say anything more. She watched the handsome man give a broad smile to the woman sitting by his side, then saw him squeeze her hand, ever so lightly.

She smiled back.

Spanish Glossary

Abajo	Down or under
Abrazos	Hugs (Mexican form of endearment)
Adelante	Enter/come in/move it
Aduana	Customs
Adentro	Inside
Almendron	Almond tree
Aqui	Here
Arriba	Up
BC	British Columbia, Canada
Baja	Northern state that borders US and Mexico
Baño	Bathroom
Barrio	Neighborhood
Basta	Enough!
Bienvenidos	Welcome
Bud	Slang for exceptional marijuana, the actual bud of the plant
Bueno	Hello/used when answering phone —or good
Buenas tardes	Good afternoon
Buenos dias	Good morning
CDMX	Mexico City

Cabrón	Ass
Café negro	Black coffee
Calle	Street
Casa	House
Ceiba	Maya tree of life
Cerrado	Closed
Cerveza	Beer
Chacá	Type of tree used for fences
Chetumal	Capitol of Quintana Roo, borders Belize
Chica	Sweetie
Chichen Itza	Famous pyramid site in Yucatán
Chicleros	Men who tap chicle trees for gum (Wrigley's)
Chiquita	Sweetie
Chinga!	Disparaging exclamation
Chit	Tree used for making palapas
Ciao	Bye (Italian but frequently used in Mexico)
Claro	Certainly
Coca	Cocaine
Cojones	Part of a man's anatomy
Cuidado	Be careful
Culiacan	City in Sinaloa state, on Mexican west coast, head of cartel ops
Dónde	Where
Dulce	My sweet (an endearment)
Ejido	Land grant, gifted to citizens by Mexican government

El centro	Center
El comandante	The commander, usually military
El dentro	Inside
El jefe	The boss
Ensenada	City in northern Baja, touristy
Esta aqui?	Are you here, is it here
FARC	Fuerces Armadas Revolucionarias de Colombia/guerillas
Federales	Mexican federal police (similar to state troopers)
Fincas	Farms/Colombia/where cocaine is processed
Go-fasts	Cigarette boats, fast motors, used in drug trade
Guapo	Handsome
Hacienda	Large villa
Hasta manaña	Until tomorrow (good bye)
Hectare	2.5 acres of land
Henequen	Agricultural product Panama hats are made from
Hermana	Sister
Hermano	Brother
Hijole!	Good grief (or stronger)
Huipiles	Maya woman's cultural dress
Jefe	Boss
Libre	Free highway/ or free
Listo	Ready, or one can be listo/very "together"
Lo siento	Sorry

Loco	Crazy
Manaña	Tomorrow
Mangalar	Mangrove swamps
Merida	City of one million in Yucatán
Mi amor	My love
Milpa	Maya cornfield
Momento	One moment, please
Mostradore	Counter in store
Motul	Pueblo on Yucatán Peninsula near Merida
Mucho gusto	The pleasure is mine
Muna	Pueblo near Uxmal pyramids south of Merida
Muerto	Dead
Narca	Female drug dealer
Narco trafficker	Drug dealer
Nada mas	Nothing more
Negocios	Business
Niña	Little girl
Ojala!	By the grace of God
Orale!	For heaven's sake
Palapa	Roof or structure made from palm leaves
Pascua	Easter
Patrón	Person in charge, undisputed leader
Pendejo	Ass
Pequeña	Small
Pibil	Maya chicken recipe
Pinche	Used as pejorative adjective

Plaza	Town square
Policia	Police
Por favor	Please
Por fin	At last
Por supuesto	Of course
Posada	Small hotel or B&B
Pobrecito	Poor baby (usually in a mocking manner)
Pronto	Right away
Pueblo	Town
Puerto Simpatico	Beach town south of Cancun
Puta	Disparaging comment on women
Puta de Madre	Disparaging remark
Que bueno	How great
Que lastima	What a pity
Que mal	How bad, how horrid
Que paso?	What's happening?
Quien esta?	Who is it or who is there
Q. Roo	Abbreviation for Quintana Roo, state where Cancun is located
Rebozos	Shawl (for women)
Refrescos	Soft drinks
Rojo	Red
Rotisseria	Rotissary (store selling grilled meats)
Salbute	Small Maya tortilla of shredded turkey, cabbage, onions
Salud	To your health (usually as a toast)
Sascab	Sand used on streets in Yucatán
Se encuentra	Where do you find?
Semana Santa	Holy Week

Shawshank	Famous prison break out movie
Silver or lead	A money bribe-payoff or a bullet to the head
Sheep-dipping	Given an alternative identity, in order to disappear
Sinaloa, Mexico	Stronghold of Culiacan Cartel activity, state on west coast
Soy	I am
Straw owner	Signs paperwork, deeds for another in exchange for cash, gifts
Té	Tea
Terraza	Terrace
Tienda	Small store
Tio	Uncle
Tipos	Guys
Tixkokob	Pueblo on Yucatán Peninsula, near Merida
TJ	Short for Tijuana, border city between Mexico and US
Todo bien	All is well
Trampa	Trap
UNAM	Mexican university
Zocalo	Square or plaza

ACKNOWLEDGMENTS

My sincere gratitude to my editor, Jennifer Silva Redmond. Thank you to Jill Logan, Jill Ronsley, Steve Radziwillowicz, Kathy Wise and Eva Hunter. Many thanks to April Schwartz, Karen Haddigan, Maryjean Ballner, Carmen Amato, Gwen Dandridge and Margie Borchers. A huge thank you to Denise Gula Weller and David Simmonds for their faith in this book and for their unrelenting support.

Thanks to Nicholas Kitchel for his digital mastery and assistance.

Thank you to Rosemarie Herrmann who never tired of hearing about the book's status.

Thank you to my BETA readers Christopher Rothgery and Jennifer Eagan.

Grateful thanks to Paul Zappella whose patience and support helped me, as always, to keep on keeping on.

Made in the USA
Columbia, SC
31 May 2018